P9-AFY-840

"YOU THINK EVERYTHING ABOUT ME IS PERFECT?"

Lisa's voice held suspicion.

"From toes to temple." Kevin was reluctant to point out the individual parts while sitting in the middle of a bed with her.

"But my hips are too big."

"Trust me, they're not."

"And my chest..."

"Is perfect."

"Now if my waist were smaller..."

"You may have a point," he said, after some consideration. "If your waist were smaller, you might not look so much like a pineapple."

She playfully punched him in the arm and he caught her to him, rolling over on top of her. The instant he felt the intimacy of their contact he knew he had made a mistake. "I think I'd better get out of here."

"What if I asked you to stay?"

"Do you know what you're saying?"

Lisa nodded, and with a soft moan Kevin lowered his head to kiss her.

ABOUT THE AUTHOR

Today, Tomorrow, Always is Georgia Bockoven's fourth Superromance, the eagerly awaited spin-off to *Little By Little.* A former free-lance journalist and professional photographer, Georgia now writes full-time, and in addition to her Superromances has written Temptations. Her fans particularly enjoy the warmth and good humor of her characters. Georgia, who makes her home in northern California, is married to a fire captain and has two grown sons.

Books by Georgia Bockoven

HARLEQUIN SUPERROMANCE

82—RESTLESS TIDE
102—AFTER THE LIGHTNING
138—LITTLE BY LITTLE
179—TODAY, TOMORROW, ALWAYS

HARLEQUIN TEMPTATION

14—TRACINGS ON A WINDOW
57—A GIFT OF WILD FLOWERS

These books may be available at your local bookseller.

Don't miss any of our special offers. Write to us at the following address for information on our newest releases.

Harlequin Reader Service
P.O. Box 52040, Phoenix, AZ 85072-2040
Canadian address: P.O. Box 2800, Postal Station A,
               5170 Yonge St., Willowdale, Ont. M2N 6J3

Georgia Bockoven

TODAY, TOMORROW, ALWAYS

Harlequin Books

TORONTO • NEW YORK • LONDON
AMSTERDAM • PARIS • SYDNEY • HAMBURG
STOCKHOLM • ATHENS • TOKYO • MILAN

Published September 1985

First printing July 1985

ISBN 0-373-70179-9

Copyright © 1985 by Georgia Bockoven. All rights reserved.
Philippine copyright 1985. Australian copyright 1985.
Except for use in any review, the reproduction or utilization of
this work in whole or in part in any form by any electronic,
mechanical or other means, now known or hereafter invented,
including xerography, photocopying and recording, or in any
information storage or retrieval system, is forbidden without
the permission of the publisher, Harlequin Enterprises Limited,
225 Duncan Mill Road, Don Mills, Ontario, Canada M3B 3K9.

All the characters in this book have no existence outside the
imagination of the author and have no relation whatsoever to
anyone bearing the same name or names. They are not even
distantly inspired by any individual known or unknown to the
author, and all the incidents are pure invention.

The Superromance design trademark consisting of the words
HARLEQUIN SUPERROMANCE and the portrayal of a Harlequin,
and the Superromance trademark consisting of the words
HARLEQUIN SUPERROMANCE are trademarks of Harlequin
Enterprises Limited. The Superromance design trademark
and the portrayal of a Harlequin are registered in the
United States Patent Office.

Printed in Canada

To the other "Lisa,"
Lisa Boyes, editor and friend

CHAPTER ONE

LIGHTNING ILLUMINATED THE RAIN on the mullioned windows in the room where Lisa Malorey had gone to seek refuge from the party. She pressed her forehead against the cold glass and sighed, her breath fogging the pane and closing off the outside world. But then, everything considered, that wasn't much of a loss. She had decided that Washington, D.C., in early winter had all the charm of a two-week-old bouquet of cut flowers. Frowning, she lowered herself to the seat beneath the window, put her elbows on her knees, cradled her chin in her hands and stared at the light creeping in from under the door.

Dammit! She had tried to tell them it was a mistake to send her there to testify. Ever since she had been old enough to get involved with projects and causes it had been the same...the more she cared about something, the less articulate she became when she tried to express her passion to others. Since her belief in the goals and ideology of the space program bordered on fanaticism, it wasn't any wonder she had fallen on her face at the meeting with the Senate Commerce, Science and Transportation Committee that afternoon.

Another bolt of lightning filled the sky behind her, making her pearl-colored sequined gown shimmer briefly in the white light. How was she ever going to go back to Houston and face all those people who had given her such a rousing send-off? Although she knew it was ridiculous to think the entire future of the space station had rested on her testimony, she was realistic enough to know she had not done the cause any discernible good with her tongue-tied gee-whiz answers. When a situation was as critical as this one, if testimony didn't help, it hurt.

A light tapping drew her attention, but before she could answer the summons the door opened. Squinting at the bright light, she saw the silhouette of a man and heard a baritone voice query, "Mind if I join you?"

In the mood she was in, the last thing she needed or wanted was company. Returning to the party and facing a crowd would be far less demanding than going one on one. "You can have the room all to yourself. I was just leaving."

"Please don't...I'd like to talk to you." He stepped inside and closed the door, and as he did so, he disappeared into the deep shadows.

"I'm afraid I'm not very good company tonight." One more what's-it-like-to-be-a-female-astronaut question and she would scream.

As he walked toward her, caught in the muted light coming through the uncurtained window, she saw that he was tall and slender. He wore his tuxedo casually unbuttoned, exposing a snowy-white pleated shirt, and his hands rested comfortably in his pants pockets, adding a further touch of casualness to the formal attire. Before the light had reached his face, he stopped and leaned against the back of the love seat that sat in front of the fireplace.

"First of all, let me apologize for intruding on your solitude—"

His voice was low and caressing, filled with an intimacy made more intense by the cloak of darkness that hid his features. Lisa sought a clue that would help her identify him from the dozen or so men she had met earlier, but nothing about him seemed familiar.

"But quite honestly, I was beginning to think you were never coming out."

"I'm not very good at parties." That wasn't true. Normally she loved parties, and it was a rare one that she didn't enjoy.

"I figured there had to be a reason I hadn't seen you at any of the obligatory soirees before now. A fresh face in an off election year is a rarity."

It wasn't so much what he said as the way he said it that made Lisa decide to stay. The words were standard, but the subtle appeal for friendship permeating his tone and manner was intriguing. "The reason you've never seen me before is more basic—I don't live here."

"Ah, so you're a visitor to our fair city. And how have you found it?"

A slow smile curved her full lips. She caught a sequin with her fingernail and gently tugged at the bit of plastic. It would be unfair to tell him that Washington had lived up to every miserable expectation she had harbored before coming. "Actually, I haven't had a chance to do any sightseeing. I came on business."

"To visit Washington and not see the sights is tantamount to going to France on a diet." He shifted his position, taking his hands from his pockets and folding his arms comfortably across his narrow waist.

Lisa stared at his hands. They were broad and blunt and powerful looking, in direct conflict with the elegance of his tuxedo and the graceful way he had moved across the room. Hands like those were rarely the kind that belonged to someone who worked behind a desk—they were more likely to jockey steel girders than wooden pencils. "Maybe next time..."

"I take it that means you're leaving soon?"

"Day after tomorrow."

"But there's still time."

Her smile was spontaneous this time, the first of its kind in several days. "What are you—president of the chamber of commerce?"

After a pause he said, "No...simply a man intrigued by a beautiful woman." He laughed. "So intrigued that he's willing to resort to the most inane conversation to keep her talking." He stood and came toward her. When he stopped he held out his hand. "Let me do what I should have done in the beginning—I'm Kevin Anderson."

Lisa put her hand in his. "Lisa Malorey."

"I'm pleased to meet you, Lisa Malorey," he said. His large hand closed around her smaller one, holding, touching in a decidedly sensuous way.

Lisa looked up and for the first time clearly saw his face. His eyes were framed by thick brows and full dark lashes, and the fine lines radiating from the outside corners told her he was a person who did not hesitate to respond to the vicissitudes of life. Strong emotions created lines like those. Since she had been a child Lisa had judged people by what she saw in their eyes and had rarely judged them wrong. Kevin's eyes were warm and guileless, but they were also demanding and contained a glimmer of...what was it...cynicism.

Kevin met her curious gaze openly, a silent invitation for her to look at him closely, to get to know him. Unaccustomed to such openness in strangers, Lisa was the first to break eye contact. "You must have come to the party late," she said, positive she would have remembered him after the most cursory introduction.

"As a matter of fact I arrived just in time to see you disappear into this room." He gave her a long-suffering grin. "After a while I began to wonder if you were ever coming out."

She had the uncomfortable feeling she was being subtly maneuvered without knowing where or why. In need of her full facilities, she withdrew her hand from his. "I should get back to the party before Mike and Caroline begin to wonder what's happened to me."

"Mike knows precisely where you are and who you're with." Kevin sat down beside her, filling what little room was left on the window seat. "I thought it prudent to check with him before chasing you in here since I wasn't sure why you had disappeared." He leaned lightly against the window. "Do you find all parties so distasteful that you hide out, or just this one in particular?"

Obviously he hadn't accepted her earlier answer. "I'm not in much of a party mood—it's been a rough week." He was sitting uncomfortably close, and if she could have, she would have moved away. Not only could she smell his cologne, she could feel the warmth of his body. Where her arm and leg touched him she felt flushed; where there was no contact, she felt oddly cold.

"I'm a good listener—you want to talk about it?"

She plucked at another sequin. Although the offer was tempting, it wasn't her style to unload her problems on people she had just met. "Thanks, but I'd just as soon try to forget the past couple of days. At least for tonight." There would be plenty of time to brood later.

"And you think the best way to succeed is by sitting in a dark room all by yourself?"

"Maybe not—but it's infinitely preferable to glad-handing with a senator who thinks his lofty position makes him irresistibly sexy despite a forty-eight-inch waist, sagging jowls and bad breath."

Kevin laughed. "So you've met Arnold Margolius. I certainly hope you don't let your opinion of Arnie color your feelings toward all politicians."

"This past week I've had enough of Arnie and his ilk to last me a lifetime. I don't care if I ever see another politician as long as I live."

"That bad, huh?"

"Worse."

"I can see I have my work cut out for me."

She eyed him, and her heart sank. "You don't mean that you're—"

He nodded.

She groaned. "I should have known. That's the way my luck has been running lately." So much for the theory about the strong athletic-looking hands.

"Tell you what—for tonight, why don't we forget who I am and who you are, find some place that has loud music and a big dance floor and lose ourselves and our problems in mindless, decadent pursuit of pleasure." When she hesitated he added, "Nothing permanent, just one night on the town."

She chewed on her lower lip while she considered her answer. "You make it sound tempting."

"But?"

She looked at him, her eyebrows arched in question. "You're really serious, aren't you?"

"I wasn't at first, but the longer I think about it, the better it all sounds."

The idea of a night away from the life-or-death intensity of the problems that had followed her around for the past week seemed like a lifeline back to sanity. But with a man she had known less than ten minutes? "I don't think—"

"Then don't—*think,* that is. This is the kind of thing that only works if there's spontaneity."

Still she hesitated.

Kevin took her hand in both of his. "Would references help?" he prodded. When she still didn't answer he glanced at his watch. "It's too late to call my folks— they're those early-to-bed, early-to-rise types—but I'm sure I could get Caroline or Mike to put in a good word for me."

She tried to summon all the sane, logical reasons for telling him no, but they kept being overpowered by her desire to say yes. She took a deep breath. "All right."

This time it was his turn to look surprised. "All right? Just like that? I don't have to continue being charmingly persuasive or give references?"

She tugged her hand free from his. "Once every year I allow myself to live dangerously. It just so happens that tonight is the night."

"I'm honored—I think." He stood and turned to face her. "I'll get our coats and meet you in the living room." When she didn't immediately get up, he added, "You're not thinking of changing your mind, are you?"

It wasn't changing her mind that had made her hesitate, it was wondering whether or not she had *lost* her mind. *Enough,* she mentally railed. A night out with a handsome stranger was just what she needed. There would be plenty of time tomorrow and for days after to wallow in depression. "No..."

"Well, then, let's go."

MIKE WEBSTER EXCUSED HIMSELF from the small group of people who had gathered around him and glanced across the living room, seeking his wife, Caroline. He finally spotted her beside the doorway, nearly hidden by the bulk of the man who held her in animated conversation. As had become his habit of late, he watched her for several minutes, looking for signs of fatigue. All he discovered was the special glow she had developed during her pregnancy. With her shoulder-length dark-brown hair piled on top of her head and the extra pounds her pregnancy had put on her normally lean frame, she looked breathtakingly beautiful. He found it hard not to stare at her like a kid with his first case of puppy love.

Suddenly, as if he had touched her, Caroline looked up and directly met his gaze. Her eyes filled with a meaningful twinkle before she returned her full attention to the man in front of her. She had told him in their intimate communication that she still had a little while to go before she would reach the "bureaucratic rhetoric overload" stage and need rescuing. A seed of warmth and well-being burst inside of him, making him feel impossibly happy. How he loved that woman.

Although he had known Caroline would make his life infinitely more worth living when she agreed to become his wife five years ago, he had never anticipated what an asset she would be to his work. She was magnificently adept at the subtle art of persuasion that he performed behind the political scenes for NASA.

After much discussion he had managed to get her to agree that this party would be her last official function until after the babies were born. As it was, even though she insisted she had never felt better, he thought they were pushing their luck. Keenly aware of how desperately NASA needed friends in congress to assure the continuation of the space station through yet another budget hearing, Caroline had insisted on this last party to try to sway a senator who was still undecided on his vote. It was only after she began her leave of absence from her broadcasting job early that he had finally relented, and then only when she agreed that the party would be catered.

Because they had tried unsuccessfully for such a long time to have a child, Mike still reeled with the knowledge that they were only months away from their dream. He was ecstatic but he was also terrified. The fertility drug had worked too well. Instead of the single boy or girl they had naively hoped for, they were expecting five. The warning lecture the doctor had given them still echoed in his mind. Multiple pregnancies were rarely carried to full term, and frequently the babies were so tiny they did not survive.

Lost in his thoughts, Mike did not at first see Lisa when she came up to him. Then, noticing her standing beside him, a patient, understanding grin on her face as she watched him watch Caroline, he slipped his arm around her shoulder. "What's up, gorgeous?"

"Cut the crap, Webster," she said. "You've only got eyes for one woman and that woman certainly isn't me."

He gave her shoulders a gentle squeeze. "But that doesn't mean I have to be blind to beauty in others, does it?"

"Uh-huh…you'd say the exact same thing if I suddenly turned cross-eyed and lost all my front teeth."

"It wouldn't matter. To me you'd still be as beautiful as you are now. Someone like you doesn't need the trappings, you have a beauty that comes from within."

"I think I'm going to be sick."

"Please don't—at least not on the new carpeting."

"Humph—that certainly lets me know where I fall on your list of priorities."

Mike chuckled. "I don't know why I even let myself get into these verbal sparring matches with you."

"Because every once in a while I let you win one."

"Come on over here," he said, steering her toward a group of people standing around a table filled with food. "There's someone I want you to meet."

She tightened her arm around his waist and turned him back in the direction from which they had come. "Sorry, Webster, you already had your chance to impress me with these people..." Just then Kevin appeared in the doorway with two coats draped over his arm.

"Ah-hah, now I understand your cocky independence," Mike said. "Someone has taken my place in your affections."

"I warned you it might happen if you insisted on continuing your thing with Caroline."

Mike walked with Lisa to where Kevin stood waiting. "I see you found her all right," Mike commented, taking Lisa's coat and holding it while she slipped her arms in.

"Just in time to keep her from leaping out the window, if I'm any judge of such things," Kevin answered, a smile playing around the corners of his mouth.

"Thank God." Mike laughed. "With publicity like that we might never have been able to sell the house." He looked at Lisa. "I suppose it never occurred to you that you might have sprained an ankle or something just as bad. A two-and-a-half-foot drop can be treacherous.''

Her eyes narrowed as she looked from Mike to Kevin, then back to Mike again. ''Especially when I was planning on going out with a swan dive.''

Kevin smiled and shook his head at the bantering that passed between Lisa and Mike. They had obviously been good friends for a long time. Or could it be that they were related and he had simply never heard Mike or Caroline talk of her before? He glanced at one and then the other. If they were related, it had to be by marriage. They didn't look at all alike. Lisa was almost a foot shorter than Mike, and her coloring was completely opposite. Mike had a distinct Italian look, whereas Lisa was the epitome of the golden California girl—blond and athletic looking, someone who appeared to have just stepped off the beach. He glanced up to see Caroline walking toward them.

''Leaving so soon?'' she asked Lisa as she came up to stand beside Mike.

''Kevin has offered to show me some of Washington's nightlife, and since it's unlikely I'll ever willingly be back this way again, I decided to take him up on it.''

Caroline smiled. ''Well, don't stay out too late. Remember you're due back here at nine tomorrow morning for breakfast.''

''Are you kidding?'' She moved toward the door. ''I would crawl over hot coals for one of Mike's famous Belgian waffles.''

''Try a cab, it's faster,'' Mike remarked, unimpressed. He took Caroline's hand as they walked out onto the front porch. She snuggled into his side, resting her head against his shoulder as they waved goodbye to their departing friends. Mike hesitated a moment before going in. "I hope she has a good time. This past week has been hard on her."

"Just how did all of this with Kevin come about anyway?"

"It was pure chemistry. Kevin saw her and was instantly attracted. He didn't mind at all when I asked him to see if he couldn't find some way to cheer her up."

"*You* arranged their date?"

Mike planted a kiss on her nose. "Not exactly. I only suggested he go into the study. Kevin took it from there."

Caroline slipped her arm around his waist and nestled closer to him. "Is that what it was that attracted you to me...chemistry?"

"That and that cute nose of yours."

She laughed. "Kevin reminds me a lot of you. Maybe I should warn Lisa just what's in store for her if she continues to see him."

Mike put his hands on her shoulders and turned her so that she faced him. "And what would that be?"

"Fishing for compliments."

"I get them any way I can."

Her voice became low and sultry. "How about if I show you what I mean after our guests leave?"

"You have the most incredible way with words." He kissed her tenderly on the lips, then held her close. "Come on inside. The last thing we need right now is for you to catch a cold."

She untangled herself from his arms and stepped back through the doorway. "You certainly have become practical lately."

"It comes with the territory. Impending fatherhood has a sobering effect."

"Mike?"

"Hmm?"

"Do you think she'll be all right? Something tells me this past week has been harder on Lisa than either of us realize, and Kevin isn't—"

"I agree...he isn't someone I would have chosen for her under normal circumstances. But I think they'll do okay."

"As long as they don't discuss politics."

"Or the space program..."

"Or any of a hundred other subjects I can think of." She hesitated a minute before going on. "Do you know, of all our friends, I can't think of two who are more opposite."

"It's only one date, Caroline, not a commitment."

"I don't know...I have a funny feeling about this." Suddenly she stopped and sucked in her breath. Her hand went to her stomach, and after several seconds she let out a deep sigh.

"Are you all right?" It was impossible for Mike to keep the panic from his voice.

Caroline managed to give him a reassuring smile. "As all right as anyone can be who has ten little feet tap-dancing on their bladder."

He pulled her close and pressed a kiss against her temple. "See—there's nothing for you to worry about. That funny feeling you just had had nothing to do with Kevin and Lisa, it was simply one of those cryptic communications you're always getting from that brood you've got incubating in there." But Mike wasn't as convinced as he sounded.

CHAPTER TWO

To BEGIN THEIR NIGHT OUT Kevin chose a bar on Pennsylvania Avenue called Jenkins Hill. The music was loud, the dance floor crowded and the drinks poured with a generous hand. In keeping with their earlier agreement to forget who they were in their mindless pursuit of pleasure, they concentrated on having a good time and were surprised at how easily it was accomplished.

It had been a long time since Kevin had done anything quite so freewheeling. It felt startlingly good and a little disconcerting, making him realize just how painfully conservative he had become over the past few years.

And then there was Lisa. Away from the party and whatever had been bothering her, she was a different person. Her face was animated and flushed from their continuous dancing, and her quips gradually took on a teasing, fun-loving quality, losing the cutting edge they had held earlier.

By the time they left Jenkins Hill they were building a foundation for a friendship that went beyond a single night on the town. Besides a shared passion for Chinese food, they discovered that they both adamantly refused to read their astrological forecasts in the daily paper and that yellow was their favorite color, although neither owned a single piece of yellow clothing.

While on the road to Kelly's Place, their second stop, they found that both of them considered sunrise their favorite time of day, and both were fanatical football fans, even liking the same, illogical team—the San Francisco 49ers instead of the Houston Oilers or the Washington Redskins.

Three bars, four hours and countless dances later they were at F. Scott's in Georgetown dancing to the big-band sounds of the 1930s and 1940s, surrounded by elegant art-deco designs and at least two identifiable Hollywood celebrities.

As they moved across the floor Kevin noted there had been a transformation in the way he and Lisa danced together. They had started out on the stiff and formal side, but now they were loose and comfortable. She fit into the planes of his body in a decidedly enticing way, and it was with greater and greater reluctance that he returned with her to the table whenever a song ended.

"How are your feet holding up?" he asked as he deftly turned her to avoid the onslaught of a self-styled Fred Astaire.

She raised her head from his shoulder to look up at him. "Right now they're fine. I have a feeling that if you asked me that in the morning, though, the answer might be different. These wispy things I have on my feet are a far cry from the boots I'm used to wearing."

"Boots?"

"Whoops—I keep forgetting the rules. Only *who* we are, not *what*."

"It's getting tough—"

"And a little frustrating."

"Perhaps we should—"

"Oh, let's not. Everything's been so perfect up until now."

He spun her around, gently pulling her closer. "That's not very flattering. What kind of ogre do you think rests behind this facade of mine?"

"If you remember, I already know what you do for a living."

"Ahhh, that's right. Which, I might add, is a little unfair."

"But then, the terms of this agreement were yours."

He gave her a slow smile. Could she possible have any idea how intriguing the air of mystery she insisted on maintaining made her? The evening had turned into something he had never intended. He found himself more than idly curious about her and had reached the conclusion that "one night on the town" was not nearly enough for them. "If I were to hazard a guess, I would say you were the foreman on a chain gang."

Lisa laughed aloud, a happy sound. "Do I come across that hard-nosed?"

"Hard-nosed isn't *exactly* the term I would have used."

"Oh? And what term would you have used?"

His gaze swept her face. "How does 'iron-willed enchantress' sound?"

She felt herself flush with both embarrassment and pleasure. "I don't know about the enchantress part, but I seem to recall the term 'iron-willed' being used once or twice in connection with my name."

The song ended and the announcer informed them that the next number would be the last of the evening. Lisa looked startled. "What time is it?"

Kevin pulled her back into his arms. "It should be about ten minutes before three."

"I had no idea it was so late."

"To be honest, neither did I."

They finished the dance in silence, neither knowing quite how to express the feeling of disappointment that the evening was nearly over. The implied agreement between them that their "date" was simply a friendly gesture and nothing more had put unexpected strictures on them. In the process they had created boundaries that neither was quite sure how to breach.

For Kevin it had been years since he had felt a desire that edged on necessity to see someone again. Not since Angela had a woman's smile made his heart quicken or her perfume made him feel light-headed. Although he had known from the beginning that the attraction he felt for Lisa was unusual for him, he was surprised that not only had it remained intact after getting to know her better, it had intensified.

The music ended, then the applause, and it was no longer possible to delay leaving. Kevin helped Lisa with her coat and they walked out into the bitingly cold night. The car was parked several blocks away and Kevin offered to walk there alone while Lisa waited in the warm lobby, but she refused his offer in favor of fresh air no matter how cold. Halfway to the car it began to rain, and in less than a minute the rain progressed from a gentle mist to a freezing downpour. This time Kevin insisted she wait for him, telling her he could get there much faster alone. He left her under an awning while he sprinted the two remaining blocks.

Lisa pulled her coat tighter around her as she stood against the building out of the wind. Thunder cracked in the distance, cars splashed through puddles in the street in front of her, and overhead the awning gave an ominous creak. She saw the headlights flash on Kevin's car and watched as he pulled into the street. Again the awning groaned beneath the heavy load of rainwater.

Kevin pulled up to the curb and reached across the seat to unlock her door. As she stood waiting for him, the canvas gave one last groan and broke loose from its moorings, dumping its contents on her. Had the accident been planned, she could not have been more precisely placed to receive the torrent. Instantly she was soaked through her coat and dress. The near-freezing water felt like cutting shards of ice as it reached her skin.

She caught her breath, unable to speak or move as she was robbed of her body heat. Finally the shock plunged her into a peculiar sort of numbness. At first she couldn't understand what had happened, then when she heard the awning slapping against the building, everything made sense.

Immediately Kevin jumped out of the car and came over to her. "Are you hurt?"

She slowly shook her head.

"Are you sure?"

This time she nodded, afraid if she unclamped her jaw she would be unable to stop her teeth from chattering. Kevin opened the car door and reached for her arm to help her inside. "I'll r-r-ruin your seat," she stammered, resisting him.

"For God's sake, Lisa, get in the car before you freeze to death out here on the sidewalk." The rain was beginning to turn to sleet as they stood there arguing.

She reached down to lift her coat and skirt so that she could step from the curb. Water oozed from the material and ran between her fingers. Again she hesitated, glancing back at Kevin. If she got in he would never be able to get the water stains out of the crushed-velvet upholstery.

Sensing the reason for her continuing reluctance, he took her elbow and forcefully guided her into the car. By the time he was back in the driver's seat, she had begun to shiver uncontrollably. He tried the heater but only made matters worse when a blast of cold air filled the car.

Lisa couldn't remember ever being so cold. Not even during the crazy tests she had taken while training to become an astronaut had she felt this miserable. And even though she wasn't absolutely sure where Georgetown was in relationship to her hotel and dry clothes, she was sure it wasn't close.

A few minutes later Kevin stopped the car in front of a group of Victorian houses. "W-w-why are w-we stopping here?" *And just when hot air had finally started to come out of the heater.*

"This is where I live."

"C-couldn't you show me some other t-t-time?"

The plaintive note in her voice brought a smile to his lips, overriding the seriousness of the situation. "We're not here for a visit, Lisa," he said. "I want to get you out of those clothes before you turn into a human icicle."

"Oh..." She sat quietly while she waited for him to come around to her side of the car but instantly recoiled when he opened the door and a great gust of cold air slammed into her.

"Come on," he urged. "Let's hurry up and get you inside."

By the time they made it into the foyer, Lisa was trembling so badly she could hardly stand. Kevin helped her take off her coat, then reached inside the hall closet and took out a sweater and wrapped it around her. It didn't help. He led her down the hallway into a room that contained a large oak desk, an old leather sofa and walls lined with books. "Wait here," he said, and disappeared.

When he returned he was carrying a bundle of clothes. "I'm sorry, but this was the best I could do. It's either these—" he showed her a pair of brown wool slacks and a long-sleeved flannel shirt "—or this." Draped across his other arm was a terry-cloth robe.

Lisa had only to remember the feel of wool on wet skin to make her reach for the robe.

"Turn around," he said. Automatically she obeyed. Without explanation he removed the sweater and unzipped her dress. The zipper ran the length of her back, stopping just above her buttocks. Besides exposing a great deal of skin, he found a tiny heart-shaped birthmark he bet few people knew she had. Taking her by the shoulders, he turned her around. "If you need any more help, call me. I'll be in the kitchen."

She clutched her dress tightly against her breasts to keep it from falling. "T-th-thanks."

"Don't mention it. Now hurry up and get into that robe."

She nodded.

Kevin closed the door behind him and headed for the kitchen to make coffee. After flinging his jacket and tie over the back of a chair, he scooped grounds into a filter and poured water into the top of the Mr. Coffee machine. As soon as the rich brown liquid began dripping into the glass pot he headed for the living room to get a bottle of whisky. By the time he returned, the air was filled with fragrant steam and Lisa was standing in the middle of the room holding her soggy dress. "Do you have a hanger I can put this on?"

He took the dress from her and gave her a startled frown. "How did you ever manage to move around in this thing? It must weigh as much as a suit of armor."

"It wasn't too bad before it got wet." A sudden shiver started her trembling again. Kevin laid the dress on the tile counter and reached in a drawer for a towel. He went over to her and vigorously began drying her hair, flipping the towel over before reaching for another. When he was satisfied her hair was as dry as he could get it, he ran his fingers through the short looping curls to fluff them and get them to finish drying faster. He then took her into his arms. "What are you doing?" she demanded, both surprised and confused by his actions.

"For crying out loud, Lisa, I'm not doing anything we haven't been doing all night. Now settle down and let me try to get you warm enough to stop shaking before you lose all of your teeth."

She held herself stiffly at first, feeling awkward in his embrace without music and a dance floor. But as soon as she began to feel his warmth penetrate the robe she started to relax. Finally, when she realized he had no intentions beyond friendly succoring, she let herself meld into the welcoming niche he provided with his arms and body, at last even laying her head against his chest. A tiny smile curved her lips as she listened to his heartbeat. Unless he had an unusually rapid heart rate he wasn't quite as uninvolved in what he was doing as he would have her believe.

Kevin too had a smile on his face as he felt her relax in his arms. Not wanting to make a move that she would misinterpret, he made none at all other than to rest his chin on the top of her head when she snuggled closer against him. Somehow she felt different than she had when they danced together. He tried to figure out why.

It was something more than the erotic yielding of her body now that she was free of all clothing save his robe. It was... "You've shrunk!"

She tilted her head back. "By three inches. Happens every time I take off those shoes."

He looked down at her bare feet. "It's not going to do any good to get the top of you warm if we don't do something about the bottom."

If she only knew him better, what a wonderful comeback she could give for that line. Instead she said, "My shoes are shot. They've danced their last dance."

Taking her hand, he led her from the kitchen to the living room, where he had started a fire. Once he had her ensconced in the corner of an overstuffed sofa with her feet tucked under the hem of the robe, he returned to the kitchen and fixed them both big mugs of Irish coffee. After making a quick detour to his upstairs bedroom, he headed back to Lisa. "Here, drink this," he said, handing her a mug.

Inhaling the potent-smelling steam, she grinned. "I thought you weren't supposed to drink alcohol when you were cold."

"You're not—if you happen to be stuck in the wilds. Special rules apply, however, when you're sitting in front of a fireplace and it's fairly certain that any danger of frostbite is over."

He delivered his lines in a deadpan manner that made Lisa laugh out loud. It wasn't often that she was bested so easily. She studied him over the rim of her cup. "Were you a towhead when you were little?"

"According to my mother and the baby pictures she claims are mine, I was so fair-haired it was hard to tell whether or not there was anything at all on top of my head." He adjusted the logs in the fire before coming over to sit next to her. "How did you guess?"

"There are still a lot of blond highlights in the brown."

"Probably from the time I spent outside this summer helping my father with the cattle."

"Is that something you do every summer?" It seemed an odd off-time job for a politician. She thought they were always on a campaign trail somewhere.

"It's something I *try* to do, but don't always succeed."

"Where is your parents' ranch?"

"Kansas." He took a pair of socks from his pocket and reached for Lisa's feet. Automatically she tugged them back. He chuckled. "You don't let go easily, do you? I don't think I've ever known anyone quite as distrustful as you are." He held one of the socks up by its toe. "See—no ulterior motive. All I wanted to do was help thaw those chunks of ice you've got under there."

She grinned sheepishly as she put her feet on his lap. "It isn't that *I'm* distrustful..."

"Oh?"

"It's that *you're* too damn sexy." Even though it was the truth, it wasn't what she had intended to say at all.

His hands hung suspended over her foot as if he was suddenly afraid to touch her. "Are you always so blunt?" he managed to ask.

She let out a heavy sigh. "Unfortunately, yes."

He thought for a moment. "Maybe not so unfortunately," he said slowly. "Bluntness can have its own appealing charm." He eased the woolen sock over her toes and heel.

"In children and very old men, maybe, but not in thirty-two-year-old women."

"Would it help if I told you I'm flattered by what you said?"

She took a sip of coffee. "It can't be the first time you've heard it."

For long seconds he stared at her. "What would you say if I told you that I think you are an incredibly beautiful woman?"

She felt a flush crawl up her neck. "Why...I...I, ah, I'd say you were a very discerning person."

"Nice try, but your red cheeks give you away. Now do you understand what I mean? I know I'm not the first person to tell you how beautiful you are, but I'm just as sure you don't always blush when someone does."

"Meaning?"

He smiled. "Who knows? Four in the morning is either too early or too late for me to solve the mysteries of life."

"I must still be operating on Houston time. I'm hardly tired."

"So you're from Houston. Is that where you met Mike and Caroline?"

"Mike and I go back a long ways...before he ever met Caroline. He used to date a friend of mine. She was totally unsuitable for him."

There was a pause in the conversation while they drank their coffee and stared into the fireplace. Finally Kevin broke the silence. "Is there anyone in Houston..." He left the question dangling.

"Are you asking me if there's a man in my life?"

"Yes..." He was still staring into the fire, his elbows on his knees, the cup of coffee cradled between his hands. As he waited for her to answer, he held his breath.

"Not right now there isn't," she said softly.

"But there was?"

His question was way beyond the rules they had set up for the evening. But then, the evening had changed. "A guy named Ross Stewart. We were engaged for quite a while before we realized marriage would never work for us. I just couldn't be the kind of wife he had decided he wanted." Slowly she ran her finger around the lip of the cup. "Before that—years ago when I was just out of college—I was engaged to a man named Eric Barker. We were almost to the altar when word came that I had been accepted for a job I wanted desperately. Eric didn't want to move to Houston—at least that's what he said. I really think it was the job he resented. The day before the wedding I made my choice— and it wasn't Eric." She smiled at the memory. "You wouldn't believe the uproar. It took weeks to return all the gifts." She looked up to see him looking at her. "Now that you know more than you ever wanted to know about my past affairs of the heart, what about yours?"

He turned away to stare at the fire. "I was married—a long time ago." He paused. "We had a daughter." Not since the accident had he willingly talked about Angela and Christine. "As for right this minute, there's no one I see steadily." He looked over to see her trying to stifle a yawn, and he set his cup on the table. "It's time to get you home."

"I'm sorry, Kevin," she said, another yawn overtaking her in midsentence. "I don't know whether it's that I'm finally warm again or that the whisky in the coffee is affecting me, but I'm suddenly so sleepy I can hardly stay awake." She started to get up, stopped and grinned. "This should prove interesting. It's going to take real panache to blithely walk through the lobby in this getup.''

"I have an overcoat you can use.''

"Oh, that should help...I can't see why anyone would look twice at a woman wearing a man's overcoat and argyle socks.''

His gaze quickly swept over her. "Lisa, men would look twice at you if you were wearing a Sherman tank.''

"Do you practice lines like that or do they come naturally?'' She stood and stretched, yawning. "I'll be back in a minute. I'm going to get the things I left in the other room.''

When she arrived at Kevin's study she took a second to look around before retrieving her shoes and purse. The shelves that lined the walls held richly bound leather law books. So Kevin was a lawyer as well as a politician. It made sense. Hadn't she read somewhere that the majority of congressmen were or had been lawyers? She turned to leave when a photograph sitting on an end table caught her eye. Walking across the room for a closer look she saw a younger, smiling Kevin standing next to a woman with dark expressive eyes and straight, shoulder-length auburn hair, parted in the middle. Between them, clinging to Kevin's leg, was a mischievous-looking child with a charm that radiated from the picture. Lisa stared at the threesome a moment longer. What had happened to destroy their apparent happiness?

She heard Kevin coming down the hall and turned to watch him enter. "Your daughter's beautiful,'' she said after he came over to stand beside her. "And so is your wife.''

"Yes, they were," he stated softly, then, as if the pensive moment had never occurred, he asked, "Are you ready?"

She wondered about his use of past tense but decided not to pursue it. "I just need to get my dress and coat."

"They're still soaking wet. Why don't you let me take them over to the Websters' sometime tomorrow when they're a little more manageable?"

"If you wouldn't mind..."

"It will help assuage my guilt for having you stand under the awning in the first place. Besides, you'll need someplace to leave my things where I can pick them up."

"That sounds perfect...." Everything was tied up in such a neat, complete and *final* bundle.

When they were at the front door, Kevin gave Lisa a pair of galoshes. They were so large she had to walk with a shuffling gait to keep from losing them, but they served their purpose and kept her feet dry on the way out to the car.

Later, at the hotel, Lisa insisted it was all right for Kevin to drop her off out front, but he insisted just as adamantly that he would accompany her to her room. He won out. Although her entrance didn't go unnoticed, there were few people in the lobby at five in the morning who paid them much attention. After a short elevator ride to the seventh floor and a long walk down a corridor, they were at Lisa's room. She opened the door and stepped inside, fully expecting Kevin to follow. He didn't. Instead he stood in the doorway and looked at her. "Lisa, I want to talk to you."

She turned and stared at him. "Okay, come in and—"

"I don't think that's such a good idea." He rubbed the light stubble on his chin. "I know we agreed that this was to be a one-night kind of thing, but I've suddenly discovered that I've changed my mind and I want to see you again."

She came back to stand in front of him. The long night had begun to show on him. His eyes were a little bloodshot, his crisply pleated white tuxedo shirt looked a little rumpled, he needed a shave, and his thick light-brown hair was on the windblown side. Yet all in all he looked enormously appealing. "I thought you would never ask," she said, her heart thumping heavily in her chest.

A slow smile curved his full lips and lighted his dark-blue eyes. It took every ounce of energy he had left not to reach out and take her in his arms. He looked at her lips and imagined their softness pressed against his own. "You really shouldn't leave Washington without seeing the monuments, you know. I give this incredible two-hour, twenty-monument tour that rivals any of the professionals."

She laughed. "Sounds wonderful. I'll bring my running shoes. What time?"

"Twelve?"

"Where—"

"In the lobby?"

"I'll be there."

To his surprise, his need to touch her had become a physical ache. If he didn't leave soon, he was going to do something about that ache that might ruin everything between them. "Tomorrow then..." He turned to go.

"Good night..." Lisa almost reached out to stop him, but instead of taking his arm, her hand closed around the doorknob. "What should I wear?" she called out softly as he moved down the hall.

He purposely looked at her from head to toe, then grinned. With his overcoat almost brushing the floor and his black galoshes peeking out from underneath, she looked like a forlorn waif. "It's going to be hard to top what you're wearing now...surprise me."

"Careful, Kevin. When I detect a challenge I've been known to do crazy things."

"Sounds exciting." More exciting than she could ever know. It was about time his life seemed worth living again.

CHAPTER THREE

ALTHOUGH LISA HAD SLEPT less than three hours, when she arrived at Mike and Caroline's home for breakfast the next morning she felt refreshed and more alive than she had since coming to Washington.

"I take it all went well with you and Kevin last night?" Caroline asked as she greeted Lisa at the front door and motioned for her to enter.

"In a manner of speaking," Lisa replied. Having an awning full of water dumped on her wasn't her idea of fun, but she couldn't fault the rest of the evening.

"I *knew* it," she said, sighing. "You and Kevin didn't hit it off, did you?"

"I'm surprised at you, Caroline," Lisa teased, picking up on her friend's disconsolate tone. "Do I look like the kind who would kiss and tell?"

Caroline took Lisa's coat and hung it in the closet. "I told Mike I thought it was a mistake for you and Kevin to go out with each other, but he insisted you would have a good time."

Lisa cocked her head to one side and stared at her. "I think you're serious about this."

"Come on with me. I'll explain while I finish squeezing the oranges."

Lisa followed Caroline down a short hallway into a large country kitchen where they found Mike standing behind a counter, testing a waffle iron with drops of water. He looked up at their entrance. "So how was the big night on the town?"

"We've already been over it," Caroline said. "I don't think she wants to go through it again."

"The evening wasn't as bad as Caroline makes it out to be. Actually I had a pretty good time."

Mike gave Caroline an I-told-you-so look as he made a circular sweep of batter across the waffle grids. He closed the lid with a flourish, wiped his hands on a towel and came around the counter to give Lisa a hug. "Don't go making anything sinister or secretive out of our interest," he warned good-naturedly. "It just so happens that you and Kevin are two of our favorite people—it's only natural that we'd be curious how things turned out now that you've finally met each other."

"Well...the date wasn't what I'd call 'typical,' but all in all I had a good time. I think Kevin did, too, or at least he seemed to. We're going to do the tourist thing later on today. He's meeting me at the hotel at noon."

Mike went back around the counter, pulled the waffle off the grids with a fork and plopped it onto a plate. "Without even trying, you've just made me feel like a first-class heel."

"I have?" Lisa said. "How?"

"I'm taking off in a few minutes to meet Cory Peters out at Andrews, and I had hoped to make up for my abandonment by taking you and Caroline to Loring Art Gallery for a reception they're having this afternoon."

"Don't worry about it." She breathed a mental sigh of relief that she would miss the reception. Mike's tastes in art leaned heavily toward the avant-garde while hers were strictly traditional. "What's Cory doing at Andrews?"

"He had a two-hour layover on his way back to Houston."

"How is he? Since he's been on that goodwill junket for NASA I haven't seen him or Ann for the past couple of months. It seems whenever I'm in Houston he's gone, and whenever I'm gone, he's there."

"I don't know how he is, that's why I'm running out on you this morning." Mike took the second waffle out and brought them over to the table. He removed the kitchen towel he had been using for an apron, gave Caroline a quick kiss and headed toward the door. "Thanks for being so understanding, Lisa. I'll make it up to you when we get to Houston. I'll let you baby-sit sometime."

She laughed. "No problem—say hello to Cory for me."

He turned his attention to Caroline, and his voice grew serious. "I want you to behave yourself while I'm gone. Leave everything and I'll clean up the mess as soon as I get back. *You* keep your feet up."

She blew him a kiss. "I promise. I won't do a thing."

When he had gone, Lisa rolled her eyes and whistled. "How long has he been like this?"

"Ever since our first visit to the doctor together. He's walked a fine line between worry and panic ever since." She added syrup to her buttered waffle. "As excited as Mike is about the babies, he's scared to death something's going to happen to me. It doesn't matter how often the doctor reassures him or tells him how beautifully I'm doing, he still fusses and fumes over the littlest things."

"Which means you're winding up taking care of him as well as yourself?"

"Not at all. He nags a little too much about putting my feet up, but I can tolerate that kind of nagging without too much difficulty."

Lisa looked at Caroline and slowly shook her head. "I can't conceive what it would be like to be expecting quintuplets."

Caroline paused a moment to think while she chewed a bite of waffle. "At times it's overwhelming...and intimidating...and more than a little frightening. The thought of having one child used to put me in a tailspin, sometimes five is almost more than I can handle. Mike keeps telling me that I'm going to make a wonderful mother, that I have enough love and nurturing in me for five more after these. Some days I believe him, others I'm racked with doubt. I feel there isn't a job in the world as important as being a parent, and yet it's always being filled by untrained people like me."

"I can't believe what I'm hearing. Could this possibly be the same Caroline Webster I know? You're letting five sweet little babies throw you when you've gone after interviews with Mafia chiefs and rebel leaders with the same fearless aplomb you'd have with a movie star?"

Caroline let out a sigh. "Let's move on to something else before you have me more terrified than I already am." She sipped her orange juice. "Tell me about your date. Where did you go?"

"Dancing until almost three and then to Kevin's house until around four. I was caught in a downpour and he took me there to dry off."

"What did you think of Kevin?"

"He's nice." She was reluctant to give her feelings voice. They were too new, like unmolded clay, substance without form. Besides, her feelings about him could easily change by that evening, after their monument tour. She was a little skeptical of the intensity of those feelings anyway. It seemed whenever she was bowled over by someone on a first meeting, something always happened to tarnish that impression when they met again. "Is he a close friend of yours?"

"Yes, he is...and has been for a long time. We grew up together in a tiny town in Kansas. We're even related, but not by blood. Whenever we were bored or had nothing else to do we tried to figure out exactly how the relationship worked, but because of all the marriages and divorces in both of our families, we were never absolutely sure we had it right. The best we could come up with was that we were either fourth or fifth cousins.

"For years—before we found out that boys and girls weren't supposed to be best friends—we were inseparable." Caroline leaned forward and absently began drawing tiny circles with her fork in the syrup on her plate. "By age, Kevin was supposed to be two years ahead of me in school, but academically he was four years ahead by the time he finished high school. He's the most intelligent person I've ever known, and he's suffered terribly because of that intelligence. When we were children, at family gatherings someone would invariably say something about Kevin's crackerjack mind and how he was going to do his parents proud one day. He hated that kind of attention and for a while thought he could hide how smart he was by failing school. He stumbled along that way until he found someone who was as bright as he was." She smiled at the memory. "When Angela moved to town and told him she equated intelligence with sexiness, he skipped two grades in less than a year. They went together through high school and college and were married a year after graduation.''

The photograph in Kevin's study flashed into Lisa's mind. ''By any chance did Angela have long auburn hair?''

''How did you know?''

''I saw a picture in Kevin's house. There was a child in the picture, also.''

''Christine. She turned four a week before the accident.''

''Accident?''

''Kevin didn't tell you?''

Lisa shook her head.

''Angela and Christine were killed in an automobile shortly before Kevin came to Washington the first time.''

Kevin's reference to them in the past tense suddenly made sense. ''How long ago did this happen?''

''Almost ten years.'' When Lisa made no comment, Caroline asked, ''What are you thinking?''

''I—'' The telephone rang, interrupting her answer.

''Darn it! There are times I would like to rip that thing out of the wall.'' Caroline struggled out of the chair and over to the phone. ''Hello. Yes...she's here. Just a moment, please.'' She turned to Lisa, a puzzled expression on her face. ''It's for you...sounds official.''

Lisa took the receiver. ''This is Lisa Malorey.''

''Lisa, this is Paul Kellogg. You're needed to copilot a launch at the Cape as soon as you can get down there.''

When Paul Kellogg had handled the astronaut emergency-training program for NASA he had been the coolest person in a crisis Lisa had ever seen. There must be something terribly wrong for him to show emotion now. Hearing the note of strain in his voice sent a chill down her spine. "What's happened, Paul?" she asked, purposely keeping her tone even.

"We've lost contact with the *Orion*."

She flinched. The *Orion* was the newest shuttle, a state-of-the-art piece of equipment that made the old shuttles look obsolete. She swallowed to try to clear the lump that had suddenly appeared in her throat. Publicly the men and women of NASA proudly pointed to the phenomenal safety record of the shuttle, privately they had all wondered when their luck would run out. There were simply too many launches now, too many orbiters in operation. The odds were bound to catch up with them sooner or later. "For crying out loud, give me some details, Paul. Don't leave it like that." The seven people aboard the *Orion* were more than colleagues; they were friends.

"I really don't have much more, Lisa. At least nothing that's going to make any of this go down easier. Cory Peters is being briefed while he's waiting for you to join him at Andrews. He'll fill you in on the details during the flight down here."

"All right, Paul." She knew it was useless to press him for further details now. "I'm on my way." The receiver felt as if it was made out of lead. Slowly, with effort, she placed it back on its hook.

"Lisa—" Caroline's voice sounded anxious "—is there something I can do?"

Lisa pressed her palms against the sides of her face, then raked her hands through her hair. She took a deep breath and turned to Caroline. "Can I borrow your car?"

"Certainly. I'll get the keys." She waited a moment before leaving, giving Lisa the opportunity to share the worry that burned in her eyes.

"There's trouble at the space station—they've lost contact with *Orion*." She said the words in a hushed tone. "Cory and I are handling the rescue." Silently she prayed there would be someone left for them to rescue.

Caroline's face paled. She nodded, started to speak, stopped, then left without saying a word. When she returned she had a brass key ring in one hand, Lisa's coat in the other. "Don't worry about the car. We'll pick it up later. If you see Mike at Andrews you can give him the keys, otherwise leave them in the flight commander's office."

"Thanks, Caroline." She took the keys and coat. "Would you draw me a map showing how to get from here to the base?"

Caroline sketched the quickest route on the back of an envelope, gave it to Lisa and walked with her out into the garage. "I'll keep my fingers crossed," she said, pressing the button to open the automatic door.

"And your toes. Something tells me we're going to need all the luck we can get." Lisa waved as she backed the car out of the garage. By the time she was on the street her thoughts were focused entirely on the seven men and women on the stranded shuttle.

She drove the first two blocks at a slow and sane speed in order to familiarize herself with Caroline's Mercedes. Then, as soon as she felt comfortable with the way the car handled, she headed down Massachusetts Avenue as quickly as her sanity and skill permitted. Less than an hour later she was in the flight room at Andrews suiting up to copilot the T-38 she and Cory Peters would fly to Florida. Pulling the last zipper of the flight suit up to her neck, she grabbed her helmet and left to make a phone call to Caroline before joining Cory and Mike. When she did join them, she found they were deep in conversation with a third man, whom she didn't recognize.

Cory acknowledged her presence by moving aside to make room for her. As soon as there was a break in the conversation he introduced her to Tyler Ramson, a friend of Mike's who had gone through the naval academy with him. They exchanged a few words before Lisa gave Mike the keys to Caroline's car and asked him if he and Tyler would mind excusing her and Cory for a minute.

Not waiting for an answer, she took Cory's elbow and steered him to a far corner of the room. She stuck her hands in her pockets and tilted her head back to look up at Cory, who stood nearly a foot taller. With his strawberry-blond hair, clear blue eyes and fair skin, he looked like the typical boy next door—Hollywood's idea of a best friend. He was well liked and respected throughout the agency, from the top brass to the men who polished the brass railings. Lisa wasn't in the least surprised that he had been chosen to be the commander for the rescue mission. He had been her friend and mentor as she went through the astronaut program, encouraging, prodding, sometimes even bullying her into being the best she could be.

"I'm sorry for dragging you away, but I didn't know whether or not to say anything in front of Mike's friend."

"That's all right. We were just swapping a few lies while we waited for you and the plane."

"Paul said you would fill me in—"

"He was a little optimistic."

"Meaning?"

"As far as I know they haven't been able to reestablish contact—" Before he had a chance to finish, a young black man in air-force blue stuck his head in the doorway.

"Your plane is ready, sir."

"Thank you," Cory replied. "Tell them we're on our way." He turned to Lisa. "Let's save the rest for later."

She stifled a frustrated groan and followed him over to say goodbye to Mike.

"Give Caroline my love," Cory said, taking Mike's hand. "And tell her that Ann has a two-page list of nannies for her to interview when she gets to Houston." He smiled, his eyes filled with the special warmth and affection of a friendship that had endured since childhood. "I swear she wasn't this excited when she was expecting herself."

Mike returned the smile. "It's a good thing you two are still in Houston. It was just about the only way I could convince Caroline to move back there with me." He turned to Lisa and caught her by the shoulders. After staring at her for long seconds, he gave her a hug and said, "Be careful up there."

She rolled her eyes and let out a groan. "How come you didn't say that to Cory?"

"Because every time I do, he gets mad at me."

Their laughter helped ease the underlying tension as Lisa and Cory left the building and headed for their plane. Once they were buckled inside the T-38, Cory in the pilot's position and Lisa directly behind him, it seemed only minutes before they were taxiing down the runway and were cleared for takeoff.

As soon as they gained altitude, Cory began filling Lisa in on the briefing he had been given about the stranded shuttle. "If you're asking me for my personal opinion," he said in answer to her continued prodding, "it doesn't sound good. But of course the official word is that we're to maintain optimism until we actually find out something different."

"I need details, Cory, not official posturing. I can take anything but not knowing. When Paul Kellogg called he was as taciturn as usual, so the only thing I know for sure is that one minute they had contact with *Orion*, the next it was gone."

"Then you just about know it all...there really isn't much more to tell. I swear I'm not trying to keep anything from you." She asked him to go over what he had already told her on the off chance he had left something out. Patiently he began again. "It seems the crew had finished work on the station for the day—I think they were doing the initial connection for the second laboratory—and they were all inside when the explosion occurred. Frank Jenkins was updating Houston on the day's progress when he was cut off in midsentence. So far the only good news we have is that the tracking stations that have reported on the *Orion* all indicate that it's still in one piece."

"What's the official word on why they're using us instead of the crew that's already at the Cape?"

"I've been told that the press releases will say it's because the *Challenger* crew is down with the flu. Personally I think it's because they didn't want to screw things up for the Consat Satellite the *Challenger* is supposed to take up with them next week. There are some powerful rear ends riding on that piece of hardware—not to mention all the media hype that's been going on. If we should fail, they'll at least be able to follow us up with a success."

"When did you become so cynical?"

"Two hours ago."

Cory was usually the cockeyed optimist. It was disconcerting to hear him say anything negative. "Who's been given the mission-specialist job?" The mission specialist would be the person who stayed on board the shuttle while she and Cory performed the actual rescue. Should anything go wrong while they were away from the ship, the specialist would be their lifeline.

"Howard Fitzsimmons."

"I've never flown with him. How is he?" She would have preferred one of the older, more experienced astronauts for a job like this.

"He's still a little green but incredibly coolheaded under pressure. That's probably why they picked him. He did a hell of a job recapturing and bringing in the Star Search Satellite last year."

As they lapsed into silence, drifting into their own thoughts, Lisa stared out at the dissipating cloud cover below them. Finally she was the one who broke their silence. "I have this queasy feeling that one of those forty thousand pieces of junk that is floating around up there has finally found itself a target." It wasn't the more than five thousand trackable pieces of old satellites, chunks of exploded rockets and miscellaneous debris that measured larger than a baseball and were detectable by radar that made the astronauts' blood run cold on sleepless nights. What they truly feared were the smaller bits and pieces created from the same sources, undetectable because of their small size, but capable of striking and destroying something thousands of times larger.

"My thoughts exactly," Cory answered, as much to himself as to her.

CHAPTER FOUR

KEVIN ARRIVED AT THE HOTEL to pick up Lisa fifteen minutes early. He contemplated calling her room, but as he headed for the house phone he decided against it, afraid he might seem too anxious. To kill time he wandered around the lobby, stopping to watch a little girl he judged to be about four years old who was trying to decide whether or not to continue eating a sucker she had dropped on the carpeting. After a hasty glance at her father, who was busy registering, hunger won out over cleanliness, and with a cursory brushing off, the candy found its way back into her mouth.

As always, whenever he saw a child who reminded him of his daughter, he felt an instant of profound sadness for what might have been. It had only been in the past few years that the sharpness of his sorrow had developed blunt edges, allowing him to remember Christine with a smile. He deeply welcomed the transition; it had been a long time coming. He sometimes wondered if the lessening of pain would have come sooner, the self-forgiveness been easier, without the solid, overwhelming feelings of guilt that had dogged him like a relentless, purposeful hunter.

Again he glanced at his watch, smiling at this unaccustomed anxiousness when he discovered there were still ten minutes to go. Brushing his tweed jacket aside to shove his hands into the pockets of his jeans, he strode toward the lobby restaurant, calculating how much time he could consume along with a cup of coffee. He went inside, requesting a seat beside a window so he could occupy his mind by watching the Saturday tourist traffic. But within seconds his eyes had glazed and he was once again thinking of Lisa.

Her dress still hadn't dried by the time he had been ready to leave that morning so he had left it behind, telling himself it was the logical thing to do, refusing to admit that he was hoping his actions had created a situation that would lead to her coming home with him again. He had liked having her there. She had filled the rooms with her presence; the place had seemed brighter, more like a real home. Perhaps it was the way she had been so completely at ease while curled up on his sofa, wearing only his robe and socks. But then again, it could have simply been that she was another person in a house unused to people. Whatever it was, he liked the way it felt to have her there and was curious to see if the feeling would return when she came again.

As soon as his watch indicated it was noon he left the table and his half-finished coffee and returned to the lobby. Every time the chime sounded indicating the elevator doors were about to open, his gaze swung up expectantly. An excruciating fifteen minutes later he was still watching and waiting. Finally, at twenty after twelve, he called her room. There wasn't any answer. He was on his way up to the seventh floor when he remembered that Lisa was supposed to spend the morning with the Websters. He returned to the lobby and called Mike and Caroline's number, one he knew better than his own. Caroline answered.

"This is Kevin, Caroline. By any chance is Lisa still there?"

"Oh, no!" she groaned. "I'm so sorry, Kevin. I got so wrapped up in watching the television coverage of the launch, I forgot to call you."

"Launch? What launch? And why were *you* supposed to call me?"

"Lisa telephoned from Andrews before she left and asked me to get in touch with you. She wanted me to tell you how sorry she was that she couldn't keep your date and to say that if you're ever in Houston, to please look her up."

"Andrews? Andrews Air Force Base? What was she doing out there?"

"Oh...I guess you wouldn't know if you've been at the hotel. Lisa is copiloting the shuttle they're sending up to rescue the astronauts at the space station."

"She's doing *what?*" Kevin struggled with the feeling that he and Caroline were conducting two separate conversations about entirely different people.

"Since I don't seem to be handling this very well over the phone, why don't you come over here. I'll start all over again while I'm fixing us some lunch."

"I'll be there in ten minutes. *Don't go anywhere.*" He replaced the receiver. Blindly staring at his fingers, which were still wrapped around the bright-red plastic, he said aloud, "She's an astronaut?" He sifted through the clues she had given him the night before, and gradually they came together like the converging boxes on a crossword puzzle.

As soon as Kevin arrived at the Websters' two-story brick house, Caroline was at the front door waiting for him. She had prepared for his arrival by fixing him a mug of coffee, which she held out in front of her as a peace offering. "I really am sorry that I forgot to call you, Kevin. Were you waiting at the hotel long?"

A smile twitched at the corners of his mouth as he took the coffee and inhaled the brandy-laced steam. "What is this? Something to soothe the savage beast?"

"Of course. When else do I give you this kind of attention?" She locked her arm in his and guided him into the family room, where the television was turned to the prelaunch coverage. Centered on the screen was the shuttle, pointing skyward atop its portable launchpad. A man's hushed voice described the tenseness of the officials surrounding him as they waited for astronauts Peters, Malorey and Fitzsimmons to appear.

Kevin moved toward the television, drawn by the mention of Lisa's name. Suddenly the picture changed, focusing on the figures of three people wearing high-top boots and one-piece fire-resistant flight suits. Kevin's gaze was immediately drawn to Lisa as she strode beside the much-longer-legged Peters and Fitzsimmons. They hesitated a moment to acknowledge someone offscreen. Lisa nodded once, turned and directly faced the camera. Kevin stared, captured by what he saw. The woman with the dancing, teasing eyes he had been with the night before had disappeared. In her place was an intense, somber-looking person who radiated an air of authority incongruous to her size. She acknowledged the assembled crowd before leaving the building behind a tall man in overalls. The astronauts went outside and boarded a van, which, the reporter announced, would carry them through numerous security checks before they reached the launchpad.

Kevin turned to Caroline. "What in the hell is going on?"

"All I know is what I've heard on the news and what I managed to get out of Mike when he called from Andrews, which isn't much. I expect him back here any time now—if they don't waylay him somewhere en route, that is. He should have more news by then."

The official version had been on the car radio as Kevin was driving over—just enough information to make it hard for him to remain outwardly calm. Despite assurances to the press that the agency was simply following prescribed procedures, Kevin knew that NASA would never send a shuttle up on a rescue mission without compelling cause. Such a grand gesture was too expensive, and sending a ship up out of turn would throw their civilian launch schedule into chaos. He lowered himself into the nearest chair and stared at the screen, mesmerized. "How long has Lisa been an astronaut?"

Caroline came over to sit beside him. "I'm not sure exactly, but it's been a few years less than Cory Peters. She came in with the group that followed Cory and Mike's."

He was having trouble trying to comprehend just who and what Lisa was. She had seemed so wonderfully ordinary the night before. And now..."Why didn't I recognize her?" He wasn't aware that he had spoken until Caroline answered him.

"Only the original women astronauts gained any real attention from the press. For a while, when Lisa first joined the program, she was a darling of the newspaper and magazine people. But the attention made her so uncomfortable she talked NASA into allowing her to keep a lower profile. She likes being able to walk down the street or to go into a restaurant in relative anonymity. The only reason she ever agreed to come up here to testify was as a favor to Mike."

"Testify?" The waters grew muddier.

"At the Senate Budget Committee hearing on whether or not to increase the funding for the space station."

"And how did it go?"

Caroline's eyes sparkled. "The funding?" she asked mischievously.

Kevin glared at her. "You're enjoying seeing me like this, aren't you?"

"I'm sorry, Kevin—I couldn't resist. I promise I'll behave. I didn't attend the hearings, but according to Mike, Lisa did a superb job. He said she was just the right combination for a partisan witness—articulate yet impassioned. Now if you were to listen to Lisa relate the story, I'm sure she would tell you that she was a tongue-tied idiot who managed to single-handedly destroy any chance the agency ever had for additional funding." Caroline paused and studied Kevin. "You do realize, don't you, that there's absolutely no way I can control myself on this. I have to say something about the keen interest you're showing in Lisa."

Kevin let out a long sigh. "I'm only surprised you didn't quiz me before you let me come inside."

"Well?"

"You're the only person I know who manages to hear wedding bells after one date."

"One and a half. And if Lisa hadn't taken off, it would have been two. When was the last time you arranged to see the same woman two times in as many days? And besides, I didn't say one word about weddings or bells." She grew serious as she reached for his hand, the playful look disappearing from her eyes. "I know what you do and who you see is none of my business, but I simply can't help worrying about you. It's ingrained. You're the second neatest guy in my life right now. Believe me, Kevin, I know what you're doing to yourself. After my divorce I spent years trying to convince myself that my life would be better if I lived it alone. And then Mike came along. Even after he proved to me that I was wrong about living alone, I couldn't give in to him. In my stubbornness I almost missed what I have now. I was like a barren desert. When Mike arrived he brought canals full of water into my life.'' She laughed at the floweriness of her words and lightly touched her stomach. "Not to mention other more obvious results of our coming together.''

"All right, all right,'' he begrudgingly admitted. "I like the woman. But for God's sake, Caroline, I've known her less than twenty-four hours. Let's not get carried away.''

She grinned. "Me? Get carried away? Perish the thought.'' Squeezing his hand, she added, "Come on in the kitchen and keep me company while I fix us some lunch. Now that I'm feeding six I've become a human garbage disposal. If it smells, looks or even crawls by me in an appetizing manner, I eat it.''

Kevin laughed and leaned over to give her a kiss on the forehead. "I'll be there in a minute.'' He couldn't leave the television just yet. He had been to the Cape to watch launches before, as a guest of Mike's and twice as the guest of one of NASA's primary subcontractors headquartered in Kansas. Each time the spectacle had been as awesome as the time before, taking his breath away with its bigger-than-life kind of show. This time, however, a new emotional dimension had been added. Never before had he personally known anyone who was making the flight. Even if he had, he doubted he would have felt the way he did now. The lump that filled his throat, the queasiness in his stomach were decidedly different from anything he had experienced before.

LISA STEPPED OUT of the van and waited for the technicians who were to escort them to the elevators in the service tower. She took a deep breath and shifted from one foot to the other, anxious to get going. Finally they were in the slow-moving elevator and out again at level 195, where they crossed the steel-grated catwalk into the room abutting the open hatch of the shuttle. The technicians who awaited them immediately went to work securing the vestlike escape harnesses that would be used to snatch them out of the orbiter in case of an explosion or fire. Once they were hooked up they crawled through the forty-inch-wide hatch door and across the middeck back wall, which, because of the orbiter's nose-up position, had become their temporary floor. After maneuvering through the deck opening and twisting to reach the special hand and footholds put there to help them enter, she and Cory jockeyed themselves into the commander and pilot's seats. Howard sat directly behind them in a temporary seat that would fold back into the wall when they were in orbit.

Once their helmets were in place, the only way to communicate with the technicians who had entered to help secure them to their seats was through the headsets plugged into the ship's intercom. Normally they would have exchanged lighthearted bantering about everything from the World Series to skirt lengths. Today a tense silence hung in the air like undischarged lightning. When the final adjustments were completed, the technicians unplugged their verbal links, gave the astronauts a sober, thumbs-up signal and left.

Lisa paused a moment to listen to the sounds surrounding her before reaching for the Velcro-backed cue cards from the flight-data file. All around her the ship hissed and groaned in preparation for flight. The noises were the comforting, normal ones created by the supercold, liquid cryogenic hydrogen and oxygen that had already been pumped into the huge external tank attached to the orbiter's belly.

The methodical countdown they would have gone through under other circumstances had been accelerated wherever possible in order to take advantage of a three-minute "launch window," hastily determined by the position of the earth, sun, space station and their desired return time.

After attaching the flight cue cards to their matching strips of Velcro on the instrument panel, Lisa turned to Cory. "Did you have a chance to phone Ann again before we left?" She knew he had been concerned about reaching her, not wanting her to learn the news of the flight from someone else.

He nodded. "She still wasn't home. I left another message on the answering machine, this time telling her to contact Mike if she didn't get back in time to return my call."

"She probably decided to do some shopping in Dallas before heading home."

"That's what I figured. Especially when I couldn't reach her at her mother's, either. What about you, Howard?" Cory asked. "Did you ever get in touch with Susan?"

"Yeah, finally. She was playing tennis."

Although he was a year older than she was, Lisa thought of Howard as younger—probably, she reasoned, because he had come into the training program three years after she had, plus the fact that Howard's round face and dimples made him look eighteen. They hadn't crossed paths very often even after the shuttle launches had started operating on the frequency of early predictions, and they had never flown together, which was unusual nowadays. With added flights to take up the hardware to build the space station, the astronauts no longer had to vie for the chance to fly as they did for so many years. Now they were kept busier than any of them had ever dreamed.

The familiar, disembodied voice of Ray Huffstead came over the intercom. While they were on the pad, Ray was their human link to launch control. Known to every astronaut for his wry sense of humor when off duty, he was all business on the air. "*Discovery*, this is launch control. Radio check, over."

The prelaunch work had begun for Cory and Lisa. For the next twenty minutes they would be kept busy checking and rechecking instruments with both launch control at the Cape and mission control in Houston. At T-minus one hour and ten minutes, Ray announced, "*Discovery*, this is control. Side hatch is secure."

They were now physically closed off from the outside world. Cory answered, "Roger, we copy." He checked the cabin pressure and found it in the normal range. Lisa went through the preflight alignment and confirmed the figures with control. Then, as if there had been no interruption in their previous discussion, she continued questioning Cory. "Do you think having a family, with its inherent responsibilities, makes being an astronaut harder on you?"

Cory glanced up at her from the instrument panel, his eyebrows drawn together in a puzzled frown. "What in the world made you ask something like that?"

She shrugged, purposely affecting nonchalance. "No particular reason. I was just thinking about the families of the crew stuck up there at the station and one thing led to another." She reached overhead to flip a series of switches off, then on again. "It seems to me if you knew there were people dependent on you, either financially or emotionally, it might color the way you did things. Maybe you'd be thinking about them when you should be concentrating on the job."

"Is that why you've never married?"

"I've never really thought about it before, but I suppose fear of being mentally or emotionally encumbered could be one of the reasons."

"Well, I've had it both ways," Howard interjected. "And as far as I'm concerned, there's no comparison. I wouldn't go back to being a 'carefree' bachelor for all the phone numbers of the Dallas Cowboy's cheerleaders."

Again Ray Huffstead's voice broke in. "*Discovery*, this is control. Ground crew is secure."

"Roger," Lisa answered. Now that the ground crew had safely retired to the fallback area, she, Cory and Howard were alone on the pad. This was the time in every launch that sent a shiver of excitement through Lisa. More than anything else, the withdrawal of personnel was a signal to her that flight was imminent.

"To answer your question, Lisa," Cory said, "no, I don't believe having a family makes my work more difficult. If anything, I think Ann and the kids make it easier. Not to mention that every time I've had the urge to listen to people who 'ooh' and 'ahh' over how wonderful I am because I'm an astronaut, the kids bring me back to earth with lightning speed." He grinned at her. "Pardon the pun."

"But don't you worry about them worrying about you?"

"I'm probably more concerned about Ann being late getting back from Dallas than she is about me taking this flight. After my appendix ruptured during my first flight and I managed to survive, she said she finally became convinced I was invincible and she was never going to lose another night's sleep because I was off somewhere doing my thing."

Lisa had no doubt Ann had told Cory she was through worrying, but she was just as sure that in private, Ann was glued to the television watching and waiting for news every time Cory flew.

KEVIN PUNCHED THE BUTTONS on the remote control, switching back and forth between the two stations that were covering the launch. He had left Caroline right after consuming the tuna-salad sandwich she had prepared, telling her he had work waiting for him at his office. He had truly intended to go there or at least that was what he told himself all the way to Georgetown. But the instant he had turned on the radio and caught the tail end of what was now no more than rehashed news about the shuttle, he headed for home and the small comfort of being able to see the launch instead of simply hearing about it.

Once home he had given up all pretense of being only mildly interested and had gone straight to the television. Still wearing his jacket, he sat on the edge of the chair, his elbows on his knees, his hands locked around the tuner, waiting and watching as the time for lift-off shortened to minutes.

"DISCOVERY, THIS IS CONTROL. H-two tank pressurization okay. You are go for launch, over."

Lisa answered. "Roger, control. We read you. It is a go for launch." She took a deep breath and settled back against the seat. Less than two minutes and they would be on their way. Again she scanned the instruments that surrounded her, taking comfort, reassurance, in their familiarity. T-minus twenty-five seconds and counting, she mentally recited, following the countdown with an internal clock, honed through dozens of launches.

"*Discovery*, this is control. You are on your on-board computer, over."

"Roger," Cory replied, acknowledging the information that the shuttle was now in control of the launch.

When it was T-minus eight seconds, thousands of gallons of water were released to fill a depression at the pad's base. The water was used to dampen the sound energy from the engine, protecting the shuttle's wings and tail from possible reverberation damage.

At T-minus five seconds, valves opened to allow the liquid hydrogen and oxygen oxidizer into the three main engines. The liquids became gases, were compressed, mixed and then ignited. There was an enormous roaring noise and the sudden feeling of motion as the ship lurched nearly two feet laterally, toward the main fuel tank in reaction to the initial ignition. At T-minus two seconds, the orbiter's computers checked and confirmed that the engines had reached proper pressure and thrust, the nose returned to its correct position, the powdered aluminum side tanks were ignited, and with enough power to light up the entire east coast of the United States, the shuttle left its pad.

Eleven seconds into the flight, still trailing spectacular six-hundred-foot-long flames, the astronauts began the roll maneuver that would put them in a heads-down position. At thirty seconds the roll was complete and they were far enough into space that the blue sky had turned a deep black. Lisa stared at the instrument panel as all around her the ship vibrated. She felt the shuddering deep in her bones, and despite her protective helmet the noise became ear shattering.

At fifty seconds and seven hundred miles per hour, the engines were throttled back to protect the shuttle's wings, tail and windshield from damage by the increasing air pressure. As soon as the air thinned sufficiently, the engines were increased to full thrust. Only a minute later they were traveling three thousand miles per hour.

At two minutes from launch and twenty-eight miles above the earth, the solid rocket boosters were exhausted. Small explosive charges separated them from the main tank, allowing them to free-fall until they were four miles above the Atlantic Ocean. At that point parachutes were deployed, slowing their descent and allowing the tanks to be recovered for future use.

With the solid booster rockets gone, the flight became noticeably quieter and smoother. It stayed that way for almost five minutes more until the ship began a shallow dive in preparation for main engine shutoff and the orbiter's separation from the remaining tank. When they were into the dive, at Cory's instruction, the computers shut down the main engines.

At the cessation of power Lisa felt herself more forward against the restraining straps. She waited the sixteen seconds for the sounds of the tank being jettisoned and the engagement of the two smaller maneuvering system engines that would take them the final distance to their orbital rendezvous. At forty-five minutes from launch and half a world away from the marshy grasslands of Florida's Cape Canaveral, the shuttle reached orbit.

KEVIN HAD GIVEN UP sitting in front of the television and had gone into the study to go over the revisions of the new Wild and Scenic River Bill that would be coming up for a vote in the Senate at the end of the following week. Despite repeated attempts to concentrate, his mind kept wandering back to Lisa. Finally he gave up all pretense of work and reached for the phone. Mike answered after the first ring.

"You're just the person I wanted to talk to," Kevin said. "What do you know about this shuttle rescue thing that I don't?"

"Right now, not much. The official stance is one of hopeful expectations. Privately, everybody I've been in touch with sounds pretty grim."

"How dangerous..." His voice trailed off.

"Is it for Lisa?" Mike finished for him.

Kevin was confused to find how intensely he cared. His feelings went far beyond the concern he would normally have had and were way out of proportion to the degree of involvement between himself and Lisa. Granted, she was interesting and beautiful and a lot of fun to be with, but none of it added up to the gut-wrenching anxiety he was experiencing. "I guess that's what I wanted to know," he answered.

"The flight itself isn't any more dangerous than any other. The actual rescue and how dangerous it is will depend on what they find when they get there." He paused. "I'm sorry, Kevin. I realize that's not much help." Mike wished he could give Kevin the easy answers he sought. A sense of guilt for having indirectly arranged the introduction between Lisa and Kevin had surfaced that morning and despite repeated efforts had refused to go away.

They were both exceptional people, alike in many ways, destructively opposite in others. For a long time Kevin had needed someone to share his life with again, but Mike had grave doubts that the someone he needed was Lisa. She was not by nature a subdued, loving companion. She was volatile, passionate and aggressive—the necessary qualities for a woman in a male-dominated field, but not highly recommended attributes for a politician's wife. Especially not a politician being groomed for the presidency. But the differences in their personalities didn't really bother Mike; what bothered him was the effect Lisa's job would have on Kevin. After losing Angela, would he be able to handle the inherent dangers Lisa faced with a job like hers?

Mike shook his head. Caroline's runaway romanticism was obviously contagious. What in the world had made him think Kevin's interest was ever going to reach the point where their conflicting personalities and careers would make any difference? But he could see that trying to make his worries disappear wasn't going to work. He was concerned because he could see himself in Kevin, could hear the catch in his voice and knew how hard someone could fall for another person after the most cursory meeting. How long had it taken him to realize he was in love with Caroline? He smiled at the memory. All of three hours. Kevin and Lisa had had an entire evening.

"Mike?"

"What...I'm sorry, Kevin, I was thinking about something else. What did you ask me?"

"How long do you figure the rescue will take?"

"Again, it depends on what they find. If it's just a matter of transferring the crew from the *Orion* to the *Discovery*, they should be home by tomorrow. If there are...complications, they won't be back until late Tuesday. That is, if they still plan to land at the Cape. They could land in California or New Mexico and come in just about anytime."

"When will you know for sure?"

"Four, maybe five hours from now. They should be reaching *Orion* in approximately forty-five minutes, give or take."

"Call if you hear anything."

"I'll do that." Mike's voice lowered and became softer. "Why don't you come over here and wait with us? It might be easier on you."

"Are you hinting that I'm acting a little crazy about all this?"

"No...at least 'crazy' isn't the word I would have used."

Kevin didn't have to ask what word Mike had in mind. Nor did he have the energy to tell him he was wrong. It was obvious that some of Caroline's wishful thinking had rubbed off on him. Kevin was only surprised that such fanciful ideas had infected someone who was usually as levelheaded as Mike. "Thanks for the offer, but I have a ton of work that needs doing around here."

"Should you change your mind, don't bother calling. Just come on over."

Kevin said goodbye and hung up. Fleetingly he wondered who he was trying harder to convince with his supposed casualness, himself or Mike.

CHAPTER FIVE

LISA PAUSED on her way to the lower deck to look out the window again at the *Orion*. She breathed another mental sigh of relief at the sight. Nowhere within her field of vision was there any sign of damage.

Cory came up beside her. "It's hard to believe there's anything wrong over there," he said.

"I wish we were in a position to see the front and left side better."

"I know...I've been thinking the same thing. When we arrived I even imagined I saw someone signaling to us through the cargo-bay windows."

"There aren't too many people I would admit this to, but I'm not overly anxious to open that hatch."

He gave her a commiserating smile. "Come on, it's time to get dressed."

Howard started to say something, stopped and tried again. "Good luck," he finally, simply stated.

Cory touched Howard's shoulder as he passed. "Thanks—I hope we don't need it."

Lisa followed Cory into the locker area, where they removed their coveralls and replaced them with liquid cooling and ventilation garments—special underwear worn with space suits, designed to keep the body at a comfortable temperature by integrating a series of water-filled tubes into the material. As soon as they were both dressed they went into the air lock. Cory checked the life-support system and closed the entry hatch.

Mounted on a pipe frame on the air-lock wall were two space suits. The one-size-fits-all garments were a vast improvement over the custom-made types first used in the space program. Where it had once taken a half hour and an assistant to get dressed, it now took each of them only five minutes working alone.

Once they were suited up they began the three-hour prebreathing period, inhaling pure oxygen to eliminate nitrogen from their blood and prevent what was known as bends to deep-sea divers. While they waited, Cory and Lisa went over the plans for the rescue, detailing even the most minor points, trying to include every possible scenario. At Lisa's request they bypassed the short nap they would have taken under normal circumstances and spent the time going over the rescue procedure once again.

Finally it was time to leave. The air lock was vented into space, the handle released and the outer hatch opened. The sound of metal striking metal was followed by a hiss as the remaining air escaped, but otherwise there was silence. Before leaving the air lock they reached outside to grab and hook the ship's thin tethers to rings on their suits. As soon as these lifelines were connected, they floated through the hatch into the open cargo bay and worked their way over to the manned maneuvering units.

After attaching the hard-shelled torso of her space suit to the unit, Lisa released the tether, unclamped the unit from the bay's wall and propelled herself away from the ship to wait for Cory.

She had left the relative safety of a spacecraft more than a dozen times before; each occasion was different and yet the same. Always there was a sweeping sense of exhilaration, tinged with an instant of bone-deep fear. Leaving the only ride home to float freely in the vastness of space required supreme confidence or sheer idiocy, depending upon who was asked.

To keep herself from dwelling on what they might find when they entered the *Orion,* Lisa filled her mind with other things. Purposely she concentrated on the reddish-brown outline of upper Africa, trying to place each of the nations and pinpoint its cities. Rarely did an opportunity like this one come along, and she told herself she should take advantage of the peaceful moment. Usually there wasn't enough time during a flight for such fanciful imaginings.

For years, with each launch, the yearning for a period in space free from experiments or duty had become a little stronger. She longed for time alone with her thoughts—to dream, to contemplate or simply to stare out a window at the wondrous sight of a new day dawning on the earth below. But there were rarely enough hours to get the scheduled work finished. It was a scene out of a black comedy that allowed her the time today. Perhaps in the future leisure hours would be alloted to space workers as they were to workers on earth. Maybe for those assigned to the space station. Again, as it did every time she thought about the personnel assignments to the station, she felt an intense longing to be one of those chosen.

Cory came up beside her. "Ready?"

She nodded.

"Let's go then."

For the first time Lisa heard a hint of hesitancy in Cory's voice. She stared at him, his face clearly visible through the large plastic half bubble. *He was as fright-*

ened as she was about what they might find. The realization hit like a bucket of cold water.

Cory's gaze shifted to the *Orion*. He fired one of the jets on his pack and moved in front of her; she immediately followed, gently landing in the *Orion*'s cargo bay beside him. After securing themselves to tethered lines and removing their manned maneuvering units, they hand-walked over to the hatch door. As Lisa reached for the handle, she and Cory exchanged meaningful glances. Silently she said a prayer.

KEVIN PACED THE NARROW PATHWAY between the overstuffed chair in front of the television and the room's lone window. He paused to draw the curtain aside and stare out into the leaf-littered backyard. His gaze swung skyward, as if he might somehow magically be able to see the shuttle.

It would soon be dark. Illogically the thought made him feel even more isolated from what was happening those relatively few miles overhead. He had given up trying to understand his runaway emotions. A lifetime of nurtured logic had abandoned him, leaving turmoil in its wake. He jammed his hands in his pockets; his eyes narrowed in thought. What in the hell was the matter with him? Where was the fearless, outspoken decisive senator from Kansas, the one who reporters liked to say knew precisely where he was going and what he was going to do when he got there?

The question jolted him into action. Stopping only long enough to turn off the television set, Kevin left the room. On his way out the front door he picked up his coat from the hall closet. Less than an hour later he was at the airport boarding a plane for Florida.

LISA TURNED the *Orion*'s hatch handle. First came the familiar clanging sound of metal on metal, then the hiss of air escaping. *Air!* If there was air on board...

"Don't get your hopes up," Cory said softly, reading her thoughts.

The surge of hope was instantly contained when she looked inside and saw that the air lock was completely black, lacking even the reassuring glow from the prototype instrument panel, new to the *Orion*. Lisa reached for her flashlight. The narrow beam created a tunnel of brightness, which she quickly passed back and forth in the small room. "The suits are gone," she told Cory, and again her heart leaped against her chest.

"Thank God," he answered.

They entered the air lock and removed their tethers before closing the hatch. Lisa turned the light on the gauges that would indicate whether or not it was safe for them to open the hatch leading into the ship. She wasn't surprised to discover they weren't working.

"We can't stop now," Cory said, giving her a nudge toward the door that lead into the main section of the middeck. "Go for it."

"Here, hold the light." She took a deep breath and reached for the handle. Before she had a chance to do anything to the door it swung open, pulling her into the cabin. The forward motion catapulted her into the welcoming arms of Frank Jenkins. Cory scrambled through, bumping into her and Frank like a wayward bowling ball. They rolled over each other in the freedom of weightlessness, a mixture of arms and legs, laughter and tears. Finally Lisa found a handhold and stopped their wild ride. The flashlight moved past her, its beam sweeping the ceiling. She reached out and caught it as it bounced off the wall in front of her.

Immediately she swung the light around the cabin, going from face to face, saying the names of the *Orion*'s crew members out loud in a joyous recital. She had never been so happy to see a group of people in her life. Their shoulders were slumped in exhaustion, eyes shadowed with fatigue, but their indomitable spirits— an attitude, an asset, as integral as any other requirement to become an astronaut—still shone through.

For all the relief, elation and welcome on their faces, the reunion was silent as the seven men and women continued to breathe oxygen through tubes attached to portable emergency packs in preparation for the transfer to *Discovery*.

Rather than straining to be heard through her helmet, Lisa pointed to her wrist and then to Frank's air pack. He held up three fingers to indicate they had been on oxygen the necessary hours, then made a circle with his thumb and index finger, telling her they were ready to leave. Lisa smiled. They had obviously been watching for *Discovery*'s arrival.

"Commander Peters—" Howard Fitzsimmons's voice broke the emotional silence "—this is *Discovery*. I have a request from Houston Control for an update on the rescue operation."

Lisa glanced over to Cory. It was only then that she realized that they had not shared the good news.

"Roger, *Discovery*," Cory said, stopping to clear the catch in his voice. "Tell Houston…" A broad smile illuminated his face. "Tell them there will be seven more for dinner."

KEVIN SHOULDERED HIS WAY THROUGH a line of reporters, greeting those who recognized him with a smile and quick assurance that he knew no more about the rescue than they did. When he finally reached the guard at the gate that led to the welcoming delegation, he felt as if he had completed an obstacle course in military basic training.

He glanced at his watch. *Discovery* was to arrive in less than half an hour. The mood of the crowd was Fourth of July and Christmas rolled into one. They had been given a present and a reason for celebration and were giving full reign to their enthusiasm. Red carpets were ready, flags were flying, a large platform with red, white and blue bunting lavishly draped across the front and sides had been put together with remarkable speed. A military band played patriotic tunes to the delight of the civilian crowd, and even though the landing was now still a good twenty minutes away, the majority of the spectators were scanning the sky in hopes of being the first to spot the shuttle.

The closer the time came for the landing, the stronger Kevin's doubts grew about the wisdom of being there to meet Lisa. Now that the danger had passed, the intensity of his feelings had diminished proportionately, leaving him wondering if he had made the right decision to come to Florida. Lisa was the first woman he had pursued this way in ten years. He had gone out with dozens of women and counted many women among his friends, but not one had produced this kind of feeling in him. He was rusty—no, it was more than rust that he felt shaking his confidence, it was fear. Did he really want this to happen now? His life was in order, had settled into a routine...was uncomplicated.

He wondered if it was possible his behavior would seem threatening, presumptuous to someone who obviously valued her freedom as much as Lisa did.

Dammit! He wasn't used to feelings of self-doubt; he sure as hell didn't need them now.

If he were to give in to his gut feelings, he would simply walk across the runway, take Lisa in his arms and let the agony he had known for the past twenty-four hours melt away with the warmth of their embrace. A disparaging smile twisted his mouth. He could just imagine what her reaction would be to his brash behavior...she'd start running and never look back.

He crossed the narrow strip of asphalt between the gate and the reception area. As a member of Congress he had been invited to join the other dignitaries who had flown in for the occasion on the stand. He walked over to the platform, shook a few hands and exchanged the standard greetings before quietly working his way to the back of the crowd, where he could watch the landing in relative privacy.

A short time later he heard a shout. "There it is." Using his hand to shield his eyes from the sun, he scanned the sky. A lump filled his throat when he caught sight of *Discovery* as it glided past the single puff of white cloud in a field of blue. The moment was imbued with misty-eyed magic. It was a morning of heroes and heroines and good guys coming in first.

A spontaneous cheer greeted the landing and then another when the shuttle door opened and Frank Jenkins appeared, his ear-to-ear grin visible all the way across the field as he exuberantly waved his arms. Kevin's gaze locked on the open cockpit door, seeking a woman with a slight frame and short blond hair. She was the last one to leave, not coming out until the others were on the ground, almost as if she was reluctant to come out at all.

Kevin's breath caught in his throat. A slow private smile moved from his lips to his eyes. God, he was glad to see her.

Lisa glanced at the jubilant crowd as she hesitated at the top of the stairs. She would rather go through the entire flight over again than face the people and the ceremony awaiting them on the platform at the edge of the runway. She closed her eyes, gulped a lungful of air, reminded herself that this, too, was a part of her job and joined the others, a broad, seemingly genuine smile in place, an enthusiastic step to her walk.

Fortunately the ceremony was kept brief—three speeches of welcome, including one that introduced the rescuers and rescuees and one that dashed all of Lisa's hopes for a quick return to anonymity. The governor of Florida expansively announced an official gala to be held the next day at the White House, followed the day after that by an old-fashioned ticker-tape parade in New York City.

Lisa gently nudged Cory. Looking straight ahead, her lips barely moving, she said, "I have a terrible headache, my throat is sore and my stomach is churning. I'm absolutely positive I'm coming down with some kind of flu. There's no way—"

"It won't work, Lisa," he replied, acknowledging his reintroduction to the crowd with a jaunty wave while surreptitiously continuing to talk to her. "The only way you're going to get out of going on this trip is if you die."

She heard her name announced, followed by loud cheering, and passionately wished she could short circuit the microphone.

"That's the spirit. Now smile and wave and pretend you're enjoying yourself. Just remember..." His voice trailed off.

Lisa glanced up to see what had distracted him. She was taken aback by what she saw. His face was suffused with a loving glow that made her feel as if she had intruded on an exceedingly intimate exchange between Cory and someone in the audience. She followed his gaze to a small group of people standing to the left of the platform and discovered Ann, Cory's wife. She had come all the way to Florida to welcome him home. She sent him a look of love that left little to the imagination. Remembering her question of the day before, Lisa smiled. Even if Ann was ever to cause Cory concern or make his job more difficult, the pluses of their relationship obviously far outweighed the negatives. She had made his homecoming truly special.

Suddenly, uninvited, an image of Kevin appeared in her mind. She shoved it aside. The last thing she needed was someone complicating her life. Just because home and hearth were good for Cory didn't mean they were good for her, too.

Finally the speeches ended. Next came the obligatory posing and smiling for the press, then the blessed shelter of the hangar where the astronauts' families had been taken for their one-on-one reunions in a semblance of privacy. Although she was exhausted and had no one in the hangar waiting for her, Lisa went with the others as a matter of form. She graciously accepted the gratitude and well-wishes of husbands and wives while fighting the urge to insist she had done nothing heroic or unusual and didn't deserve the attention.

As soon as she felt she could leave without being noticed, she headed for the exit, seeking what she knew would be one of the last opportunities for privacy that would come her way for several days. Telling the guard she had to use the bathroom and, if anyone should inquire, she would return shortly, she slipped out a side door and started down a long hallway. Before she had gone a quarter of the way, someone turned the corner in front of her and began walking toward her. She stopped and stared in surprise.

"Lisa?"

It wasn't an illusion. Kevin Anderson was really standing in front of her, not ten feet away.

Kevin hadn't meant to run into her this way. He had left the platform after seeing how hesitantly she accepted the accolades of the crowd, not wanting to make her homecoming any more difficult than it already seemed to be. Now, seeing the stunned look on her face, he wondered if it wouldn't have been wiser if he had disappeared all together.

"What...are you doing here?" she managed to say at last, inordinately pleased to see him.

He tried to think up a convincing lie, but none came to him. He shrugged. "It was easier than waiting at home."

She felt like butter dropped in a hot skillet. "I'm glad," she answered honestly. He looked as if the day since she had seen him last had been hard on him. Although he was now clean-shaven and his hair had been freshly combed, his eyes were even heavier with fatigue than when he had left her at the hotel.

"I'm glad you're glad. Frankly I was a little worried about the reception I might receive." A *little* worried was a gross understatement.

She gave him a puzzled frown. "I don't—"

"Is there somewhere around here we can go to talk?"

Lisa hesitated, listening to the commotion behind her. From the laughter and celebration she could still hear, she judged it would be awhile yet before she was missed and anyone would start looking for her. "How does a cup of coffee sound? You look like you could use one."

"You're right. But then, so do you."

She gave him a tired smile, walked up beside him and took his arm. "I haven't had much sleep lately. First I had this wild date and almost drowned with this really crazy guy up in Washington, then I got stuck in a shuttle with a bunch of people who couldn't stop talking."

"And now you're headed back to Washington..."

She opened a side door and guided him into a small lounge. "But at least I'm safe from any more possible drownings. The crazy guy who took me on this wild date just happens to be in Florida now." Taking two Styrofoam cups from a stack, she filled them with coffee and handed one to Kevin. "If I remember correctly, you take yours black."

"Only when laced with whisky." He reached around her for the cream.

She went over to the low-slung sofa and with a weary sigh, sat down, stretching her legs in front of her and crossing them at the ankles. Fighting to keep a silly grin from making its way onto her lips, she rested the cup against her mouth. She couldn't believe how pleased she was to see him. It had been a long time since anyone had gone so far out of their way for her. It felt good—almost too good.

A warning bell sounded. He was a politician, wasn't he? Didn't politicians make a point of showing up at crowded functions for the good public relations it would bring them? The thought hurt way out of proportion to the circumstances. "Have you managed to get in any interviews since you've been down here?'' she asked, forcing a lightness to her voice she didn't feel. ''I couldn't believe the press corp that showed up for—'' The devastating look he gave her made her swallow the rest. His eyes were filled with a combination of fury and pain.

He placed his cup on the counter. ''I think I'd better be leaving,'' he said evenly, struggling to contain his keen disappointment at being so completely mis-understood.

''I'm sorry,'' Lisa said. ''Please don't go. I had no right to say something like that to you.''

''Then why did you?''

Why indeed? Maybe because she had always be-lieved the best offense was a good defense. She had learned early that when it came to her relationships with men it was easier to handle disillusionments if you pre-tended they didn't matter. Then again, maybe she was just tired and a little envious of the celebration going on in the hangar next to them. No matter how many times she insisted she loved her freedom, there were occa-sions like today when it would have been nice to have someone waiting for her, too. ''I don't have an expla-nation—only an apology.''

He stared at her. For all of the bigger-than-life drama she had just been a part of, she looked remarkably small and vulnerable. He let out a sigh. ''Accepted.''

''Thanks. I owe you one.''

He pulled a chair over to sit beside her, straddling the seat with his long legs and resting his arms across the back. ''So how was it?''

''The rescue or the drowning?'' Her eyes picked up a mischievous sparkle.

"Since I happened to be privy to the *near* drowning, why don't you fill me in on the rescue."

"Actually, everything was pretty textbook. We used the personal rescue enclosures to transfer the crew from *Orion* to the *Discovery*. They worked just the way we had been assured they would. Other than a few comments about feeling like human basketballs, everyone said they weren't all that uncomfortable during the trip. The only injuries to the *Orion* crew members were burns on Sandy Williams's arm when she was fighting the fire on the lower deck and Frank Jenkins's hand when he touched some hot metal."

"So it was a fire that caused all the problems."

"Right now it appears to be a combination of things. Frank said everything started with an explosion in one of the flight-deck computers, followed by a fire. When they tried to transfer the downed computer functions to the redundant system, another fire occurred. After the third explosion and fire he decided to shut everything down except the emergency life-support systems and wait for us." Lisa reached up to rub the back of her neck. "We probably won't know precisely what caused the problem for a couple of months. They'll debrief everyone from the *Orion,* of course, but that will only produce speculation. To get any solid answers, extra flights will have to be worked into the regular shuttle schedules and special crews will probably have to go up to see whether or not repairs are possible. If they can't get the shuttle back here, I'm not sure what they'll do with it."

"An expensive proposition any way you look at it."

Lisa leaned forward, propped her elbows on her knees, and held her cup between her hands. She looked at Kevin over the rim. "The timing couldn't have been worse. If we don't get the funds approved that are being considered in Congress now, I'm afraid the whole program is going to fall apart.''

Kevin bit back the answer he normally would have given to such a statement. NASA, like so many other government agencies, didn't need more money; they needed to put a stop to the excesses that had them paying three hundred dollars for a hammer that could be purchased for twelve at a local hardware store. He decided it was best to change the subject. ''You didn't seem overly excited about returning to Washington. I was sure I saw you wince when they announced your itinerary.''

She had been dreading the trip—until now. ''I'm not big on those kinds of parties.''

''I know...you told me.''

''Will you be at the White House?'' she asked impulsively, suddenly caring very much what his answer would be. She had a feeling that with Kevin around, she would find most anything more pleasant.

''Would you like me to be?'' He hadn't considered going. Under most circumstances he would have purposely avoided going. Now, because of her, he felt differently.

''It would be nice to see a friendly face in the crowd.'' Why couldn't she just come out and tell him she would like to see him again?

''If you're interested, my offer to show you around Washington is still good.'' He made a valiant attempt to sound casual.

''You mean the twenty-monuments-in-two-hours tour?''

''With a possible dinner thrown in if you'd like.'' His heart sounded like a base drum in his ears.

"How could I say no to an offer like that? Now all we have to do is figure a way to get me out of the White House."

"Leave everything to me. I'm an expert when it comes to escaping parties."

She smiled. "I remember."

CHAPTER SIX

LISA STOOD IN A CORNER of the East Room at the White House, holding a glass of white wine and listening to a thin, redheaded woman dressed in a green silk dress tell her how wonderful she was. How, Lisa wondered for what had to be the hundredth time, was one supposed to reply to a compliment so grandiose? A simple thank-you seemed egotistical, a denial an invitation for further flattery.

She had finally settled for something in between, telling the woman that she just happened to have a job that brought her to the attention of others, but in reality it was no better or worse than most other jobs. It sounded good and seemed modest enough, but it wasn't quite the truth.

Lisa loved her work and wouldn't have traded it. She was doing exactly what she wanted with her life—something she had discovered few others could say. There had been sacrifices along the way, some more painful than others, especially when it came to personal relationships. For a reason still unclear to her, she had never been able to find a man who was secure enough in himself to handle who she was and what she did for a living. She knew there were men who were capable of coping with wives more famous or aggressive than they were, or who could deal with the problems that came with highly demanding jobs, because the majority of the other female astronauts were married and, for the most part, quite happily. After Eric Barker and Ross Stewart, Lisa had accepted the fact that she would probably forever remain single, finally even convincing herself she preferred it that way.

"Are you ready to blow this joint?" Kevin whispered, his breath caressing her ear.

Lisa spun around. When she saw Kevin's intimate, conspiratorial smile, a flood of warmth washed over her. "Where have you been?" she asked, the woman in green instantly forgotten.

"Am I to assume this show of concern means you've missed me?" She looked fantastic—fresh and animated, her eyes sparkling. She was wearing a blue-and-white wool dress, conservative and simply cut. It accentuated the curves of her body more erotically than a sheer gown could have done. Kevin was captivated.

"Of course I've missed you. If you recall, you promised to save me from all of this." She motioned with her hand, indicating the lavishly decorated high-ceilinged room, considered by many to be the most beautiful in the White House, and the crème de la crème of Washington celebrities, from top cabinet members to Supreme Court judges to the president himself.

"I take it the praise heaped upon you has been excruciatingly painful?" He was amazed at the way she made him feel—like walking through a field of fresh-mowed hay and watching the sunrise on a spring morning all rolled into one. The instant he had come into the room and found her, everyone else had disappeared.

"Almost unbearable."

"I'll try to remember not to say anything too nice to you this evening."

She laughed. "Just don't call me a heroine—even if I happen to save your life."

A man wended his way through the crush of people behind Lisa, forcing her forward until she was standing toe-to-toe with Kevin. He could feel her warmth through the light-wool suit he was wearing, and the sensation was incredibly seductive. He ached to touch her but couldn't come up with a sane reason to do so. Had she been no more than a casual acquaintance he could have kissed her in greeting as easily as he would have shaken someone's hand, but she had become too important for him to treat so casually. "Does Cory know where you're going? I would hate to have him send the troops out looking for you."

"He isn't exactly thrilled that I'm cutting out on the festivities, but he said he understands." She could smell the after-shave he had used that morning. It was a clean fragrance, unpretentious and compelling, much like Kevin himself.

"Well, if you're absolutely sure you want to leave all this adulation, I'm ready."

"Does this mean you plan to treat me like I'm just plain, common, ordinary folk?"

He grinned. "I'm sorry—what did you say your name was?"

"You're a man after my heart, Kevin Anderson."

He stared at her. His demeanor changed and he grew thoughtful. "You're right," he said, only then realizing that her heart was precisely what he was after.

The laughter left her eyes. She swallowed. She was at a loss for words. Could he be serious? The look he gave her told her he was deadly serious. Again she swallowed, unable to find a way to answer him.

Kevin took her arm and put it through his. "It was just a friendly warning, Lisa. I didn't mean to scare you."

At least she found her voice. "You didn't—at least I don't think you did. You just surprised me."

"You couldn't be half as surprised by this as I am." His expression was guileless. "Believe me, I had every intention of pursuing you with a hell of a lot more subtlety, but I'm afraid I'm out of practice when it comes to romancing someone—it's been a long time." He skillfully led her through the crowd, nodding and smiling to those he knew while gracefully sidestepping those who looked as if they would like to stop and talk. When they arrived at the side door, Kevin hesitated. "Last chance—are you sure you want to leave?"

She reached for the doorknob. "I'll race you to the car."

THEIR FIRST STOP was the National Archives. Taking her hand as they walked up the steps, Kevin said, "This place is a bonus on the tour. It really doesn't qualify as a monument, but since we were so close I thought we should stop by." They went inside and up another short set of stairs into a room lined with temperature- and humidity-controlled glass cases. In the center was the original copy of the Declaration of Independence. On either side were papers to and from the leaders of the War of Independence.

Lisa stopped to read one that caught her eye—a letter from the infamous spy, Benedict Arnold. The letter had been written to George Washington and asked that Arnold's wife be taken care of after he was hanged for treason. Her country's history had never seemed so poignantly real to Lisa as it was at that moment. A man who had been nothing more than a name in a history book became flesh and blood. She looked up at Kevin, who stood close beside her, reading over her shoulder.

"I felt the same way the first time I came here," he said, seeing the look in her eyes. "It was after a particularly frustrating session on the Hill...I was a freshman representative and had been bombarded by lobbyists for both sides of a new bill because I couldn't make up my mind on how I wanted to vote. I was looking for something that would make me feel that what I was doing here in Washington was important."

"And did coming here help?"

"Immensely. My problems and doubts became insignificant when I compared them to the ones faced by the people who wrote these papers."

"Sometimes it's a lot easier to be part of a movement when the enthusiasm is running high and the freshness is there to spur you on than it is to be a part of it when the movement has settled into a routine."

He smiled. "I'll take a winter in my house in Georgetown over one in Valley Forge with Washington's troops anytime."

"You have a point." She moved on to the next glass case. "I thought you were a senator," she said, responding to his statement about being a freshment representative.

"I am now, but I started out in the House when I first came out here almost ten years ago."

"And have you learned to like what you do?" He hesitated so long Lisa glanced up to see if he had heard her.

"Sometimes," he finally said. "On the rare occasions when I can convince myself that my being here makes a difference."

It was not the answer she had anticipated. Aware of the back-breaking effort required to gain a Senate seat, she had automatically assumed that those who ran for office would do so because they felt the same way about their jobs that she did about hers. "Then why are you here?"

He stepped to the side to let a man with three children in tow pass. "It's a long story," he said quietly. "I'll tell you about it someday."

The opportunity for private conversation ended with the arrival of a bus load of school children.

The next stop was another "bonus," Ford's Theater. The building where President Abraham Lincoln was shot was located in a rather run-down section of town, tucked away on a side street. Kevin took Lisa to the museum below the theater to show her the Lincoln memorabilia and the diary of John Wilkes Booth, his assassin.

"I first came here to the theater to see a musical," he told her. "Then I came back the next day to see the museum. I've been back here several times since."

"I can understand coming here once or twice, but why several times?"

"I guess it does sound a little morbid." He reached for her hand, and the gesture seemed natural. As their ease in being with each other grew again, the earlier awkwardness slipped away. "Maybe it's because I've never been able to understand violence and I come here looking for answers. How many places are there where a museum has been dedicated to both the assassin and his victim?" He led her back out onto the street. "Basically I'm a simple person trying to understand a complicated world, one in which I've been given the job of trying to make laws for the people who live there."

"You're not very happy as a politician, are you?" she asked intuitively.

He gave her an embarrassed smile. "What's happy?" He stopped and took a deep breath. "I sound like a character out of a Tolstoy novel. Forget what I just said. I'm supposed to be showing you a good time, not depressing you."

"Do you really want to put a smile on my face?"

"Name it."

"Feed me."

He laughed, appreciating how easily she lightened the mood. "If that's what it takes, I'll have you grinning from ear to ear before the night's out. I know a hundred good places to eat in this town."

They got into the car and headed up Pennsylvania Avenue to the Capitol. The first couple of blocks were spent in companionable silence while Lisa sorted through the clues Kevin had given her to his personality. She considered both his offhand remarks as well as the two places he had already chosen to take her and tried to blend them with the discreet inquiries she had made about him that morning. From several sources she had learned that although he hadn't been in Congress all that long, Kevin had managed to become one of the most respected people there. Honesty and dedication were two words that had cropped up time and again in descriptions of him. Several of the people she talked to had spoken of Kevin in terms of presidential material, though others had said he would never make it that far because he refused to play the necessary political games.

Cory Peters had filled her in on Kevin's reputation as a congressional watchdog while they were flying in from Florida that morning. Cory was without a doubt the most politically aware astronaut Lisa knew, mainly because of his wife Ann's avid interest and her own plans to run for local office one day, and after listening to him, Lisa felt a little embarrassed she had never heard of Kevin before. He was the most vocal senator when it came to excessive government spending, and he had a perfect record of refusal whenever it came to voting new funds for the space program. She would have liked to ask him about his reasoning but decided to try a safer subject.

"Is there anything about my job that bothers you?" she asked impulsively, immediately wishing she hadn't. She tried to pretend it was simply an idle question.

"The whole idea of space flight terrifies me—I'm afraid of heights."

"That's it? That's all that bothers you?"

"Have you ever seen Kansas? Just about the only things above sea level are the grain elevators."

She shook her head. "Now that I know how *you* feel about being an astronaut, how about telling me how you feel about *my* being an astronaut."

He pulled up to a red stoplight, turned and stared at her. "Something tells me this is some sort of a test."

"Don't try to analyze the question, just give me your honest, no-holds-barred answer."

"You'll have to give me a minute to think about this one." He pulled into the middle of the intersection, waiting for several cars to pass before turning left. "Since up until this past week the safety record of the shuttle was nearly flawless, I suppose it would be un-fair—"

"What do you mean *nearly*?"

"All right," he backtracked. "You have me on that one, the record was flawless. Anyway, with a safety record better than traveling on a freeway, I hardly have the right to complain there." He made another turn, this time onto the Capitol grounds. When she didn't respond, he glanced over at her. Seeing an expectant look still lingering, he shrugged. "Sorry—I can't come up with anything else on such short notice."

"What about women astronauts in general?" she asked, fighting the suspicion that he was placating her.

"You're going to have to help me out on this one. I don't know many women astronauts in general."

"Give me your best shot at stereotyping a woman astronaut," she persisted.

"This is important to you, isn't it?"

"Very."

He lapsed into thought. The car inched through the early evening traffic, soft music came from the radio and somewhere in the distance a horn honked. "Aggressive..." he began. "Sure of herself, intelligent, most likely brash at times, intolerant of mistakes of her own or stupidity in others, idealistic, myopic—"

"Myopic?"

"Don't interrupt—I'm on a roll. Let's see...she would probably be isolated at times or at least have thefeeling she was isolated from the mainstream of life because of the uniqueness of her profession. She'd be defensive, with a tendency to try too hard to be one of the boys—"

"That's how you see me?"

"That's what I assume would be a part of you." He winked at her. "If you noticed, I said nothing about beauty, only brains. Would you like me to describe how I see the only woman astronaut I happen to know personally?"

"I think we went over that territory already at your house the other night. Once is enough, thank you." She turned and looked out the window to keep Kevin from seeing how easily her cheeks had crimsoned. It was then that she noticed where they were. "I thought we were going to get something to eat."

"Trust me. In these hallowed halls is the Senate restaurant, a place that serves the world's best bean soup. Nowhere is their a better first course to a meal."

She gave him a whimsical smile. "Bean soup seems an odd specialty for a restaurant that caters to a group of people who cloister themselves all the time."

He returned the smile. "Ah, the stories I could tell."

"Please don't!"

He hesitated getting out of the car, letting the pleasure of her company reach the innermost parts of him like a summer rain after months of drought. Finally he turned to her. "I'm glad you're here," he stated simply.

"Me, too."

BY THE TIME they had finished eating and left the restaurant it was dark. With the sun gone the temperature dropped dramatically, making Lisa acutely aware of the inadequacy of the thin raincoat she had taken with her that morning.

Noticing how she huddled against the cold, Kevin put his arm around her shoulders as they walked back to the car. "Do you want to go back to your hotel to get a coat?"

"I'll be all right. From now on I'll just move faster." She was afraid if she went back to the hotel and was seen by someone from NASA there would be no getting away again.

"Are you sure?"

She snuggled against him. "Uh-huh."

"Remember, we still have twenty monuments to go…"

"I'm a lot tougher than I look."

"Well, I'm not," he said, stopping and pulling her into his arms. "Watching someone freezing to death has never been my idea of fun."

She tilted her chin up to look at him. "I don't want you to get the idea that I'm complaining about the present arrangements, but if you're that concerned about my freezing, it doesn't make much sense for us to be standing out here in the wind when we're less than five feet away from the car."

His eyes narrowed as he stared down at her. "You can add pragmatic to that list of stereotypes."

"Why, what a nice thing to say." She grinned, then stood on her toes and gave him a quick kiss.

Kevin's breath caught in his throat. A band tightened around his chest. With only a simple meeting of their lips he was instantly and completely lost to the world around him. He wanted Lisa. His hands wanted to touch the curving arch of her bare back; his eyes longed to see the unbound beauty of her breasts. He wanted her with an intensity and single-mindedness that dumbfounded him. He wanted her, was enchanted by her, felt he was falling in love with her and was absolutely sure that if he told her his feelings, he would scare the hell out of her.

If he was to give in to his instincts, he would return her kiss, thoroughly, completely losing himself in the meeting of their lips, without regard to the cars passing by, the pedestrians walking around them or the policeman on the corner. He would kiss her deeply, passionately. He would take her home with him and kiss her again and again until they were both breathless with desire…and then he would make love to her with all the skill and tenderness that was inside of him.

He would shout his joy at finding this fantastic person; he would hold her close and whisper the wondrous way she made him feel when she smiled. Instead he said, "You're right. It doesn't make much sense to stand out here in the cold." He walked with her to her side of the car, unlocked the door and waited for her to get inside.

Lisa slumped against the seat. She was sure Kevin had been about to return her kiss. What had stopped him? Could she have misread his signals so completely? She shivered against the cold, made more intense by the loss of his body heat. By the time he was beside her, her teeth had started to chatter. She gave him a wisp of a smile. "Is there any chance the monuments we're going to see are indoors?"

He could think of a dozen ways he would like to warm her and none of them had anything to do with putting more clothes on. "Where are you staying?"

"At the same hotel. I never got around to checking out before I took off for Florida."

Kevin stepped back out of the car, took off his coat and handed it to her. "Here, wrap this around you for now."

"I can't take your coat—you'll freeze." She was astounded. Kevin's behavior was straight out of another era. He opened her doors, held her coat, treated her as though she were a Victorian lady who might swoon at the slightest provocation.

"It's all right. If you recall, I live here. I'm used to the cold."

"If that hypothesis were true, Eskimos wouldn't run around all bundled up in fur. Now take this back." She tried to hand him his coat.

"Look, this isn't a point of honor, simply a gesture of goodwill. Your teeth are snapping together like a dog chasing a mailman—mine aren't. Now cover up."

Seeing his logic, she relented and pulled his coat over her lap and up to her chin. "I can't say I'm too crazy about the comparison."

"Just a little down-home sageness I pull out every once in a while. There's a veritable wellspring under this facade of sophistication."

She scooted across the seat to sit next to him, snuggling into his side. "Well, you've certainly impressed me."

He held her a moment before letting out a deep sigh. "I hate to complain, but you can't sit there."

"Why not?"

"No seat belt."

Her eyes narrowed. "Are you for real?"

"I'm afraid so," he said, a pained expression on his face. As soon as she had moved over and had the seat belt in place, he started the car.

Lisa purposely looked at him as he drove off the Capitol grounds. Studying his profile, she noticed he had a small bump on his nose and wondered if it had been broken. She speculated on whether it had happened in a football game or a fight. More likely—considering the rest of his looks—it had happened tumbling out of a hayloft while chasing a girl in ruffles and gingham. She decided she liked the way he wore his hair, parted on the side and swept back over his ears with a wave that dipped across his forehead. And then there was the hollow behind his ear. It was the perfect size and shape for nuzzling. She imagined herself doing the nuzzling and liked the imagery.

Her attention was drawn to his hands and the graceful way they moved along the steering wheel. His hands had been what first attracted her to him in the Websters' study. They were powerful looking yet gentle, the hands of a lover, hands she sensed would cradle and stroke and caress with infinite care.

When she realized where her thoughts were leading, a tiny smile twitched at the corners of her mouth. She wondered what he would think if he knew what lusty things were going through her mind. Would they scare him? She wished she had the nerve to find out. It was an odd contradiction in her personality that her boldness in every other area didn't follow through to her dealings with men. For all her bravado she had never been able to take the initiative in a relationship.

She decided to give it another try. Clearing her throat, she said, "If it's closer to your house than my hotel we could go there. I wouldn't mind wearing something of yours—again." Nor would she mind sitting in front of his fireplace, or curling up on the couch, or...

For an instant Kevin wondered if she was able to read his mind. He had been daydreaming of taking her to his home, but not for the reason she had suggested. "Actually we're pretty much right in the middle. Going to the hotel isn't out of the way at all."

"How nice..." So much for subtle seduction. He had missed her point entirely.

To keep his mind from wandering to fantasies that would only make the present more difficult than it already was, Kevin began a tour-guide recitation that lasted all the way to the portico of the hotel. What he didn't know he made up, pointing out buildings of supposed great historical value that were in reality tenements scheduled to be torn down.

When they arrived, Lisa sat and stared at the front door. "Would you mind driving me around to the restaurant side? There are some people I would just as soon not run into right now."

Kevin glanced at his watch. The reception had broken up more than an hour ago. "I didn't think—"

"That's all right. I'm sure I can slip in and out again without anyone seeing me."

He drove around to the side entrance. She took a deep breath, handed him his coat and reached for the door. When he started to get out with her, she told him not to. "You stay here and keep the car running for our getaway." She would be much less visible without a six-foot-three-inch companion.

Kevin watched her slip inside while groaning over his stupidity for taking a chance and returning to the hotel. His sophistication, savoir faire and just plain common sense had taken a nose dive since meeting Lisa. The longer he was around her, the more tongue-tied and adolescent he felt. At this rate he'd be incapable of speech and tripping all over himself by the end of the week.

Lisa scanned the restaurant for familiar faces before crossing the foyer to the hotel entrance, where she paused again. She spotted Sandy Williams by the registration desk, her arms covered by long sleeves with white bandages peeking out the ends. So they had come right back to the hotel as she had feared.

She started across the hallway that was behind the indoor fountain and fully visible to the front desk but hidden from the bar. It wasn't Sandy she was worried about spotting her; it was Cory. He had been given the job of "mother hen" for the trip and was responsible for making sure everything ran smoothly. She waited a moment, trying to get a feel of the area between her and the elevators. Finally she made a dash for it, arriving just as a set of doors slid open and Cory stepped out.

"Boy, am I glad to see you," he said, grabbing her arm and steering her over to a quiet corner. "Don Meyers has been looking all over the place for you. He's lined up a Sunday supplement that's anxious to do a piece on you. The interviewer has been cooling her heels since the reception."

"What ever happened to appointments and going through channels?" Despite her anger she knew she was cornered and it was useless to argue. The request wasn't one she could easily ignore. Don Meyers wasn't just another NASA official; he would be highly influential in the final determination of the crew assignments to the space station, a job Lisa wanted so badly she could taste it.

"He told me the interview was particularly important because the magazine would reach newspapers in states where we need the support."

"Then why use me?" she groaned. "I give terrible interviews."

His mouth curved in a commiserating smile. "But, my dear Lisa, you are missing the point. All of that doesn't matter anymore. You happen to be hot stuff right now. The world has had enough of heroes. We need a few honest, good heroines."

"I don't suppose there's any chance it would be something short—"

Cory shook his head. "She came well prepared—photographer and all." He slipped his arm around her shoulders and walked her back to the elevators. "It's a good thing you decided to make it an early evening. Meyers was looking for someone to hang when he couldn't find you and he had locked his sites on me.''

"But I didn't decide to make it an early evening. You caught me on my way up to get a coat. I was planning on leaving again.''

"I didn't see—"

"He's in the car waiting for me.''

"Do you want me to tell him?''

"No, I'll do it. You can go up and tell Meyers I'm on my way.''

He gave her shoulders a squeeze. "Atta girl.''

She glared at him.

"Atta *woman*?''

Despite herself she smiled. "I don't know how Ann puts up with you.''

"Old habits are hard to break.''

KEVIN'S HEART SANK when he spotted Lisa coming toward him wearing the same coat she had been wearing before. Obviously she hadn't made it to her room unnoticed. He got out of the car to meet her.

"I'm sorry,'' she said. "I never should have tried to come back here.''

He forced a smile. "The tour isn't all it's been cracked up to be anyway.''

"And here you had me all excited about going.''

"Next time you're in town, we'll try again.''

"I don't suppose there's a chance you'll be coming to Houston...''

"Not anytime soon, I'm afraid.'' *Damn!* They couldn't really be saying good-bye. He couldn't let her leave like this.

"Be sure to call me if you do.''

"I will..." He decided to go with his instincts and started to reach for her to at least kiss her good-bye when he heard someone calling her name.

"That's Cory," she said, willing him to take her into his arms. "I think he's worried I might skip out on him after all."

Kevin nodded. "Well, I guess I'd better let you go then. Good luck tomorrow."

"I don't suppose there's any chance you're going to be in New York?" Did she sound as if she was wheedling?

"I wish I could, but there's an important vote coming up tomorrow and I have to attend the session."

"I understand. It isn't as if New York were all that close that you could just hop up there for a visit." Again she heard Cory call her name. "Thanks for the soup," she said, still stalling, unable to let go.

"Anytime." What in the hell was the matter with him? She had just as much told him she wanted to see him again. Why was he standing there like a cretin?

"Well, I guess I'd better go." She couldn't put off leaving any longer without seeming painfully obvious. She turned and started to walk away.

"Lisa?"

She swung back to face him. "Yes?" She saw a complex mixture of runaway emotions in his eyes—doubt, desire, confusion.

He came toward her, stopped, put his hands on her shoulders and lightly touched his lips to hers. "It's been fun. Thank you." It had been more than fun; it had been a marvelous reawakening. He felt truly alive for the first time in longer than he cared to remember.

She reached up to touch his face, and he took her hand and held it. "I wish I didn't have to go," she said softly. "Quite a change from two days ago, huh?"

"Washington has that effect on some people."

Again Cory called her, his voice developing a desperate edge. "It isn't the town I'm talking about." She reached up, put her hand around his neck and brought him to her. The meeting of their lips was explosive with promise, eloquent with unspoken meaning. They stared at each other for long seconds before Lisa turned and ran across the parking lot.

Kevin stood and gazed at the doorway long after she had gone inside. He had never believed someone could fall in love in just a few days. Love needed room to grow; it was process that took nurturing and long-term care. What he was feeling for Lisa couldn't possibly be love. But if not love, what then?

Stunned by his thoughts, he returned to his car. It had been so long since he had felt this way about a woman that he had assumed he never would again. Over the years, like an oyster protecting itself from a painful intrusion by building a shiny protective shell, he had softened the aching loneliness and his deep-seated need to intimately share his life with someone by feigning acceptance. With ridiculous ease Lisa had shattered his shell.

As he drove out of the parking lot he glanced up at the hotel. He would give her a week to get home and back to work and then he would call. He grinned. Maybe four days would be enough.

CHAPTER SEVEN

AT FIVE O'CLOCK the next morning Lisa left her room to go downstairs to the lobby to meet the other astronauts and their families for the fight to New York. Morning was usually her best time of day but today she would have traded a ticket to watch the 49ers play in the Super Bowl for one more hour of sleep. The interview had seemed to go on forever and then there had been a phone call to her father in California. They had talked for more than an hour before she learned her brother was at her father's house waiting to talk to her, too.

By the time she had exchanged the latest family gossip with her brother and his wife and had talked to her three nieces, it was too late to call Kevin. It was probably just as well, she reasoned, standing her luggage carrier against the back wall of the elevator; she wouldn't have known what to say to him anyway. She had spent the remainder of the evening convincing herself it would be plain dumb for them to allow something to get started. She was never in Washington and he had no reason to go to Houston. They would never see each other. She folded her arms across her chest and propped her shoulder against the elevator wall. What a rotten time to be practical when what she really wanted to do was forget everything else and have a crazy whirlwind wildly romantic affair.

The elevator's bell sounded and the doors slid open. "Good morning," Cory said. "I've been waiting for you. How'd it go last night?"

"I assume you mean the thing with Ms Dankin, interviewer par excellence? Well, that all depends on whether you were curious about before or after I let it slip out that Don Meyers is sleeping with George Quigman's wife."

"You didn't!"

"Or would you rather hear about Ms Dankin's reaction to my telling her that I thought the design chosen for the space station was politically motivated and wouldn't last ten years before we had to replace it with something larger."

"Lisa, I hope you're—"

"But the real fun came when I asked her if she'd had a sex-change operation. Did you happen to get a good look at her? She's a strange woman." No longer able to keep a straight face, she put her head down and stepped around him, pulling her two-wheeled cart behind her.

After recovering his composure Cory followed, quickly catching up with her. "You had me going there for a while," he said, his voice revealing he wasn't absolutely sure whether she was putting him on or not.

"What gave me away?"

"The one about the sex-change operation."

She looked up at him and winked. "That was the only one that was the truth."

"Excuse me—" A young man wearing the hotel's distinctive kelly-green uniform came up to them. "Are you Lisa Malorey?"

"Yes…"

"A package arrived for you last night. The gentleman who brought it said not to disturb you but to make sure you knew it was here before you left this morning.

Ask for Mary at the registration desk. She can help you."

"Thank you." She and Cory exchanged looks, hers a puzzled frown. "Who do you suppose—"

"If I were to hazard a guess—" his voice indicated he felt there was no real mystery involved "—I would say the senator from Kansas has taken a shine to you. At least that was the way it looked last night in the parking lot."

Lisa's heart gave a funny little skip. "Watch my luggage for me." She went over to the desk. A gray-haired woman wearing a name tag that read Mary Wilson came over to her. "My name is Lisa Malorey. I understand you have a package for me."

The woman went into a back room and came out with a silver shirt box that had a red ribbon wrapped around it, then tied in the center with a bow. Lisa thanked her and went over to sit on one of the high-backed mauve chairs that were scattered around the indoor fountain. She turned the box over, looking for a card. There wasn't one.

"Aren't you going to open it?" Sandy Williams asked, coming across the lobby and sitting beside her. She had put her long black hair up in a French knot, making her look a lot closer to her twenty-eight years. When she wore it flowing down her back she was asked for identification every time she tried to order a drink. Sandy was a good friend of Lisa's, probably her best friend. As the only two female astronauts who were still single they frequently went places together, especially whenever the evening involved the possibility of shoptalk.

"I suppose so," Lisa answered, only peripherally paying attention to her friend.

"Would you rather be alone?"

"What?" She blinked. "No—stay. I'm just a little surprised that someone sent me a present, that's all."

"You mean it's not your birthday?"

Lisa didn't bother answering. Sandy knew very well that it wasn't her birthday. They had celebrated their birthdays together less than two months earlier; it was her way of fishing for information.

"Maybe it's something from the Greek god who stole you away from the reception yesterday..."

"It's impossible to keep any secrets around here."

"Why would you ever want to keep someone like him a secret? He's a real fireworks-and-brass-band kind of guy."

"You make him sound like a hunting trophy."

"Not a bad parallel. It takes about the same amount of work to get either one." She reached over to pull lightly on the ribbon. "You going to open this or not? I just saw Meyers get off the elevator, which means we should be taking off any minute now."

Lisa tugged on the simple bow and the ribbon came off. She caught the sides of the box between her hands and let the bottom slip free from the top to land in her lap. Inside she found a note.

Lisa—
I thought it was about time one of us owned something yellow.

Kevin

She folded the tissue paper aside and found a scarf the color of freshly opened buttercups. She ran her hand over the knit material. It was wonderfully soft and yielding to her touch.

"Looks like alpaca," Sandy announced, holding the corner of the scarf in her hand. "There's nothing like it—costs a fortune, but it's worth every penny."

Lisa pulled the scarf from the box, pressed it against her face to feel its softness more closely, then loosely wrapped it around her neck. "What do you think?"

"It's smashing. But then quality tells." She bent over to retrieve the box, which had fallen to the floor. "Why a scarf?"

"To keep me warm."

"That's it? No hidden meanings?"

A smile lighted her eyes. "None that I know of." It pleased her immensely that Kevin had remembered yellow was her favorite color. Just then she looked up and saw Cory signaling to her. "Time to go," she told Sandy, slipping Kevin's note in her pocket.

TWELVE HOURS, a breakfast, one parade, a luncheon and a reception later, Lisa reached into her pocket and found Kevin's note. The reception was winding down, and she and the others were waiting for transportation to their hotel, where they would change clothes for a black-tie dinner later than night. While she waited she listened to a man whose name she hadn't caught tell her how much easier it was for women to get ahead in today's world than it was for men. Lost in her own thoughts, Lisa nodded absently and turned Kevin's note over, curling it around her finger, using it to mentally transport her back to the previous night.

When she returned to Houston she was going to have to spend some time thinking about him. Right now he was only a mass of feelings to her—albeit wonderful, warm, exciting feelings. Whenever she thought about him, her heart beat faster and a smile hovered around her lips. The possibility they might never see each other again had become a big black cloud threatening the sunshine of their meeting. What if, with one thing and the other, even with the best of intentions, he never got around to coming to Houston? With Mike and Caroline moving soon, her readily available reason for going to Washington would leave with them.

Ann Peters came up to stand beside her. She had flown to New York with the astronauts and their families that morning. Ann's black hair, laced with gray, was cut stylishly short, and her trim athletic build belied the fact she had given birth to three children. She was one of the handsomest forty-year-old women Lisa had ever known.

"Pardon me for intruding," Ann said sweetly to the man espousing his theory of reverse discrimination to Lisa, "but there's someone who's been waiting all afternoon to meet Lisa, and I promised him a personal introduction if he'd help me with tickets for a play I've been dying to see. I do hope you don't mind," she added, possessively taking Lisa's arm.

"No...not at all. But if you really need tickets—"

"It's all been taken care of. Thank you anyway," she said over her shoulder, steering Lisa to the other side of the room.

"Who—"

"No one. You looked like you needed rescuing, so I did my duty."

"Bless you," Lisa said with a sigh, leaning against the wall to take some of the weight off her feet. "It was all I could do to keep my temper when he went from the problems of the world in general to telling me that women astronauts were being given preferential treatment merely because they're female." Her eyes flashed with repressed anger. "I'll bet that man has never been within a thousand miles of Houston, and yet he felt he had the right to lecture me about what goes on there.''

"Whoa, I'm on your side, remember?''

"Sorry...I didn't mean to vent my spleen on you.''

"You're probably just exhausted. You've been through a lot lately. Why don't you try to take a nap when we get back to the hotel? We're not due to go out again for three hours.''

"It isn't fatigue that's getting me down.'' Lisa wearily rubbed her temples, her actions contradicting her statement.

"Oh?''

She eyed Ann. Maybe telling someone what was bothering her might help put it into perspective, and there was hardly a better person than Ann. "Do you know Kevin Anderson?''

"The senator?''

Lisa nodded.

"Not personally, but by reputation. Cory's met him a few times at the Websters'. I know he likes him a lot despite their differing political views.''

"So do I—like him, that is. I don't know too much about the political thing but the other...well...'' She shrugged expressively.

"I see...'' Ann said thoughtfully.

"Well, I wish I did. I've never been this confused about anyone in my whole life.''

"It sounds serious.''

"That's just it. I can't decide whether it is or not. We met for the first time four days ago and yet I feel I've known him forever. He's a terrific guy, warm, friendly, with a neat sense of humor. We like a lot of the same things...''

"And how does he feel about you?''

"I don't know." She reconsidered. "That's not exactly true. I know he likes me, just not how much or in what way. He's had a dozen opportunities to make a pass and hasn't. Frankly, I'm not used to men who treat their dates platonically."

"Then Kevin must be a refreshing change."

Lisa smiled. "Yes...he is." The smile faded. "And he's in Washington and I'm in Houston. It's madness to let—"

"Distance didn't stop Mike and Caroline when they were going together. And believe me, you two couldn't have half the problems working things out that they did."

"But Mike had a reason to go to Los Angeles."

"And you have a reason to go to Washington— Kevin."

"I don't know," she said slowly.

Ann shook her head. "Can this possibly be the Lisa Malorey I know?"

"I've worn my heart on my sleeve too many times in the past to do it again so easily." She hadn't meant to say that. She preferred her friends to think of her as strong, certainly not vulnerable.

"So you're going to let someone like Kevin slip away because of a couple of jerks who didn't deserve you?"

Lisa gave Ann a knowing smile. "You're really good at this. Who do you usually practice on?"

"If you recall, I have two daughters and a son who is always in love."

There was a movement by the door that led outside. Lisa looked up and saw Sandy signaling to them that the limousine had arrived. "Maybe a nap will help," she said to Ann as they began working their way back through the crowd.

"Lisa...don't cheat yourself."

She had to lean over to hear Ann above the boisterous well-wishing crowd.

"Don't let this thing between you and Kevin fall to the wayside because you're afraid to get hurt again. From everything I've heard and read about Kevin Anderson, he's worth sticking your neck out for. That is if—and I'm afraid where you're concerned it could be a big if—you can accept his political philosophy." When Lisa didn't immediately answer, Ann went on. "Even though he has an old-fashioned honesty and caring about people that is pretty hard to find in politicians these days, his ideas and goals are diametrically opposed to yours. But I'm sure you already know all that."

Lisa put her arm across Ann's shoulders and gave her a quick hug. "Thanks, Ann. I promise I'll think about what you've said."

An hour later, scrunched down in a tub full of steaming water with only her head and feet exposed to the air, Lisa could think of nothing else. Again and again she went over the reasons she should leave well enough alone, go back to Houston and forget she had ever met Kevin Anderson. They made sense, were logical and even compelling. On the other side of the argument stood the first man who truly seemed capable of liking her exactly the way she was. He was fun to be with, handsome, sexy, *unmarried*—something rare enough in itself anymore—and obviously interested in seeing her again.

She flicked the lever over the faucet with her toe to empty the tub, stood up and reached for a towel. Her decision was made. She had spent the past three days giving her all for NASA; she had earned a night off. Not bothering to dry herself but stopping long enough to wrap the large blue bath towel around her to keep from freezing, she trudged into the bedroom and picked up the phone to call Cory. He sounded as tired as she had felt earlier. "Cory, this is Lisa. I want to talk to you about something." She said the words in a rush, afraid she might weaken in her resolve.

"I already know. Ann told me. She said you were coming down with something and wouldn't be able to join us for the banquet tonight."

Lisa heard the muffled sounds of a hand being placed over the receiver. "Did I get it right?" she heard Cory say, his voice sounding as if it was coming from far away.

"You got it right," Lisa answered, smiling. "Tell Ann she's a doll."

"Take your time getting back to Houston. I've checked and you don't have anything scheduled until Friday. In the meantime, if you should happen to need me for anything, Ann and I are going to stop in Washington for a couple of days to visit the Websters."

Cory's unexpected collusion made her feel guilty about running out on him. "Are you sure you won't get into trouble if I'm not there tonight?"

"Personally I'd like to see everyone walk out. Meyers went way overboard on this thing. NASA's not going to win any new friends if the people they send to represent them fall asleep during the welcoming speeches."

"I'll get a petition going as soon as I get back."

Cory laughed appreciatively at the long-standing joke the astronauts used whenever they were particularly frustrated about something. "Save the first space for me to sign."

"I'll see you Friday. And Cory...thanks."

"My pleasure."

She hung on to the phone for a long time after she had replaced the receiver. Now that the pathway was cleared, she was suddenly not as confident as she had been before.

KEVIN NUDGED HIS READING GLASSES back up the bridge of his nose, stretched his arms wide and let out a tired sigh. He glanced at the clock on his desk. It was already almost midnight and he still had a stack of papers to go through before morning. Sleep had eluded him the night before as he tossed and turned, going over and over in his mind how he should have handled his date with Lisa. Finally, at five in the morning, he had given up trying and had gone into his study to review some papers until it was time to leave for work.

Earlier that night he had tried to make it home in time to see if there was coverage of the parade in New York on the evening news, but he had been delayed by a call from the White House. He had missed his second chance when he worked right through the late news before he remembered to turn on the television.

Seeking relief from the onset of a headache, he dropped his chin to his chest and rolled his head from side to side. When that didn't work he got up and went to the kitchen for aspirin. He was reaching for the bottle when the doorbell rang. Again he looked at the time, frowning in puzzlement, wondering who would be coming to see him so late.

LISA STOOD on the small concrete porch and watched the taxi drive away. She said a silent prayer she had not made a horrendous mistake coming to Kevin's unannounced. Because it was so late she had come straight from the airport to his house. Her luggage by her side, she was sure she looked as if she was there to stay. As she waited for him to answer the bell her courage flagged, seeping from her like water from a cupped hand, until she was ready to make a dash for the disappearing taxi, convinced she should have called him from the hotel. It would have been so much more sensible to go to the hotel tonight and call in the morning, she inwardly groaned. But it was too late for such reasoning now. The door was opening.

Kevin stood in the doorway and stared, too surprised to perform the social functions associated with greeting a guest. Lisa appearing on his doorstep was tantamount to rubbing a magic lantern and having a wish come true—neither of which he had believed could ever happen. "Lisa?" he breathed, finally summoning the wherewithall to say her name.

"In the flesh," she answered, forcing the words past the lump in her throat.

"What are you doing here?"

"I was on my way to a banquet and took a little detour."

She was wearing the scarf he had given her. The yellow made her hair look golden. "Come in—"

"I have my luggage with me," she said self-consciously. "I came here straight from the airport... it was so late..."

It had taken awhile but it was beginning to dawn on Kevin just what was happening. Lisa had skipped out on the New York festivities to come to Washington to be with him. The knowledge momentarily stunned him, draining him of all feeling, and then what she had done raced through him, touching, warming, electrifying every corner of his being. By coming to him this way she had traveled far more than the two-hundred-odd miles that had separated them. How could he hesitate going the rest of the way? Confident where he had been unsure of himself before, he unconsciously let his instincts take over and gently he reached for her. Cradling her head between his hands, he brought her to him and kissed her.

A soft moan came from Lisa as their lips met. This was the dream she had nurtured since leaving New York. The feel of his mouth pressed to hers was everything she had imagined—and more. She was swept up and carried away from everything ordinary and familiar, like an autumn leaf caught in a violent storm.

Kevin's hands combed through her hair to cup and hold the back of her head, then moved on to wrap around her shoulders. She stood on her toes to return the pressure of his kiss. Her mouth opened in invitation; his tongue tenderly tasted her sweetness.

He drew her to him, holding her, reveling in the way she felt in his arms. It had been so long since he had held a woman this way. A deep burning ache, one that had been held in check for nearly a decade, burst in him. He was a man who had been meant to share his life, not spend it alone. The past years had been lived in an emotional solitary confinement. With Lisa he had at last been set free.

Lisa felt Kevin's release in the unrestrained way he held her and in the passion of his kiss. She didn't fully understand what had happened to precipitate the change but she deeply welcomed it. In coming to him she had worn her heart on her sleeve; he had responded with consummate understanding.

"I wish I could tell you what it means to me that you're here," he said, looking deeply into her eyes.

"I think I know," she answered softly, feeling the passion in his words in a place inside of her that responded in kind.

"Come in the house. Let me get you something hot to drink—it's freezing out here."

A tiny happy laugh bubbled to the surface. "After that greeting you can't possibly think I'm still cold."

He lightly touched his lips to hers. "What a nice thing to say," he murmured, her words sending yet another swell of longing through him. He reached for her suitcases at the same time she did. For an instant both their hands were wrapped around the leather straps. Finally Lisa yielded and let him carry the bags inside. Kevin took them into the living room and put them beside the coffee table. He sat on the arm of the overstuffed sofa and pulled her to him, drawing her between his outstretched legs. His arms around her waist, hers around his neck, he eyed her steadily. "To avoid fighting over luggage or checks or who opens the door for whom in the future, maybe we should get this thing settled between us right now. Because I'm an old-fashioned kind of guy, raised by old-fashioned, plain-speaking people, I tend to do certain things that are sometimes misunderstood in today's world as having hidden or even sinister meanings."

He started unbuttoning her coat. "Just because I happen to hold your chair for you in a restaurant or insist on paying for the meal or get up to greet you when you first enter a room doesn't mean I don't think you are my equal in every way. Doing these simple, polite things are ingrained in me. *Not* doing them causes paroxysms of guilt, not to mention making me feel bad."

Lisa smiled. "Sounds okay to me—as long as you're flexible enough to let me take you out once in a while."

"It will be a new experience for me, but one I think I might learn to enjoy." He could imagine a hundred new things he would like to learn to share with Lisa. He slipped the last button of her coat through its hole, then reached up to take it from her shoulders. When he saw how she was dressed, he froze. She was wearing a sweater made of the same material and of the same color as the scarf he had given her.

"Do you like it?" she asked, hoping he would intuitively understand what she had done.

"The sweater is beautiful," he said slowly. "The woman who chose to wear it for me, beyond description. Where—"

"In a store window on the way to the airport. I ran inside while the taxi driver circled the block. The only one they had left in my size was on the mannequin, so I had to wait while they removed it and wound up missing my plane. That's why I arrived in Washington so late and appeared on your doorstep bag and baggage in tow."

"You mean you weren't planning on staying?" He tried to ignore the way the sweater clung to her breasts, sensually outlining their fullness.

"Not here..." she said, embarrassed he had thought she would show up unannounced and expect him to take her in. "I have a reservation at the Hilton."

"Is there a reason you don't want to stay with me?" The thought of her leaving created an empty feeling inside of him.

"I...uh...," she stammered, not sure she was ready for the commitment staying with him would necessarily imply.

"I have a guest room," he said gently. When she didn't immediately answer, he went on, "The guest room has an inside lock and I don't have a key. You would be perfectly safe—"

"That's not the reason, at least not the whole reason. I just don't think it would be a good idea for me to stay here in your house, Kevin. We've known each other less than a week—'' she shrugged expressively ''—and here we are...'' She couldn't find the words to finish.

''How long would we have to know each other for you to feel comfortable with such an arrangement?''

Before he had even asked, she realized how full of holes her argument was. ''Maybe it isn't the actual days and hours as much as it's the way I feel about you.''

''Which is?''

She had never been very good at putting feelings into words, as she had proven disastrously at the Senate budget meeting the previous week. ''I'm not sure. It's crazy. All I can think about when we're not together is what it would be like if we were. There's something you should know about me, Kevin. Maybe it would help you to understand why I'm not exactly ecstatic over the prospect of falling in love with anyone again.'' She hadn't meant to mention the word love, but as usual the direct line from brain to mouth had taken over and she had blurted out something that would have been better left unsaid until they had known each other longer. She shifted her weight to her other foot and took a deep breath.

''I've been down that road twice already and it wasn't much fun afterward when I found out I'd made a mistake. And there's no one else to blame for what happened because both times it was me who made the mistake. I got so caught up in the whole business of falling and being in love that I refused to see that the men I chose to lavish these feelings on were totally unsuitable for me. They were terrific guys and both of them eventually made happy marriages to women who were nonthreatening, who chose to make the center of their life home and hearth and who were content to walk in the shadows of their husbands for the rest of their lives.''

Kevin had watched her carefully as she spoke, seeing the hurt, the confusion in her eyes while listening to the defensive tone in her voice. "And you're afraid you've zeroed in on someone who's just like them all over again?"

She nodded. "I know you've told me you're not intimidated or threatened by a woman like me, but words are easy."

"And you need proof?"

Again she nodded.

"How would I go about proving something like that to you?"

"Time..."

His heart went out to her. She wanted time to know him better without realizing that the time she proclaimed she needed would only deepen the feelings that had already begun to grow between them. In the end it would be too late for her to escape unscathed. Because he knew her fears were groundless, it was easy to give her what she needed. "Isn't it possible that staying here would create the perfect opportunity for you to get to know me better?" he asked, not insisting, only suggesting.

Why was she fighting him? "Separate rooms?"

"Until you tell me differently."

"I only have two days. It does seem foolish for us to spend even a little of them traveling back and forth to a hotel."

"Would you like to see your room and check the lock out before you make a final decision?"

She responded to his teasing with a soft smile. "That won't be necessary."

He stood and slipped his arm around her shoulders. "I insist." He guided her to the stairs, then reached for her hand and led the way. At the landing they turned right and went down a short hallway to the back of the house. Kevin opened the door and stood back to let Lisa enter first.

She caught her breath in surprise. When he had mentioned a guest room she had expected something utilitarian at best, certainly not anything as charming and elegant as this—nor anything that looked as if it had come straight out of the nineteenth century. A four-poster double bed covered in an antique-lace spread dominated the large room. In one corner there was a washstand complete with pitcher and bowl and in the other an elegantly carved armoire. Matching ecru lace covered the window and skirted a dressing table, and highly polished oak floors warmly reflected an old-fashioned gaslight that had been fitted for electricity and hung from the ceiling.

Seeing her confusion, he answered before she had a chance to ask him about the room. "I lease the house from a family who left their furnishings. I put everything of theirs into storage except for what was in this room and the law books downstairs, which I use occasionally."

"The books aren't yours?"

The tone of her voice as well as the question perplexed him. "No—"

"Then you're not a lawyer?"

"No. You thought I was?"

"I just assumed."

Of course. She had seen the books in his study that first night. The conclusion would have been obvious. "Are you disappointed?"

"Not at all. Relieved is more like it."

Kevin laughed. "And why would that be?"

"My uncle is a lawyer. He's probably my least favorite person in the world." She walked over to the window to look outside. "If not a lawyer, then what?"

"You mean what did I do before I became a politician?" He wasn't surprised she didn't consider what he did a career; many people didn't. To them, holding an office was something someone did in addition to their "real" job and at the whim of the voters.

"Or what would you go back to after you quit."

"I'm afraid it's not very glamorous."

She turned away from the view of a small, precisely laid-out backyard, her curiosity peaked. "Oh?"

"Ranching has always been my first love."

"Then what are you doing in politics?"

"It's a long story."

Lisa stared at him. There was a strange mixture of sadness and acceptance in his eyes. "Don't you think now would be a good time to tell me about it?"

Finding the words for something he had never spoken aloud would be difficult. His first inclination was to try to put Lisa off by telling her he'd save the story for another time. To do so would be far easier than dredging up old and painful memories. But did he have the right to ask her to love him without being open and honest with her in every way?

Not knowing where to begin a tale that essentially encompassed all that he was, he arbitrarily chose a point. "Since I was a child, people have seen me differently than I've seen myself. They've wanted things for me that I didn't necessarily want and dreamed their dreams for me without taking mine into consideration. First it was teachers and then relatives and then finally my parents who yielded to the pressures of others and subtly, and at other times not so subtly, insisted it would be a shame to let a fine mind like mine go to waste running a ranch. No one knew exactly what to do with me, but they all thought they knew I had no business limiting my reach when I had this 'God given' gift.''

Caroline's comments came back to Lisa. She pictured Kevin as a child fighting back with the only weapon available to him—his intelligence. The pressures must have seemed unbearable to a little boy to make him resort to purposely failing school.

"When Angela moved to town," he went on, "she convinced me it was all right to be who I really was and that eventually, after I went away to college and still demonstrated my first love was the land, everyone would leave me alone." What he would say next hurt because it sounded like an indictment of someone he had once loved and needed as much as the air he breathed. But he owed Lisa the truth, no matter how painful or uncomfortable the telling. "The only problem was that Anglea, too, eventually got caught up in the idea that I was destined for 'bigger' things than ranching.''

With a graceful movement of his lanky frame he sat down in the chair beside him. Lisa came over to join him, sitting on the floor on a lamb's-wool rug. She laid her arms along his thigh. Kevin curled his broad hands around her arms, gaining a quiet strength and comfort from touching her. Long seconds passed before he began again. "Angela's father was a wealthy grain broker, his phenomenal success of his own making. He was the kind of man who enjoyed manipulating people from behind the scenes. It was only after Angela and I were engaged that I learned he wasn't overjoyed at the prospect of her marrying an ordinary rancher. But Angela had a stubborn streak wider than her father's. He eventually yielded, even giving us his blessing when she told him he would never see his grandchildren if he didn't.

"The year after we were married, three sections of land that abutted my parents' place came up for sale, and with their help I scraped together enough money to make the down payment. A blizzard hit five years later and decimated both of our herds. Without cattle to sell I couldn't keep up the payments. My father's position wasn't much better. When Angela's father found out how desperate I was, he arranged a private meeting with me. He told me he'd help me to hang on to the ranch if I'd be willing to run for the congressional position against a man he'd been trying to get out of office for years." Kevin paused. He took a deep breath, releasing it slowly. He looked down at Lisa. His hands tightened around her arm.

"I'm sorry, Kevin," she said, trying to apologize for demanding he tell her something that resurrected such painful memories.

He reached over to touch her hair, letting a lock curl around his finger. "By then it wasn't just Angela and me. We had a daughter, Christine. When I decided to go along with his proposal, I told myself it was strictly for Angela and Christine. If it were just me I had to look out for, I would have given up and started over rather than do his bidding. But I know now it was as much for myself as it was for them, probably more so. I desperately wanted to keep that ranch, and running for office was the only means left open to me. I had tried everything else. I rationalized the long-term effect running for office would have on my life with the belief that there wasn't a chance in hell I would win. Voting for my esteemed opponent was as much a tradition in our district as Grange dances on Saturday nights." The last was punctuated with a self-deprecatory laugh. His voice softened. "Angela took to campaigning as if she had been born to it. Christine even got into the act."

Lisa cringed. Because of what Caroline had already told her she knew what was coming next.

"A week before the election the strategists decided we should split forces. I was to work the northern end of the district and Angela would work the east. The polls said I was so far behind there wasn't a chance for me to catch up, but I figured I owed Angela's father my best shot for coming through on the loan, so I headed north." He took another deep breath. "I was in the middle of a speech on federal subsidies to farmers—it's funny how something like that will stick in your mind—when word arrived that there had been an automobile accident. Christine and Angela's father had been killed. Angela was taken to the hospital, where she died on the operating table an hour before I could reach her. The sympathy vote their deaths instigated put me in office with a victory more lopsided than any the district had ever recorded."

Lisa rose to her knees and moved between Kevin's legs. She wrapped her arms around his waist and gently held him. "You must have wished you could have died with them," she said, her cheek resting against his chest.

He pressed the side of his face into the fragrant softness of her hair. "For a long time there was a numbness that kept me from feeling anything. It wasn't until much later that an overwhelming feeling of guilt set in."

She tilted her head back to look up at him. "Why guilt?"

"A hundred small reasons, one big one. Angela and Christine would never have been in that car if I hadn't been so eager to sell myself to own a piece of land."

"And you've been punishing yourself for that ever since then?"

"Not quite. It took a while, but I finally managed to forgive myself." He reached up to hold the sides of her face, staring intently into her eyes. "If you're worried you've hooked up with a man who has ghosts that are still haunting him, don't. Angela and Christine were a part of me once, and they will always be a part of me, but I learned to let go of them a long time ago."

She met his gaze, studying his face as intently as she had listened to his words. "I believe you."

Slowly he came forward until their lips met in an infinitely tender kiss. "I think it would be best if we called it a night and started fresh in the morning."

She didn't want to let him go and would have made love to him then and there if he had asked her, but she realized he was right to postpone their coming together for the first time until the time was theirs alone.

CHAPTER EIGHT

THE NEXT MORNING Kevin woke early, took a shower and went downstairs to fix breakfast. He had slept surprisingly soundly despite knowing Lisa was only a door away. He felt as if the five hours had been ten. Because he rarely had more than toast and coffee in the morning, he was unsure what to fix for Lisa, finally settling on the addition of orange juice to his usual fare with a promisory note for more later stuck in a napkin ring. He took the tray upstairs and lightly tapped on her door.

"Come in," she called, the tone of her voice letting him know she had been awake before his knock.

"How did you sleep?" he asked, coming into the room. She was sitting up in bed, running her hands through her hair. Her smile of welcome made him catch his breath in pleasure.

"As if I were home in my own bed." She met his gaze and felt a warmth flow through her. He looked wonderful—rested and refreshed, as if he had just returned from a much-needed week's vacation. He was wearing a pair of jeans and a red polo shirt that hugged his chest and arms and clearly showed that his years behind a desk had not softened him. His hair was still damp from a shower and looked darker than usual, his eyes more blue. Noting the tray, she said, "I don't think I've ever had breakfast in bed unless I was sick."

"It's hard to tell from outward appearances that you've led such a deprived life." She folded the blanket over her lap and he noticed the imprint on the bright-pink nightgown she was wearing. In the center, over her chest, was an owl surrounded by the words, Give a Hoot, Don't Pollute. He pointed at the owl. "I'm glad to see that."

Automatically Lisa's hands flew up to cover her breasts, even though logic told her there was no way she could be exposed. She blushed with embarrassment when she realized what she had done.

Restraining a laugh, Kevin put the tray on the dressing table and went over to her. He sat on the edge of the bed and reached for her hands. "I was talking about the sentiment expressed on your nightgown," he told her, a smile on his lips.

She closed her eyes and groaned, wishing she could disappear into the mattress.

"Government costs—all governments, from federal right down to municipal—could be cut dramatically if people would just pick up after themselves," he purposely pontificated.

Lisa opened one eye and peered at him. "Not to mention making the countryside look a lot better." He was trying to make it easier for her. She might as well cooperate.

"See..." He leaned over and lightly kissed her. "We've found another bit of common ground already today, and it's only seven-thirty."

Lisa inhaled the wonderfully clean smell of him, suddenly not caring in the least about owls or economies, only the way his lips felt against hers. Too quickly he left to get her tray. "What time do you have to go in today?"

Kevin placed her breakfast over her lap. "I don't. I called and had my secretary cancel everything for both today and tomorrow."

"Can you do that?"

"I never have. But I've never had such a worthy cause before." Lisa reached up to tuck a curl behind her ear. Kevin watched the guileless movement, noting the way her nightgown tightened across her breasts and her nipples pressed against the fabric. He was not nearly as detached as he would have her believe. The desire she had reawakened in him had been gnawing at his midsection more than any hunger he had ever known.

"I'm honored." When she saw he was going to sit in the chair on the other side of the room, she patted the bed beside her. "Sit here and help me eat some of this toast. You've made enough for a small party."

Kevin gave her a crooked grin. "That's just about the best invitation I can ever remember receiving."

"Toast?" she asked innocently.

He took a pillow out of the armoire, propped it against the headboard, took off his shoes and carefully sat down next to her while she held the tray steady. "Of course toast—what else?"

She held up a piece for him to take a bite. "So what shall we do today?"

He took a minute to chew and swallow, wondering what she would say if he told her exactly what he would like to do with her the entire day—the entire two days. "There's a terrific exhibit on space flight at the Smithsonian."

She wrinkled her nose at him. "How boring. Who wants to know what's in space when we haven't even explored everything right here on good old earth?"

"Hmm...I can see you're going to make this hard on me. There's always the gem collection—"

"Any monuments at the gem collection? Seems to me there was something said a while back about monuments." She offered him the last bit of her first piece of toast.

Kevin ignored the toast and took her fingers into his mouth instead, gently holding and caressing the sensitive tips with his tongue.

Lisa drew in a surprised breath. "There's more if you're still hungry," she said, taking her fingers from his mouth, trying to hide just how devastating an effect he had had on her. He caught her hand and turned it over. Slowly he leaned forward and pressed his lips to her palm. She felt the contact down to her toes. "I meant more toast," she said. Her gaze settled on the hollow behind his ear. She had a compelling desire to run her tongue across the smooth skin she saw there...and to catch his earlobe between her teeth...and to have him touch her... "Kevin?"

He looked up at her, his lips still pressed to her palm. "Hmm?"

"What are we doing?" If he wasn't going to make love to her, she wanted him to stop fooling around. She could only take so much.

He reached for the tray and set it on the floor. "I'm not sure what you're doing, but I'm enjoying myself more than I have in a long, long time."

"Tell me why."

At first he thought she was kidding but then realized there must be a doubt lingering from what he had told her about himself the night before. She needed to know he was falling in love with her, that she wasn't simply a woman who had happened along when he was ready to love again. He cupped her chin with his hand, running his thumb across her lips. "If you were to ask any given number of my friends or acquaintances here in Washington about my sense of humor, they would probably say I don't have one—yet you can make me laugh without even trying."

"And quite unintentionally most of the time."

He smiled and shook his head. "It's my turn to talk, you'll get yours later." Leaning back against the pillow, he pulled her to him. She curled up beside him, snuggling against his chest, her arm flung across his waist. "We've known each other less than a week and yet I feel we've always known each other. The things I have left to learn about you seem like treasures waiting to be opened. When I first found out how you make your living, I was a little in awe about the whole thing. That lasted about half an hour before I discovered I wasn't thinking about what you did anymore, I was thinking about who you are. You're a complicated mixture of sometimes contradictory elements. One of those elements is your toughness. You carry it around like an impenetrable shield. But there's a compelling vulnerability that comes through, too. You're intelligent, but I have a feeling you're not smart enough to realize just how intelligent. Courageous...I've read articles about the training program astronauts go through and I—"

"Stop! You're making me sound like Wonder Woman, a girl scout and the new Jane Fonda all rolled into one."

He ignored her. "You also happen to be one sexy lady. Sometimes your hair reminds me of harvest wheat the way it catches the light. You have an incredibly sensual mouth, especially at certain times when you're deep in thought and your lips are partially opened and you touch them with your tongue. And your eyes, they're the main clue to the imp that lurks inside the serious woman.'' He ran his hand along her arm as he paused to consider. ''If I were to change anything at all, I think I'd like it if you were a little taller.''

''You and me both. There's a definite conspiracy in this world against short people.''

''But my reasons are totally selfish. If we should ever want to spend any time kissing while we're standing up, I'd probably wind up with a crick in my neck.'' He pressed his lips to the top of her head. ''Otherwise I wouldn't change a thing about you.''

''Meaning you think everything about me is perfect?'' she asked suspiciously.

''From toes to temples.'' He was reluctant to point out the individual parts remaining or to dwell on them any more than necessary while holding her in his arms, sitting in the middle of a bed, when she was wearing nothing but a nightgown.

''You're wrong about being perfect, Kevin...my hips are too big.''

''Trust me, they're not.'' The way they flared gently from her waist was decidedly enticing, especially when she walked. She had a way of moving that was unlike any other woman he had ever known. Just thinking about it was enough to set his mind wandering.

''And my chest—''

''Is perfect.'' Her breasts were full yet not too large. He had measured their weight in dreams, imagined their touch in his hands over and over again.

''Now if my waist were smaller...'' She waited for him to say something. When he didn't she looked up and found him peering at her through hooded eyes.

"You may have a point," he said, after some consideration. "If your waist were smaller you might look more in proportion, not so much like a pineapple."

She laughed and playfully punched him in the arm. "And here I was all set to tell you how handsome you looked this morning."

He caught her to him and rolled over on top of her. The instant he felt the intimacy of their contact he knew he had made a mistake. The playfulness that had put them into that position vanished as they stared deeply into each other's eyes. "I think I'd better get out of here and let you get dressed," he said, struggling with the words. He wanted her so badly he could hardly speak.

"What if I asked you to stay," she answered, barely above a whisper, feeling the intensity of his craving for her and responding with one as deep.

"Do you know what you're saying?"

She nodded.

"Are you sure?" As much as he wanted her, his overwhelming need was to have her want him in return.

Again she nodded.

With a soft moan of pleasure he lowered his head to kiss her. Their lips met and parted, their tongues touched and caressed. Kevin rolled to his side and then to his back, taking her with him. "Lisa...it's been so long," he said, a catch in his throat giving voice to his fears. "Be patient with me." His hands coursed the length of her back, stopping at the swell of her buttocks before fanning out to caress her hips. He pressed her against him, fitting the planes and curves of their bodies together in an erotic melding.

He wanted their lovemaking to be perfect for her, he wanted to give her pleasure such as she had never known, but he was unsure of himself. He had made love to one woman in his life and had no real idea how to please another. It would be so easy to simply take the satisfaction he ached for, to use Lisa as a release for the pent-up desire that tore at him, but he couldn't. Their lovemaking would be no good unless it was good for both of them.

He reached up to grasp the sides of her face, to make her look at him. "Lisa, I need your help...I don't know how to make this—"

Intuitively she understood what he wanted to tell her. She pressed her fingers to his lips and gave him a tender, understanding smile. "You've been reading too many magazine articles about the modern woman, Kevin. Just remember that basically we're all put together pretty much the same and I'm sure you'll do fine on your own." She lowered her mouth to his and kissed him. It was a deep, inviting kiss to tell him she was as much a part of their lovemaking as he was. "If not," she added a little breathlessly, "I'll be sure to let you know."

"With an offer like that, how could I go wrong?" He kissed her lips and then her chin, her cheeks, her temples, her eyes. "As I recall, this whole process works better without clothing," he said, reaching for her gown and slowly pulling it up over her hips. Where his hands touched her bare skin he would have sworn an electrical charge passed between them.

He rolled to his side and sat up. Untucking his shirt, he took the hem and pulled it over his head, deciding it might be easier for her if he was the first to undress.

Lisa sat up beside him. "I believe that's my job," she gently chided.

He smiled. "Should I put it back on?"

"No...just leave the rest to me." She motioned for him to put his feet on her lap. When he did, she wriggled her hands up first one and then the other pant leg and slowly pulled his stockings over his calves and off his feet. Unable to resist, she ran her index finger down his instep and gave him a satisfied grin when he jumped. She had never trusted people who weren't ticklish.

The stockings tossed on the floor, she reached for his belt. It was a struggle to get the thick leather through the brass buckle but she persisted, refusing to ask for his help. Next came the buttons on his jeans, provocatively placed and impossible to undo without intimately touching him. Lisa took her time, purposely stumbling with the task, reveling in Kevin's sighed pleasure. When she had finished, he stepped from the bed to complete the rest.

With his jeans and underwear gone she openly looked at him, an appreciative gleam in her eye. "You must have spent a lot of time in a gym working off your frustrations—you don't look half bad for an old man of thirty-six."

"That's the best you can do after all I had to say about you earlier?" He was surprised at his own lack of shyness as he stood still for her appraisal. The only people who had seen him naked in ten years were the physicians who handled his annual checkup.

Oh, she inwardly sighed, she could have said a lot more—if her mouth hadn't suddenly turned to cotton and she weren't already on the verge of trembling with desire for him. Kevin had the kind of build that had always appealed to her. There was quiet strength in his muscles, a gracefulness in the way he moved. She liked the light matting of hair on his chest and the narrowness of his waist. "I'll work on it and get back to you later."

Lowering himself beside her, Kevin brushed a curl aside and pressed his lips to her temple. His breath caressed her ear, and his tongue teased her lips. She responded to him like a poppy to sunshine, opening her arms in welcome. He buried his face in her hair and whispered words of love, tender words lacking meaning by themselves but expressing volumes to a receptive Lisa.

She started to pull her gown off, wanting to know the feel of his flesh against her but Kevin stopped her. "That's my job," he said, echoing her earlier words. Slowly he raised the gown, letting his hands mark the journey along her sides. She lifted her arms to help him and her gown quickly joined his clothing. For a long time he looked at her. After a while a private smile lighted his eyes. "You put my feeble powers of imagination to shame."

She returned his smile. "Dare I ask just what you were imagining?"

"It loses something in the translation." Hesitantly at first he reached out to her. The backs of his fingers touched her collarbone, then began a downward journey to the gentle swelling that marked the beginning of her breast. Her skin was as smooth as finely sanded cherry wood, so much softer than his own. Wherever he touched her she became an intoxicating drug, one that was released into his fingertips and raced to his mind, leaving him reeling with its effects and craving more, always more.

With infinite tenderness he cupped the undersides of her breasts in his broad, flat hands and brushed her hardened nipples with his thumbs. Shyly he lowered his head to caress a nipple with his tongue. She combed her fingers through his hair, pulling him closer, whispering his name over and over again in a litany of passion. His fingers traced small circular patterns on her sensitive inner thigh, moving ever closer to a place she ached to have touched. When he unerringly found that place, she raised herself up on the bed so that she was kneeling, allowing him an ease of movement that made her light-headed with the force of her desire. Quickly the need for release came to her in a raging demand. She caught her breath. "Now, Kevin," she murmured, not knowing whether or not she had spoken the command aloud.

He lowered her to lie crossways on the bed and covered her with himself. She moved beneath him, welcoming his body into the cradle of her own. His hips fit against hers and with a gentle thrust he was inside. As they moved together in pleasure so intense it bordered on pain, he listened to the soft sounds she made, to the rhythm of her breathing. When he sensed she was ready, he moved his hand between them and again touched her. She cried out his name as they traveled the final distance together.

CHAPTER NINE

LISA STOOD IN THE DOORWAY to the kitchen, an egg in one hand, a fork in the other, watching Kevin bring in wood to start a fire. Fresh from her shower, she was still wearing her robe and had a towel wrapped turban-style around her head.

Closing the door with his foot, Kevin glanced up to see her looking at him. At the sight of her a physical pain shot through his chest and he caught his breath. He was like a man who had been unaware of his hunger until a meal had been placed before him. As irrational as the thought was, he wished with all his heart they could go on as they were now. The knowledge she would be leaving in a day was torture. A house that had never seemed lonely before would seem cold and cavernous when she left.

"Are you all right?" Lisa asked, concerned by the way he was looking at her.

He gave her a reassuring smile. "I'm fine," he said. "I just had a little catch in my back." It was an easier explanation, less complicated.

"Probably the result of too much unusual activity." She winked at him. "You'll have to let me bring in the wood from now on."

"And save myself for more important things?"

"You got it."

He gave her a quick kiss as he passed her on his way into the living room. *God, she made him feel good*. He finally understood why Tarzan always beat his chest and let out that funny sound whenever Jane was around. He chuckled, wondering what Lisa would do if he acted in kind. Never mind what Lisa would do, he could just imagine the reaction among his fellow senators if they should ever find out he had even contemplated such a thing. The hard-nosed young senator from Kansas? Never!

Lisa came into the room. She stood beside him, pressing her legs against his back as he kneeled in front of the fireplace. "I need some help on this brunch thing. Just how hungry are you?"

"Ravenous."

"Does that translate into a two-, three- or four-egg omelet?"

"Three."

"Hash browns?"

"Of course."

"Fresh fruit?"

"Definitely."

"I assume you have all these things?"

"Mrs. Mayfield makes sure the cupboards are always full." He placed several pieces of kindling over crinkled newspapers.

"So that's who takes care of this place. I didn't think you did everything yourself."

"Do I detect a bit of female chauvinism? Is it possible you think a man is incapable of taking care of himself without—"

"Do you or do you not have a housekeeper?"

"Yes..."

"Then I rest my case."

"Not so fast. Only the Washington house has a housekeeper. When I'm in Kansas I do all the work myself." He struck a match to the paper.

"You have a house in Kansas, too?"

He stood. "Of course. Where do you think I go when Congress isn't in session?"

"I don't know. I didn't think." She stuffed the egg in one pocket and the fork in the other, then put her arms around his waist. Tilting her head back to look up at him, she said, "Is it the same place?"

He knew what she was asking. She wanted to know if he still lived in the house he and Angela had shared. "Yes, it's the one that came with the three sections of land. I still own them, too." He became thoughtful, considering how much he should tell her, what she might feel was important to know. "Because Angela died after her father, she became the sole inheritor of his estate. When she died, everything passed on to me." His voice was neutral, accepting. "Eventually I gave a large portion of the money to different charities. The rest I use occasionally to make things a little easier for my parents. But for the most part the money just sits. Right now I have no use for it. Maybe someday I will." His first impulse upon learning he had become a multimillionaire because of the accident had been to give the money away as quickly as possible. It wasn't until after much soul-searching that he came to realize that receiving the money wasn't an indictment of guilt. Part of his self-healing had centered around his inability to think of the money as he would any other, and only when he could do so did he follow his earlier instincts and give any away.

With all of her heart Lisa wished she had known Kevin then and could have helped him. "You mean when you leave all of this behind?"

"Uh-huh."

"You'll be too old and doddering to know how to spend it," she teased.

"God, I hope not."

It wasn't the words but the fervent tone that alerted her. "So it's true. You really don't like being a senator."

"I feel that what I'm doing is important, and when I manage a victory it brings a sense of satisfaction."

She was intrigued that someone would continue in a job he didn't like. She couldn't imagine doing the same. "Why are you called a watchdog?" She was curious to hear his feelings about his reputation.

He smiled. "You've been talking to someone about me." For some reason he liked knowing she had.

"As a matter of fact, several someones. All of whom had basically the same thing to say. They told me you were honest and had integrity, and I should avoid discussing politics with you at all costs if I wanted our relationship to go anywhere."

"And I see you always listen to your friends' advice."

"Back to watchdog."

"It means I make it a point to find things in government spending that are out of line and try to do something about them." He checked the fire and found it burning nicely. Guiding her over to the sofa, he added, "Such as an eight-thousand-dollar, ten-cup coffeepot ordered for an air-force cargo plane or a $544-million cost overrun on a nuclear submarine." He sat down and reached for her to sit on his lap.

"Wait a minute," she squealed, jumping up. Carefully she extracted the fork and egg from her pockets and laid them on the coffee table.

Kevin laughed. "I'm sure glad you remembered. I shudder to think of the damage you might have done with one and the mess you could have made with the other." He pulled her to him and nuzzled her neck.

She squirmed around to look at him. "Oh, no you don't. You're not getting off so easy...back to telling me all about you."

"Are you absolutely sure you want to talk about me when there are so many more pleasant things we could be doing?"

"I'm positive."

"And persistent." He let out a resigned sigh and leaned back against the sofa. "If you recall, when we were at the National Archives I told you how I used to spend time going to different places around town to try to get a feeling that one man could make a difference. Well, during my search, something totally unanticipated happened to me. I developed a feel for what this country is all about—at least what it was about two hundred years ago. When I had been in Congress long enough to understand how dangerously close we are to financial ruin and collapse because of the national debt, I decided my small contribution to my country would be an attempt to try to do something about it—if only by being a thorn in so many sides that someday, somewhere, someone listened and joined me."

"And so you arbitrarily vote against all government spending, no matter what the cause?" she asked evenly.

"That's not quite true, but close enough." Obviously the people she had been talking to had also filled her in on his voting record for the space program. "If there's no longer a government, Lisa, it doesn't matter how altruistic or far-reaching its goals once were," he answered just as evenly, detecting the quick anger in her eyes and the way she held herself stiffly in his lap.

"Not everyone on the Hill shares your views about imminent disaster, I take it."

"Economists and their theories are like religions and churches—you go to the one that preaches what you want to hear."

"And the church you attend preaches doom?" Her anger was becoming more pronounced, her patience shorter. She was fighting for something she believed in as surely as she believed the earth was round.

"I like to think of it as hope for the future."

"By sacrificing everything in the present?"

"Not everything."

"Oh? What would you single out to save?"

"The programs for the sick and elderly..."

"And?"

Kevin felt as if he had been given a piece of ice that held a wondrous promise for their future but only if he could keep it from melting in his hand as he held it. "Lisa...are we going to let what is basically only a difference of opinion come between us on today of all days?" he asked softly.

The poignancy in his voice touched her, detroying the anger that had been building. "No," she answered. After several seconds she gave him an impish grin. "Not if *you* don't want to."

He brought her to him and gave her a kiss. What started out as a peace offering soon took on a deeper meaning as lips parted and passions reignited. Lisa was the first to pull away. "Whew," she breathed, fanning herself with one hand while readjusting her turban with the other. "I'll bet when you were in college you carried one of those signs that said, Make Love, Not War."

"It's the company I'm keeping," he replied, taking her by the waist and pulling her backward until they were lying side by side on the sofa. He took the towel she had wrapped around her head and threw it to the floor.

There was no mistaking the look in his eyes or his intentions. The hesitancy he had shown earlier was gone from their relationship forever. "By any chance, are you planning on blaming this midmorning dalliance on me?" she said, demonstrating her willingness by reaching for the buttons on his shirt. Before he could answer, she touched her lips to the hollow behind his ear and with her tongue traced a line to the base of his throat, where she felt his racing pulse.

"If you want the credit," he murmured into her fragrant still-damp hair, "it could certainly be arranged."

"We'll have to discuss it later."

"Sounds good to me." He held the back of her head and drew her to him. His tongue tasted her mouth in an urgent erotic rhythm, and she responded with a low moan. Soon they were lost to everything but their growing need for fulfillment. "Do you want to go upstairs?" he asked, saying a silent prayer that she didn't.

"Upstairs?" she answered through a fog of passion. "What upstairs?"

He smiled.

BY THE TIME THEY ATE it was early afternoon and the fare had changed from omelets to sandwiches. Finishing the last of his ham and cheese on rye, Kevin took their plates to the sink. "I've decided where to take you this afternoon."

Her eyebrows rose in question.

"Mount Vernon."

"George Washington's home?" Her lack of enthusiasm was evident in her tone of voice.

"Not only is it a nice drive, there's something there I want you to see. On the way back we can stop for dinner at an outstanding Chinese restaurant I know in Alexandria. This place serves the best pot stickers and *mu shi* pork I've found anywhere." He put his fingers to his lips and kissed them. "You'll be impressed, I promise."

"Is the dinner a bribe because of the other?"

He laughed. "Trust me—you'll enjoy Mount Vernon."

"Uh-huh."

Kevin was right; she did enjoy Mount Vernon—and the drive there along the parkway that ran parallel to the Potomac River. He added to the enjoyment by relating anecdotes of the first president both before and after the revolutionary war.

As they walked down the tree-lined path that led up to the house, Kevin told her of a young Washington, a third son born of his father's second wife. Because of his birth order he received little formal education, and his future seemed unpromising. When they walked through the fields and gardens and rooms of the two-story wooden house where Washington and his family had lived, Kevin spoke of the love the nation's first president had held for his home, a home he had inherited from his brother's widow after leasing it from her for sixteen years.

When they left the house they walked the hundred or so yards down the hill to the Potomac River. "For six years after the war," Kevin said, "the colonies floundered without a strong central leadership. Realizing what was happening, the men who were selected to do something about this problem met in Philadelphia in 1787 and revised the Articles of Confederation into the constitution of the United States. Washington served as their leader, and even though he preferred the planter's life there at Mount Vernon, he reluctantly agreed to serve as the country's first president. He never enjoyed the position and eagerly awaited the time he could return there.''

Lisa looked out across the Potomac to Fort Washington Park. ''Why do you suppose he took the job in the first place?'' What Kevin was telling her contradicted what she had learned as a child in school. She had thought Washington served as president because he wanted to, not because of a sense of duty to his new country.

''Because he believed in the ideals and the idea.'' They started back up the hill. ''Another thing that fascinated me when I did my studying on Washington— something that had never occurred to me before, was how much he must have suffered with his teeth. Although his false teeth have become legendary, it never crossed my mind that he would have spent much of the war suffering with toothaches.''

They reached the garden gate and Kevin held it open for Lisa to enter. ''The more I learned about Washington, the more real he became to me. As with all real men, his successes were accompanied by many failures. In his personal life he suffered unrequited love for Sally Fairfax, the wife of his best friend. And although he dearly loved children, he died without producing an heir of his own.''

The museum they headed to next was located in one of the outlying buildings. Because of the season, few people had accompanied them on the tour through the house, and there was no one in the museum. As they walked around the room, reading the literature and looking at the clothing and artifacts, Kevin added more details, always personalizing what they were seeing.

"Can you imagine how hard it must have been for someone who had been raised with a tradition of loyalty to a country and its king to abandon that life? The sacrifice in friendships alone must have been staggering—not to mention relatives. And what if they had failed? Everything Washington had built here at Mount Vernon would have been confiscated by the Crown. He would have been disgraced and branded a traitor. But he had a cause he believed in and was willing to lose everything to support that cause."

Lisa stopped and leaned against a wall, putting her hands behind her and pressing them against the cool wood. She looked at Kevin through narrowed eyes. "All of this has to be leading up to something."

"I'm not trying to convert you to my cause, Lisa," he said, "only to give you the means to understand why I feel so strongly about what I'm doing. I happen to think the ideals people like Washington fought and died for are worth saving. Maybe the way I'm going about it won't work, or I could find out in the end that I've been jousting with windmills, but while I'm here I have to try. It gives me a purpose."

Despite a growing understanding of the forces that motivated him, she couldn't separate his idealism from the knowledge that if he was to win, there would be no space program. It wasn't just that she would be out of a job. The whole idea of the program—the goals, the achievements, the long-range benefits for everyone— was something she believed in with as much fervor as

Kevin believed in what he was doing. "Is there no middle ground for you?"

"Of course there is. But it's not one anyone wants to hear."

"Try me."

"If we could just hold the line on, and in some instances cut, spending—"

"And if agencies would stop paying ten dollars for a twenty-five-cent bolt..." She let out a frustrated sigh. "You can't actually believe there's enough padding in NASA's operation for us to be able to cope with inflation and a budget cut and still go on the way we are now."

"I've been trying to avoid naming names."

"Why? We both know you're talking about NASA." She felt torn between her burgeoning feelings for Kevin and what he stood for. How could she love a man who would, if he could, destroy the other passion in her life?

"Lisa, you're being rather myopic about this." There was a plea for conciliation in his voice. "NASA is a small part of the overall picture. I've never singled them out above any other government agency."

Her chin dropped to her chest, and she stared at the tips of her shoes. She couldn't shake the feeling that they were the elected representatives of their respective sides and what happened between them would determine the outcome of their private war. "I seem determined to do battle with you on this, don't I?"

He cupped her chin with his hand and made her look at him. "You're probably still smarting from the Budget-Committee meeting."

She gave him a smile. He wasn't trying to do anything except help her to understand him. In his way he was struggling to give her another part of himself, and she kept throwing it back at him. "You can say that again."

"You're probably still smarting—"

She put her arms around his neck. "You know, there's a real streak of Kansas corn in you."

"It seems to come with the territory." He lightly brushed his lips over hers.

"What do you suppose old George would say if he knew what lusty thoughts I'm having right now?"

"Somehow I think he would approve. I know I do." He refused to consider the possibility that they might not always be able to set aside their differences so easily. With each passing hour his feelings for Lisa deepened, became more of an integral part of his being. They could not let what was basically one philosophical difference separate them.

She took his hand. "Listen," she commanded, tilting her head slightly as if to hear something from outside. Kevin did listen but heard nothing. He shook his head and shrugged.

"You can't hear that?" she asked incredulously.

He tried again. "No..."

"Well, I can. And it sounds just like Chinese food calling our names."

He blinked, then laughed aloud. If a lifetime was indeed composed of hills and valleys, he had started on his way to climbing a wondrous peak the day he met her. He gave her a hug filled with joy, their differences forgotten.

LISA KNEW IMMEDIATELY upon entering Kevin's favorite restaurant that he had chosen a winner. The Dancing Dragon was a hole-in-the-wall where diners were greeted from the kitchen as they entered. The young

Chinese girl who seated them knew Kevin by name and showed no surprise that he was there with a woman. When she left to get them their tea, Lisa propped her elbows on the table, put her chin in her hands and pointedly stared at Kevin. "How did I get the impression you didn't go out with women very often?"

He gave her a genuine look of surprise. "I don't know."

"You do go out with women then?"

"Not on a weekly basis and rarely with the same woman twice in a row, but I do go out. Surely you didn't think I was a social recluse."

"I don't know what I thought."

"You're confused about what happened this morning," he said, suddenly understanding what had precipitated her statement. He reached for her hands; they disappeared into his own. "I happen to be one of those men who have no interest in sleeping with a woman he doesn't love." Seeing a skeptical look in her eyes, he added. "We're not as rare a breed as you might suppose."

"Name me one other—"

"Mike Webster."

She had only to summon a mental picture of Mike to know Kevin was right. "Well, someone has been giving you guys a lot of bad press because this isn't the way you're depicted at all."

"Does the idea bother you?"

"What? Fidelity?" A flip answer was on the tip of her tongue. It was the way she would have normally dealt with the subject of fidelity. She bit it back and forced herself to dig deeper for the way she really felt. "It doesn't bother me at all...I like knowing I'm this important to you...it makes me feel special." She felt herself grow warm as a flush hit her cheeks. "It isn't as if I were all that experienced myself. But then that's still expected from the female of the species." She had slept with two men before Kevin, both of whom she had planned to marry.

Kevin noted the fresh color in her cheeks and squeezed her hands. "Being old-fashioned isn't so bad. Who knows, things may head back our way someday and we'll be the trend setters."

"As long as the pendulum doesn't swing too far. There are some things I would hate to see come back."

The waitress came for their order. They took turns naming their favorite dishes and wound up ordering far more than they could possibly eat, justifying their indulgence by telling each other the leftovers would make a great lunch the next day. When they were alone again, Kevin refused to let Lisa ask any more questions about him until he had asked some about her.

"Let's start with some basics," he said. "I think it's about time I knew where you were born."

"Seattle, Washington."

"Raised?"

"Same place until I was ten and my father accepted a teaching position at the University of California in Berkeley. He was a physics professor. I'm the product of a single-parent household. My mother died when I was two, leaving my brother and myself in the care of a man who barely knew he had two children. To familiarize himself with his new role, my father quit teaching for a year and studied David and me." As always happened when she spoke of her father, Lisa's eyes lighted up. "He told us we were the toughest subjects he'd ever tried mastering. He also told us he'd never enjoyed anything more. We were a crazy household of mismatched socks and music lessons and forgotten dinners that turned into late-night snacks, but there was always an abundance of love and mental stimulation.''

"What does your father do now?"

"He's still teaching."

"And your brother?"

"He works in San Jose, about an hour and a half drive down the road from Berkeley, for a company called Apache Computers. He's one of the geniuses who keeps them one step ahead of everyone else.'' Lisa looked up to see their waitress coming with their pot stickers. She smiled at Kevin. "The feast begins."

Lisa took one of the plump, meat-filled Chinese pasties with her chopsticks and dipped it into the small bowl filled with ginger, soy sauce and chili oil that had been placed between them. She brought it up to her mouth and caught a drip with her tongue, then licked her lips before taking a bite.

"My God, Lisa, you're the only woman I've ever known who could turn me on by the way she eats."

She ignored him. "Well, you were right about the pot stickers—they're fantastic." Again she licked the sauce from her lips.

Kevin chuckled. Her sensuality was as natural and guileless as her personality. If only they could find a way to completely clear the path between them. For him it was a simple matter of agreeing to disagree. For Lisa it was much more. A terrible premonition hit him. Something was going to happen that would make it impossible for them to overcome their conflicting ideologies. The feeling was so real, so powerful, it left him speechless.

Lisa reached for his hand. "Kevin...what is it?"

He grasped her hand and held it tightly. "Nothing," he said softly, refusing to give credence to his fears by giving them voice. Regardless, for the rest of the evening he was unable to shake the uneasy feeling.

LATE THE NEXT NIGHT Lisa and Kevin were at National Airport waiting for her to board her plane to Houston. For the first time she wasn't looking forward to going home. It had been impossible for them to make definite plans as to when they would be able to see each other again because of the work load she knew she would face when she returned and the bills that were coming up for vote on the Senate floor. It seemed so trite to say she would write, so inadequate that he would call. Although no verbal declarations had been made, they both knew they were in love. It was almost as if it was necessary for a certain amount of time to pass to legitimize their feelings before either of them could say them aloud. To make any kind of commitment so soon was unthinkable.

Walking with Lisa to where she would board her plane, Kevin couldn't shake the feeling that he shouldn't let her go. But it was ridiculous to think he could make, or even should make her stay. She had a life, a job she had to go back to. What they had started this past week was only a beginning. Their relationship needed time and space to grow. The logistics alone would be a formidable obstacle they would have to overcome.

What in the hell was the matter with him? What was he doing searching for sane and sensible reasons why they should be apart when what he really wanted to do was take her in his arms and never let her go? He took her elbow and pulled her with him to a little alcove out of the flow of traffic. "Lisa..." He adjusted her yellow scarf, which she had worn loosely wrapped around her neck, stalling, unable to find words to express feelings that were tearing him apart. "I love you," he finally, simply stated.

She stared at him for long seconds. "*Now* you tell me. I was beginning to think you were having second thoughts about us." She threw her arms around his neck and held him close.

"How could you think that?"

"You've been acting so strangely, as if—"

"I just didn't want to face saying good-bye."

"And I thought it was because you didn't know how."

"With you I don't—I much prefer hello." In the background he heard the final call for her flight. For a second he considered delaying her until she had missed her plane so they would have at least a little more time together. But as quickly as the thought came, it disappeared. "Come on," he said, taking her hand. "We don't want you to miss your plane."

After he saw her safely on board, Kevin went to the observation area to watch her plane take off. He continued to watch until its lights disappeared into the myriad others dotting the sky, then he went to his car and drove home. As he had known it would, the house seemed cold when he opened the door. He considered building a fire but discarded the idea in favor of a snifter of brandy and bed.

It was the middle of the night and he was still lying in his bed awake when the telephone rang. He picked up the receiver after the first summons. "Hello."

"I forgot to tell you that I love you, too," Lisa told him.

Later, when sleep finally came to Kevin, it was peaceful and filled with dreams he had not dared to dream for a long time.

CHAPTER TEN

THE MORNING LISA ARRIVED back in Houston she went to work without any sleep. She had her hand to her mouth, stifling a yawn, when she ran into Cory, who was coming out of an office that fed into the hallway. "I'm on my way to the debriefing," he said. "You want to come along?"

It wasn't necessary for either of them to be present. The men who would try to put the puzzle together long distance had already quizzed them at the Cape. But Lisa was as curious as Cory obviously was to discover what had gone wrong on the *Orion*. Their lives might depend on knowing someday. "Are you sure they're going to let us in?"

"This is the eighth time they've had those people under hot lights. I can't see where we would cause any discernible distraction."

She walked alongside him, taking two steps to his one stride. "How was your visit with the Websters?"

"Fantastic. It's been a long time since we've all been together. I'm really looking forward to their move back here."

"Have the people moved out of the house they bought?"

"I'm supposed to check on that for them tomorrow." He held the door for her as they left the building. "And how was your visit with the senator from Kansas?"

"We had a stimulating two days discussing our divergent views on additional funding for the space station, among other things."

Cory laughed. "I'll just bet you did." He carefully looked her over. "It couldn't have been too bad. I don't see any lasting injuries."

They walked awhile on the concrete path, then cut across the lawn. "You seem rather blasé about Kevin," Lisa remarked. "Why is that? It strikes me that everyone here should consider him an enemy."

"You can't fault a man for his beliefs, especially not one like Kevin Anderson. Besides, there are times I'm not all that sure he's so wrong. You'd have to have your head stuck in the sand not to realize that this country's going to be in big trouble sooner or later with a national debt that grows by millions every day."

Lisa let the reference to someone having their head stuck in the sand slide by her. She already felt guilty enough about her lack of political awareness without letting Cory add to that guilt. "Are you trying to tell me you support him?"

"Support is probably not the term I would use. 'Begrudgingly agree with him in principle' would be a better way to express how I feel. I recognize the problem, but I can't quite buy the solution. I'm no different from everyone else who agrees the cuts have to be made...somewhere, just as long as they're not made in my own backyard."

She hadn't anticipated an answer like that from Cory, who was every bit as dedicated to the space program as she was. But then it also seemed a little incongruous that Kevin was as involved in Caroline and Mike's lives as he

154 TODAY, TOMORROW, ALWAYS

was. He and Mike were completely at odds when it came to the goals of their jobs. As NASA's political liaison, Mike was in Washington to get more money for the space program while Kevin worked to see that he didn't succeed. Feeling as if her thoughts were taking her around in circles, she decided to leave politics alone for a while and change the subject. "Have you heard any new speculations lately about what happened up there?"

"Nothing creative. Everyone seems pretty sure it was a computer malfunction, but no one can figure out why the redundant units would go out, too."

"What about the *Orion*'s scheduled flights? Have they decided what they're going to do about them?"

"For crying out loud, Lisa," he groaned, "I've only been here since six o'clock this morning. Give me a little time."

She tossed him a glance and a crooked smile. "You're slipping, Cory. I can remember when you would have been calling for information from Washington."

"Ann told me she wouldn't speak to me if I did." They arrived at the two-story barracks-style building where the *Orion*'s crew was to undergo yet another set of questions designed to prod their memories for a clue to the mystery of the explosion.

Lisa carefully opened the door and slipped inside, taking a seat in the back of the room. Cory followed, accidentally kicking a chair and alerting everyone to their presence. Ten pairs of eyes turned and looked at them. "We thought we might be of some help," Cory said, his voice authoritative. "We'll just sit back here, and if there's anything we can add we'll do it later."

The two men at the head of the table conferred a second before nodding their approval.

"Nice going," Lisa whispered.

Cory grinned. "You have to be quick on your feet when you have kids. It's given me great practice."

The hours passed quickly as they sat and listened to the retelling of the accident. Whenever a question was asked it would be answered by each crew member according to his or her impression of the event, and piece by piece the drama unfolded. Hearing the answers delivered in crisp unemotional sentences gave an eerie sense of reality to the events. Lisa easily imagined herself on board, reacting to the first emergency with the calmness bred from repeated drills. She felt the growing tension as the crew's efforts to rectify the problem by shutting down and switching to backup units created yet more fires. She understood the helplessness the commander had felt when he ordered all systems except basic life support shut down. She could only empathize with the crew's feelings from a distance as they waited for rescue, wondering how long the rescue would take.

Like all of the astronauts, Lisa had worked with the new shuttle extensively, both in mock-up and on the pad. She had visited the plant during its construction and consulted with engineers about everything from the placement of the computer panels to considerations of function versus comfort for the internal design. The *Orion* and her sister ship, *Pegasus*, still under construction, made the earlier shuttles seem like Model T's compared to Porsches—both would get you there, but the ride along the way would suffer considerably in comparison. This accident was a terrible blow, especially now, not only to the program as a whole but to the advancement of space vehicles in general.

Finally someone signaled for a lunch break. After having spent the previous three hours in a relatively cool room, Lisa was surprised to find herself covered with perspiration when she rose to leave. As the others filed out, she borrowed a handkerchief from Cory.

"Are you coming down with something?" he asked, concerned.

"Just an overactive imagination."

"I felt it, too. That ship could easily have been their coffin." He held the door and waited for her to leave. "Let's do something cheerful—this kind of talk I don't need. It was bad enough listening to them without adding to it ourselves."

Cory's plans were quickly revised when they walked outside and discovered the others waiting for them. Lisa begged off going to lunch, saying she had a headache—which, as she discovered while walking back over to the training hangar, wasn't far from the truth. Her job on her next scheduled shuttle flight was the operation of the remote manipulator arm for the retrieval of an African communication satellite that had gone haywire. Because of the delicacy of the operation she had decided it prudent to arrange as much time with the simulator as she could get.

As she walked the quarter mile to the hangar she thought about her phone call to Kevin. She had almost been able to physically feel his response to the words when she told him she loved him. It hadn't been an easy phone call for her to make. It wasn't that she doubted she loved him; she just couldn't shake the feeling that it was too soon for them to be making such statements to each other. The events of the past week seemed a blur, but the time she had spent with Kevin stood out in sharp relief. Because of her sense of unease about the whole thing, she had almost added a "now what?" to her declaration of love. Where *did* they go from there? More important, where did she want their relationship to go?

The logical, eventual step for two people who loved each other would seem to be marriage—or some arrangement in which they lived together at least part of the time. After abandoning the idea of commitment of any sort two years earlier, it was hard to think of herself subscribing again—and so easily.

"Hey, what's your hurry," Sandy Williams called out breathlessly, running to catch up with her.

"Sorry," Lisa said, "I didn't know you were following me."

She fell into step beside Lisa. "I couldn't face another sandwich and carton of milk so I thought I'd chase you down and see if you could tell me anything about this guy who's been raking us over the coals for the past two days. Someone said you'd worked with him before."

"Which one?" she asked, immediately attuned to Sandy's seemingly casual inquiry. "As I recall, there were three." She knew all three men slightly for various reasons.

"The tall redhead."

He was the psychiatrist who was there to analyze the crew's reactions to stress after the fact. "I worked with him about two years ago, but it was only for a short time. He was doing a study on the psychological profile of women astronauts or some such thing."

"Then you didn't go out with him?"

"On a date?"

"Of course a date. What else would I be talking about?"

Finally it dawned on Lisa exactly what Sandy was after. "So the guy appeals to you, huh?"

"You might say that."

"Are you going to ask him out?" Sandy wasn't the timid type who waited around for a man to ask her. If she was interested, she pursued.

"I already have. We're going to Sundowners tomorrow night."

"Sounds like a fait accompli. What do you need me for?"

"I thought you might be able to tell me whether or not I had made a mistake. I've never gone out with a psychiatrist before. I'd hate to spend the evening feeling as if everything I did or said was being analyzed."

Lisa laughed. "It's a little late to be getting cold feet now, don't you think?"

"Ever hear of the twenty-four-hour flu?"

"You mean one of those fortuitous illnesses that happen to come along every now and then just when you need them most? I've had a few of them in my lifetime."

"Well? Can you help me or not?"

"Probably not as much as you'd like, but I'm sure I can come up with a few impressions if I work on it awhile. Why don't you give me the rest of the day to think about it and come over to my place for dinner tonight?"

"Sounds good. Only I'll bring the food. How does pizza sound?"

"It sounds fine," she said. Pizza was far from her favorite but it was Sandy's passion. At least she wouldn't have to cook. This way there would be time when she arrived home for a nice long soak in a steaming hot tub. They decided on seven-thirty before Sandy headed back the way she had come and Lisa continued on to the hangar.

KEVIN LEANED BACK in his chair and stretched. A muscle had started to knot between his shoulder blades, and the tension would soon make its way up his neck if he didn't stop a minute. He couldn't believe the paperwork that had piled up in his office in only two days. It would take well into the next week to make a dent in the mounds on his desk.

The intercom buzzed. He reached over to press the button. "Yes?"

"Senators Arnold and Tabori are here to see you, sir."

Kevin searched his memory for some recollection of an appointment with these two men—the most impor tant and powerful in the Senate. Since such an appointment wasn't one he would be likely to forget, he assumed there couldn't have been one. Yet that seemed highly unlikely. A surprise visit from either of these senators was unheard of. "Send them in, Nancy."

He glanced around the office and decided it was too late to try to clear any of the mess or to make himself look more presentable than he was. Tossing his glasses on top of the clutter, he went to the door in his rolled-up shirt sleeves and tie askew and welcomed the esteemed senators from opposing parties to his office.

Impeccably dressed as usual, Osgood Arnold entered first. He was closely followed by Charles Tabori, who had made three-piece pin-striped suits his trademark. Both men were gray-haired and in their sixties, but the similarities stopped there. It would have taken two Taboris to make up one Arnold, but Tabori made up in commanding presence what he lacked in size. No one ever made the mistake of underestimating him twice.

After the formalities were dispensed with, coffee declined and pleasantries exchanged, Osgood Arnold went straight to the point. "As you are undoubtedly aware," he told Kevin, "Felix Larkin is in failing health. Since it's doubtful he'll be able to complete his term, it seemed prudent that we plan ahead for that eventuality in order to avoid messy complications when the time arrives."

Kevin didn't need an interpretation. The good senators were headhunting for potential replacements for the committee and subcommittee positions Felix Larkin's resignation would create. The only puzzling part was, why him? He hadn't ingratiated himself to anyone; no one owed him any major favors. Rather than beat around the bush, he eliminated the next half hour of conversation by saying, "What position are you here to talk to me about and why me?"

Tabori answered. "The Commerce, Science and Transportation Committee, because you would be a compromise that would forestall a lengthy fight for the position. Your voting record and stance on key issues closely parallels that of Larkin's, so the balance on the committee would remain intact. Both parties would be satisfied, as would the White House."

The position he was being offered was one of power and carried an enormous amount of prestige. It was almost unheard of that such a position would be offered to someone serving his first term in the Senate. He leaned back in his chair, his elbows on the arms, his hands making a tent in front of his face. Thoughtfully he tapped the tips of his fingers against his chin. "And in exchange?"

"We would expect your support for Thurman Wallace for the Ways and Means Committee."

Although Wallace would not have been Kevin's first choice for the job, he didn't have any major reservations about the appointment. "That's it?"

Arnold readjusted himself in a chair that was too small for his bulk. The antique piece of furniture groaned in protest. "Surely you didn't think we would waste our time and yours by coming to you with unreasonable demands."

"Such things aren't unheard of in these hallowed halls. What you've offered me is a plum that many of my colleagues would like to pick."

"Well, you can rest assured that such is not the case this time." Arnold started to rise. "Shall I assume this would mean your answer is yes?"

The supreme confidence in Arnold's voice rankled Kevin. "I'd like some time to think it over." The response was unexpected, and neither Arnold nor Tabori could cover his surprise immediately.

Kevin accompanied the two senators to the door. "Thank you, gentlemen," he said as he watched them cross his outer office. When they were gone he turned to Nancy. "Hold my calls for the next half hour. I have some thinking to do."

"Anything you'd like some help with?" she asked, a hopeful gleam in her eye.

"Not right now—maybe later." If word was to leak out about the possibility of his appointment, he didn't want it coming from his office. He knew there would be wild speculation about Arnold and Tabori visiting him—he had no doubt they had been seen entering his office. But the appointment they had offered was so far from the realm of possibility he felt confident it would miss the gossip mill. If his hypothesis proved correct, it would allow him to consider the job unpressured.

He returned to his desk, leaned back in the chair and propped his feet up on the windowsill, the paperwork that had plagued him earlier temporarily forgotten. He considered the committee position. On the positive side, the job would give him the power to implement some of the savings programs he had been fighting for since coming to Washington. The thought excited him. To finally be able to do something after almost ten years of trying would justify all the work he had put in, the sacrifices that had been made to put him in office in the first place. It would be like paying off an old debt, one he had never thought possible to repay.

On the negative side...he flinched. A week ago there wouldn't have been a negative side. An image of Lisa filled his mind. He heard her voice and listened again to the words she had spoken during the phone call that morning. She loved him. And he most certainly loved her. Everything should be so simple after that.

LISA EASED HERSELF into the tub full of hot water and rested her head against a rolled-up towel. With a fatigued sigh she closed her eyes. A dozen concerns and problems that had cropped up at work that day fought for her attention, but the instant a fleeting image of Kevin appeared, they all faded. Now that the two of them were apart she could think of a hundred questions she wished she had asked him when they were together. Some were nonsensical questions, others were more important—things she felt they should know about each other before their relationship deepened any more. In the privacy of her own home, all alone with her thoughts, she could admit that something in her would be destroyed if she was to go through with Kevin what she had gone through with Ross Stewart and Eric Barker. Few people knew what a devastating blow it had been to her when she felt forced to back off from marrying them. After Eric she had sincerely believed she would live the rest of her life alone, had even come to accept the idea.

She sat up and added more hot water to the bath, dipped a washcloth, leaned back and pressed it to her face. She was exhausted; the water lulled her. Just before she drifted off to sleep, an insightful thought flashed into her mind. She realized that she had so easily gone along with all that had happened between her and Kevin the past week only because she didn't really believe any of it. Their interlude had been a delightful fairy tale, one she had needed to put some spark back into her private life. As long as she realized that, she would be all right when the fairy tale ended.

In her dream Lisa chased a bright light. The faster she ran, the more elusive the beautiful, beckoning glow. Its compelling promise of warmth and happiness kept her going each time she fell. She raced over hills and valleys, always running. Suddenly, in the distance, she heard chimes. Over and over the chimes sounded, calling to her, demanding she leave the light and come to them. When she could ignore their summons no longer, she awoke and realized she was sitting in a tub full of tepid water, listening to the doorbell. "I'm coming," she shouted, grabbing a towel.

By the time she reached the front door, Sandy was halfway down the walk on her way back to her car. Lisa called to her from behind the door. "I took a nap," she offered by way of explanation when her friend returned.

"I don't blame you with the hours you've been keeping lately," Sandy replied, entering the apartment with a pizza box balanced on one hand. "Next time leave a note on the door."

"The nap wasn't planned. I was in the tub at the time."

Sandy glanced at Lisa as she stepped from behind the door. She was clutching the towel she had hastily wrapped around her, and there was more skin exposed than covered. "So I see. I don't think I've ever been that tired. You're lucky you didn't drown."

Lisa considered Sandy's statement as she closed the door. "I wonder if that's possible. It seems to me you'd wake up as soon as your face hit the water."

"It's kind of a moot point, don't you think? If you didn't wake up, you'd never know about it." Sandy set the pizza on the counter. She stood there, hands on hips, patiently waiting. Finally she said, "Are you going to eat like that?"

Lisa looked down at her towel. She was sorely tempted. So far that day she had had a glass of milk and three graham crackers and she was starving. The cold air finally won out. "Give me a minute. I'll throw something on and be right back." She returned in less than a minute, dressed in an orange floor-length quilted robe and the pair of bright-blue bunny slippers her niece had sent her for her birthday.

"I think I just lost my appetite," Sandy groaned, looking at her.

"Close your eyes, you'll be fine." She went to her tiny, one-person kitchen and pulled two plates from the cupboard. Most of the time, whenever she was there alone, she liked her apartment. It was ideal for a single person, compact and easy to keep clean. Periodically, whenever she had guests, she thought about moving to someplace larger so she could entertain more than five people at a time without having them falling all over one another. But she never seemed to find the time required to go out looking, so what had started out as temporary shelter after she had broken up with Ross had by default become permanent.

She had dressed up the basically nondescript living room with an Oriental chest and matching chair and a white sofa accented with lime-green throw pillows. She had a television, but it was broken and was currently in a closet, out of the way until she remembered to have it fixed. Standing with her head in the open refrigerator, she called out to Sandy, "I have beer, wine, milk, diet cola and some questionable-looking orange stuff in a plastic container. What sounds good to you?"

"Red or white wine?" She pulled out a bar stool from under the counter and sat down.

"White—a California Chablis."

"Do you suppose it's all right to drink white wine with pizza?" she asked, her voice serious.

Lisa laughed. "I won't tell, if you don't."

"Fair enough."

While Lisa poured the wine, Sandy slipped wedges of a combination pizza on their plates. Lisa noticed her friend moving slower than usual and asked how her burns were healing.

"They're not bad. I hardly think about them anymore."

Lisa gave her a disbelieving frown. "Did someone suggest you'd come across well if you handled this thing stoically or was it all your own idea?"

Sandy let out a resigned sigh. "Neither—I just try not to think too much about my arms. It's easier that way.

The doctor told me I shouldn't scar too badly, but there are some areas between my wrists and elbows that sure look nasty."

Lisa handed Sandy a napkin along with her wine before sitting down on the bar stool next to her. "I can't tell you what it felt like to open that hatch and find all of you still alive." She said the words softly but was unable to keep the powerful emotions from her voice.

Sandy grew serious. "And I'd be hard pressed to try to express what it felt like when we saw you arrive." She started to take a bite of her pizza, stopped and returned it to her plate. "For a while it was pretty bad up there—nothing like the simulations we've gone through."

Lisa didn't want to hear what she knew Sandy wanted to tell her. For Sandy, recounting the emotional side of the accident would be a catharsis; she would come away feeling better for sharing with someone the hell she and the other crew members had gone through on the *Orion*. For Lisa it would be the destruction of a myth she had clung to since becoming an astronaut. A myth that had made her believe that those who flew the shuttles were invincible—that somehow they were not controlled by the fears and anxieties that plagued everyone else and were therefore exempt from any situation that would create those emotions. But because she loved her friend she listened, assuming the role the wives and husbands of the other astronauts would take on, accepting the destruction of the myth, losing an innocence she had thought impossible to lose.

"After the third fire," Sandy went on, her voice little more than a whisper, "I was beginning to have serious doubts we would make it home at all. We all concurred with Frank's decision to shut down, but no one liked it. We couldn't shake the feeling we were quitting and were therefore letting everyone back home down. But the worst part was sitting there in that acrid-smelling room in the dark, not knowing what was happening down here while constantly being reminded of our tenuous position. While we were trying to kill time, someone speculated on the effect our fiasco would have on the increased funding being requested from Congress now." She ran her fingertip around the rim of her glass. "Some maiden voyage, huh?" She let out a self-deprecatory snort. "We were supposed to wow the good senators with our Buck Rogers's feats, not come home with our tails between our legs."

"Don't worry about the effect you had on the senators," Lisa commiserated. "I beat you there."

"That's right. I forgot you'd gone up to Washington to testify. How'd it go?"

"Now's not the time to talk about it."

Sandy peeled a slice of pepperoni from a piece of cheese and chewed on the edge. "I've read lots of stories where the writer describes the taste of fear," she said quietly. "I always thought it was just poetic license. Take my word for it, it's not. For a while I honestly believed we were all going to die up there. Odd things went through my mind at the time. I pictured Frank's kids and Margaret's husband and my father and imagined how they would react to the news. No one else, just them. I tried to remember if my sister was listed on my insurance policy and whether or not she'd forgotten that I told her she could have that antique gold bracelet of mine she's always loved." She glanced at Lisa, giving her a quick, embarrassed smile. "I'm sorry—I promised myself I wouldn't do this to you and here I am running off at the mouth with the tiniest provocation."

"I'd tell you some fantastic lie that none of what you've said has affected me, but you'd know it was a lie. Just know that if the situation had been reversed, I would have turned to you, so there's no need for you to apologize."

Sandy took a deep swallow of wine. "Have you heard they've extended *Challenger*'s flight by two days so the crew can work on *Orion* while they're up there?"

"No." It was the logical thing to do but still a surprise. "When did this happen?"

"I'm not sure when the decision was made, but the announcement came out just before I left the center. Cory caught me as I was heading for my car and told me that based on the debriefings they've put us through this past week, it was decided to have *Challenger*'s crew remove the panels where the main fires took place and bring as much of the hardware as they can load up back here for analysis."

Lisa refilled Sandy's wineglass. She expressed aloud the fear that had been haunting her. "God, I hope when all this is over we don't wind up with another piece of space junk. Especially not with the cost overruns they're having with the second type-II shuttle, which I understand is now projected to be two years away from completion instead of the eighteen months were were told three weeks ago. If something positive doesn't happen soon we could all wind up on the unemployment line."

"On that uplifting note, I think I'll stick my pizza in the microwave. You want me to do yours, too?"

"No thanks. I prefer mine cold anyway."

When she returned to her stool, as if by some unspoken mutual consent, they ceased talking about the accident and its possible ramifications. Instead they ate their pizza and drank wine and discussed the tall redheaded psychiatrist Sandy had a date with the next night. Later, when they had moved into the living room, Sandy persistently prodded Lisa with questions until she admitted that Kevin was someone very special to her. She accepted Sandy's gentle teasing about walking down a path she had sworn never to travel again and acknowledged her well-intentioned warning to be careful with a simple "I will."

Without either noticing, the hours slipped away, the wine disappeared and finally, reluctantly, they agreed they should call it a night.

Lisa was in the kitchen cleaning up when an overwhelming need to hear Kevin's voice struck. She missed him terribly. She stopped a minute to think about her feelings. The idea that she could miss Kevin was ridiculous. They hadn't been together enough for her to really miss him. Missing someone implied a familiarity, something they hadn't yet established. It was too soon. She stared down at the crumbs in the sink and forced herself to reconsider precisely what she was feeling. Dammit, she reasoned, responding to the emptiness she felt, logical or not, she missed him.

She tossed the dishcloth on the counter and headed for the bedroom. Before she had a chance to pick up the phone it rang. A delighted smile curved her mouth. There wasn't a doubt in her mind who was calling her. "Hi," she said, picking up the receiver, her voice silky and warm.

"I'm sorry it's so late," Kevin said. "I thought about waiting until morning to call, but couldn't." He had reached his decision not to call her until morning on the drive home, and it had lasted all of thirty seconds after he'd entered the front door.

"It's all right. Actually, I was just getting ready to call you."

That pleased him immensely. "How was your first day back to work?"

"Fine. And yours?"

"Hectic." He had decided it was best to wait until he had made his final decision about the appointment before telling her about it. "I know now why I never take time off."

"Not even vacations?" When were they ever going to see each other?

"Oh, I think I could be enticed..."

"And how would one go about such enticement?"

His voice lowered to a husky whisper. "If the one happened to be this special someone I know, all she would have to do is ask." He shook free of his overcoat and laid it on the back of his desk chair.

"Tomorrow?"

He smiled. "What about the second of November?"

"That's over two weeks from now." Disappointment edged each word. She hadn't really expected they would see each other any sooner, but expecting and knowing were miles apart. "Why then?"

"Congress adjourns on the first. I thought we could meet somewhere midway between Washington and Texas...say, my place in Kansas."

"Sounds like a lovely idea. Let me see what I can do. I haven't taken a real vacation in over three years, but with everything that's been going on around here, now isn't exactly the best time for me to leave. If I can't get any real time off, I'll try to get them to let me go for at least a couple of days."

"If you can't get away at all, I'll come down there. One way or another we'll see each other on the second of November."

"How long will you have off?"

"Until January 3."

"Two whole months?" she gasped, teasing him. "Not bad fringe benefits. No wonder so many people want to run for office."

"It sounds better than it is. The people back home don't consider my two months among them as vacation time for me. I'm usually kept pretty busy with meetings. And then there's always special appearances at social and charity functions."

"And when you're not doing your political thing with your constituents, you're busy helping your father with the ranch?"

"You remembered." His voice indicated his delight that she had.

They continued making tentative plans until the thoughts Lisa had had in the bathtub before drifting off to sleep came back to her. As if it would help to legitimize the feelings that were growing in her, she had a compulsive need to know more about him. "Kevin...can I ask you some things I've been mulling over in my mind? They're nothing special, just some random thoughts."

Her sudden change in tone let him know that the questions she wanted to ask were far more important than even she might realize. "Fire away. I'll tell you anything but what I did with all that Chinese food we had left over from dinner."

She felt awkward asking him about children because of Christine, and yet it was important for her to know. "How do you feel about children?"

"Whose?" he hedged, surprised by the question and a little taken aback by its implications.

She hadn't realized until she had said the words aloud how they might sound to him. "Don't get me wrong. I'm not suggesting...what I mean is...oh, I've done it again," she groaned.

Kevin leaned back in his chair and smiled. "Are you trying to say you don't want me to get the impression you're rushing things between us, but you'd like to know where I stand and how I feel about the possibility of having children of my own again?"

She felt like an idiot. "That about sums it up."

"Eventually I would like to have children," he said slowly. He wanted to be as honest with her as he could, but it wasn't something he had seriously considered lately. "Christine was a joy. She brought a specialness with her that was all her own. I reveled in being a father. In a way, raising a child is like being allowed to visit childhood again yourself." When she didn't immediately reply, he added, "However, I think maybe I'd prefer doing it the old-fashioned one-at-a-time method rather than the way Mike and Caroline are going about it. But then who knows?"

"And what about Santa Claus? Would you have your children believe in him?"

Her question threw him. "Yes..."

"Good. So many people I know have decided that Santa Claus is a harmful fantasy. I just wanted to know how you felt about it." She propped a pillow against the headboard and leaned against it, sticking her feet straight out in front of her and letting her toes touch so that the heads of the rabbit slippers snuggled companionably. "Where would you go on vacation if you could go anywhere in the world?"

"Hmm...another question I haven't given much thought to before. Let's see..." He struggled with an answer to a question rarely contemplated. "If we had lots of time—a couple of months—I would like to explore Alaska or Australia. I've also heard New Zealand is beautiful, and of course there's always Europe. And then there's Japan and China, not to mention—"

"In other words you're not averse to traveling." She was inordinately pleased that he had used the word "we."

He ignored her interruption. "Now, if we only had a couple of weeks, I'd probably pick a deserted tropical island where we could swim in a lagoon that had water so clear you could count the specs of sand on the bottom...where we could lie naked in the sun and make love under the stars."

Lisa drew her legs up to her chest and leaned her head on her knees. She closed her eyes and drifted with Kevin's voice to his island.

"We would be completely free of everything that tied us to the world we had left behind—clocks, newspapers, radios. We would sleep and eat and make love without consideration to time or place or circumstance. I would learn your body until I knew it as well as I know my own—where you're ticklish, where you like to be touched before making love, where afterward, how you feel about the heart-shaped birthmark on your—"

"You noticed."

"Oh, I not only noticed, my love," he said, a catch in his voice, "I can't seem to keep the memory from haunting me at the most inopportune times."

"Do you know where there's an island like—"

"Do you have two weeks?"

"I will have...someday."

"Then I'll find the island."

She had no doubt that he would. To leave everything behind—the worries, the problems, their seeming differences—didn't sound like a vacation; it sounded like paradise. "I'll hold you to that," she said softly, wishing with all her heart they could leave tomorrow.

"I promise you, Lisa," he said, as if he had been able to read her thoughts. "We'll have our time on that island."

"I take promises very seriously, Kevin."

"I hoped you would. That's why I made this one to you."

She asked him several more of the questions that had occurred to her in the tub, and he answered them honestly and openly. They laughed about some of them and were quietly thoughtful about others. Finally, an hour later, she asked her final question before they said goodnight. "What did you do with the Chinese food that was left over?"

He laughed. "I ate every last bite of it."

ALMOST A WEEK LATER, when Lisa arrived home from work, she was surprised to find a large, thick manila envelope from Kevin in her mailbox. It was unseasonably cold for Houston, and because she hadn't dressed appropriately that morning she had spent a great deal of energy simply trying to stay warm while walking to and from meetings that had taken place all over the Johnson Space Center. Consequently she was tired and a short step away from cranky. The anticipation of *Challenger*'s return in two days had created an almost palpable air of tension throughout the center. So much rested on the findings and how quickly they could be obtained.

As she walked the narrow pathway to her apartment, she tilted the envelope toward the porch light to look more closely at Kevin's bold handwriting. His strokes were sure and strong and revealed a touch of impatience. In the upper left-hand corner he had signed "K. Anderson" above his address. There wasn't any indication that he had used his franking privileges to mail the package to her, and it didn't surprise her in the least that his integrity included something as inconsequential as paying the postage himself if his mail was personal.

She tucked the package under her arm and dug in her pocket for her apartment key. Once inside she switched the light on and hung her purse over the doorknob before heading to the kitchen for a knife to open the envelope. She spilled the contents out on the counter. When she saw dozens and dozens of pictures and articles in various sizes and shapes that had been clipped from newspapers and magazines, her eyebrows drew together in a puzzled frown. She shook the envelope again and a white piece of note paper fell out. She unfolded the paper and immediately recognized Kevin's handwriting.

Dearest Lisa,

For the last few nights, whenever I haven't been able to sleep because of thinking about you, I've left my bed and gone into the living room to sit by the fire and search for ways to tell you something about the man you say you've fallen in love with. It's my understanding that these things—falling in love and getting to know someone—usually happen the other way around, but I'm not about to complain. Loving you first only makes each new thing I learn about you make me love you all the more.

My suitcases are packed for Kansas; my folks have opened the house and are valiantly restraining themselves from inundating me with questions about you. They have invited us for dinner—every night you're there, to be precise—but I told them not to count on more than once or twice. The weatherman said it looks like snow, so pack lots of warm clothes, or we'll have to spend all our time indoors. Forget what I just wrote. I'm sure, if necessary, we'll find plenty to keep us busy should we have to stay inside.

Love, Kevin

Lisa refolded the note and looked down at the first picture. It was of a man hang gliding over a deep valley. Kevin had written across the bottom: "I've always wanted to do this, but I'm not sure I could even stand on the edge of a cliff, let alone jump off one." Under that picture was an article from the *Washington Post* about animal research. In the space around the edge were Kevin's comments. "The callousness and cruelty and senselessness of so many of these so-called researchers makes me sick. We're a long way from solving the problem, but we're working on making it harder for things like this to happen." Next was a magazine picture of the shuttle *Discovery* sitting on its launchpad "The woman I love runs around in one of these. Pretty nifty, huh?"

There was an article from *Time* about an imminent famine in an East African country. "We have to do something for these people before their children begin dying or another entire generation suffers brain damage from malnutrition. As a caring nation we shouldn't have to see distended bellys or hopeless faces before we are moved to help.''

An advertisement for a diet soda showed a leggy woman lounging beside a pool. "I was a member of the swim team at Yale for a few years—won a few, lost a few." She hadn't known he'd gone to Yale but wasn't surprised. And something, intuition maybe, told her that he had won far more competitions than he had lost.

A full-page color ad for a product that Kevin had cut off the bottom of the picture showed a man standing in the middle of a greenhouse full of orchids. "I've always been fascinated by orchids and thought someday I might try growing them myself." Below the picture of the orchids was one of a tropical island. Lush forest surrounded a pristine horseshoe-shaped beach. The water in the lagoon was so clear it hardly seemed there at all. Lisa touched the picture with her fingertips, as if by doing so she could touch Kevin and feel what he had felt when he had found the photograph. She read the concise statement at the bottom. "Someday soon...I love you."

She gathered the remaining clippings and took them into the bedroom to read, to assimilate, to wonder over, the last thing she would do that night before going to sleep.

CHAPTER ELEVEN

KEVIN GATHERED the final stack of correspondence awaiting his signature before the close of the current session of Congress and began skimming the letters. Nancy never made mistakes in typing or grammar so he didn't bother looking for those. What he was looking for was the occasional tactical error in how he should handle a particular person or problem that sometimes showed up in his dictation. He was almost through and ready to head for the airport and Kansas when Nancy buzzed him. "Senators Arnold and Tabori are here to see you, sir."

"Send them in." He had told both men he would have an answer for them before he returned in January and couldn't imagine why they had stopped by now. He went to the door to meet them. "Senators..." He shook Arnold's beefy hand and then Tabori's delicate one. "What can I do for you?"

Tabori answered. "Felix Larkin died an hour ago. I'm afraid we cannot give you the time you requested to think over your answer."

"We want to head off the inevitable infighting for the position and possible bad blood it would create by being able to tell those who need to know that the position has been filled," Arnold added.

"And you need to know today?"

"That's correct," Tabori said.

"Within the next half hour, if at all possible," Arnold expounded. "We still have his other positions to fill."

To delay giving his answer even the half hour wouldn't change anything. He had delayed giving an answer in order to question Lisa about her feelings, to find out whether or not she would be able to effectively separate who he was from the job he would take on. It hadn't been something he felt comfortable about trying to handle on the phone so he had postponed telling her anything at all until they could be together. For them to have ideological differences about funding for the space program was one thing. To suddenly be given the power to put his words into actions was something else again.

Still, the longer he had considered the position, the more it had appealed to him. Finally, after all the years he had spent in Congress, he would have a powerful forum for his pleas for sanity in government spending. It could be the beginning, however small, to an eventual turnaround. "I won't need that half hour, gentlemen. I accept your offer."

They beamed their pleasure. "Congratulations, Senator Anderson," Osgood Arnold said. "You've made a wise decision. I have a feeling this is only the beginning of many good things that will come your way."

Kevin accepted their well-wishes, wondering what they would say if they knew how little he cared about climbing the political ladder they spoke of. When he closed the door behind them he took a minute to reflect on what had just happened. A deep-seated sense of unease knotted his stomach. He had one week to convince Lisa that they could separate their private and public lives; he only wished he felt more confident about his powers of persuasion.

As the weatherman had promised, it snowed the day Kevin arrived home in Kansas. Large feathery flakes drifted down as he left the commuter plane had had boarded in Kansas City. He smiled broadly when he saw his parents coming toward him. They had driven forty miles from their ranch to be there to meet him. After a long hug Rose Anderson stood back and eyed her son. "You look better than I've seen you look in years," she marveled.

"She's right," Kevin's father, Harold, chimed in. "You haven't had that look about you since...well, since longer than I care to remember."

"And the same goes for the two of you. That vacation Mom talked you into taking was long overdue."

"We'd have gone sooner, but with one thing and another it's just impossible to find the time to get away," Harold said. "You can't have forgotten how it is on a ranch."

"Don't worry about your dad, Kevin. He'll be a little quicker to leave next time," Rose said. "He's discovered there are some things in this world worth seeing before he gets too old to enjoy them. Now he's getting worried he won't make it to all of them." Rose placed her arms through those of father and son. From a distance the two men might have been mistaken for brothers. Kevin favored his father's side of the family and its strong Scandinavian heritage. For generations the men in the Anderson clan had been rawboned with strong square jaws, blond hair and deep-blue eyes. His mother's background was a European blend—the quick temper and flashing eyes of the Irish, the fair, clear skin of the English, the strong bone structure of the Germans and a personality that included a large dose of French flirtatiousness. She could still turn a spark into a fire in her husband of almost forty years by simply walking through a room and giving him a suggestive wink.

"It's good to be home," Kevin said, covering his mother's hand with his own. "Every time I get on a plane and head this way it feels like someone is lifting a weight off my shoulders."

"You say that now, but you'd soon grow bored if you stayed around here too long." Harold held the door for them as they entered the area where they would wait for Kevin's luggage.

"I think you're wrong, dad. But then even if I did, it would be a good kind of boredom. A hell of a lot better than listening to some senator's impassioned speech from the floor about a bill that stinks of special interest. You wouldn't believe how long-winded some of those people can get with the proper provocation."

"Well, it's all conjecture anyhow," Rose said, staring at the luggage belt as if she could will it into action. "The people of this state will keep you in the Senate listening to those dull speeches till you're an old man, and it's the young ones who are complaining about you."

She meant what she said as a compliment, but the thought of growing old doing what he was doing now was a pleasureless one. As usual he didn't argue the point. The pressure his parents had put on him was a loving, unintentional result of their pride in his success. With each election he had continued to gain more and more voters until it had reached the point that the opposing party was reluctant to put anything but minimal money and effort into trying to defeat him.

"Here it comes," Harold announced, seconds before the belt began moving.

Rose glared at him. "How'd you know that?"

He gave her a mysterious wink along with a quick hug. "I keep telling you, woman, I've got a sixth sense about these kinda things."

Kevin smiled. What his mother never seemed to realize was that if she, too, stood a foot taller, her ability to "sense" things would be on a par with her husband's.

The ride to the ranch was a time for catching up on local gossip and sorting through family news. Rose twisted around in her seat so she could look at Kevin while they talked. "Caroline and Mike stopped by for dinner when they were in town last week. My she's getting big—and so fast. Looks good, though. Said she wanted to get as much visiting in as she could before the babies are here 'cause she figures there's not going to be much time after they arrive. You wouldn't believe what a change these babies have made in her parents. Her pregnancy is the best thing that's happened to those two since their divorce twenty years ago. They're actually back talking to each other again."

"You're kidding. I didn't think anything could get those two to ever be civil to each other again." Kevin glanced out the windows to the fields filled with snow. "I'm sure going to miss Caroline and Mike now that they've moved back to Houston."

"It's always hard to let go of friends. That Mike sure is a nice man. Handsome, too. Much better for Caroline than that first fella she married." Rose clicked her tongue and shook her head in disgust. "I just don't know how anyone could have done such a thing to someone as sweet as that Caroline is. Imagine him sleeping with her best friend—and in her own bed of all things."

"It's past history now, Rosie. Done and over with. Caroline's got herself a man who worships the ground she walks on and is about to have a family to boot." Harold gave her knee a quick squeeze. He glanced up at the rearview mirror and caught Kevin's attention. "Is there anything you wanted us to know about this friend you've got coming to visit?"

Kevin laughed. "I've got to hand it to you, dad. It took longer than I thought it would for you to get around to asking me about her."

"Now if you'd rather not tell us—"

"Hush up, Harold. Of course he wants to tell us."

The remainder of the trip was spent discussing Lisa Malorey.

LISA STARED OUT THE WINDOW of the small commuter plane at the thick blanket of snow covering the ground. She absently folded and refolded her ticket stub while the man beside her softly snored. As usual, she was not as comfortable being a passenger as she was a pilot, and she was anxious for the flight to end.

Her heart-racing enthusiasm to be on her way that morning had been dampened by a sobering phone call from Cory. He had told her of the tentative solution to the mysterious fires aboard the *Orion* and it couldn't have been worse news. Somehow, either between or after or during the extensive inspections performed by NASA while the construction of the *Orion* was going on, corners had been cut. Wherever compartments or components were sealed or would be unlikely targets for future inspections, cheap material had replaced expensive. When asked for an explanation, the primary contractor had informed NASA officials that the substitutions were the only way he could keep the cost overruns from reaching unacceptable levels.

When news of the discovery leaked out to the public there would be hell to pay. Heads would roll in every corner of NASA's far-reaching network. Where guilt couldn't be laid, pressured supervisors would look for scapegoats. Not only was the *Orion* now a useless piece of junk, so was her sister ship, still under construction. The shuttle program would be hard pressed to continue as it was, let alone expand. And without new vehicles to accommodate the increased work load created by an operating space station, the priority of finishing that station would disappear.

The entire shuttle program would never be dropped. The air force would see to that. But now that the European Space Agency was snapping at NASA's heels with its own satellite-launching program, the only unique thing NASA could offer prospective clients was the retrieval and repair of satellites that had broken down or missed their orbit.

The plane circled the small landing field once before lining up with the runway. In minutes they were down and taxiing up to the main terminal. Lisa searched the small crowd standing behind the chain link fence and spotted Kevin. Although she knew he couldn't possibly see her, it seemed as if he was directly meeting her gaze, sending a message of love, modifying some of the hurt and worry simply by being there.

Never had she been as anxious to leave a plane and never had the procedure progressed more slowly. After interminable minutes the steps were rolled out and attached and the door opened. Impatiently she waited for those nearest the door to gather their belongings and leave. Normally not the kind to insist on her turn, she did so today. As soon as she hit the last step she flew across the strip of concrete and into Kevin's waiting, welcoming arms.

Kevin held Lisa to him, marveling that she could feel even better in his arms than he had imagined as he had lain awake that morning. Unable to express his joy in words, he told her in a kiss. Her lips were warm and yielding as she responded with a passionate eloquence. "My God, I've missed you," he said, burying his face in her hair.

She laid her head against his chest, her face pressed against the snow-dampened wool of his coat. She realized he had been standing outside waiting for her plane, every bit as anxious for her to arrive as she had been to get there. The tiny lingering question about the wisdom of loving him melted with the gentle totality of the snowflakes that landed on her nose. "I've missed you, too—more than I dreamed it was possible for me to miss anyone."

He kissed her again, an infinitely tender kiss of promise. "Come on," he told her, "let's get you inside where it's warm." When they entered the waiting room, Kevin noticed several curious stares directed their way. He leaned close so that only she could hear him. "The odds are pretty good that your arrival and who you came here to meet will make it around the county before nightfall. I hope that won't cause you any problems." In his happiness to see her, he hadn't considered the possible ramifications of the greeting they had exchanged. When he was home, it was sometimes too easy to forget his "public" image and the way the most innocent gesture or remark could be misinterpreted. For Lisa the pressure to be cautious in her words and actions must be burdensome, if not more so. And although Washington society might look the other way about their affair, the people he had grown up with in Kansas were not as liberal.

"Perhaps I should say something about coming to visit your parents loud enough for everyone to hear." The situation amused her, but she realized it could be damaging to Kevin to have any kind of scandal, no matter how mild, attached to his name.

He gave her a lopsided grin. "You can't possibly think something like that would work."

Giving him her best Mae West imitation, she drawled, "Well, how about if I tell them I was hired by a special-interest lobby group who flew me in from Las Vegas for the weekend just to keep you company." She plucked at his jacket button. "If you get my meaning."

Kevin laughed aloud. "There's not a doubt in my mind they'd believe every word."

Just then a young girl Lisa guessed to be around eleven or twelve approached them. "Excuse me, Mr. Anderson," she said shyly. "Would it be all right if I asked Miss Malorey for her autograph?"

The girl looked vaguely familiar to Kevin. He glanced across the waiting room and spotted her mother, a woman he had gone to high school with. She gave him a shy smile and fluttering wave. Turning his attention back to the girl, he said, "I think it might be better if you asked her yourself." He spoke the words gently, sensitive to the timidity in her behavior.

"Would you mind, Miss Malorey? I know celebrities hate it when people ask them for their autographs, but it would sure mean a lot to me. You see I want to be just like you when I grow up. I have pictures of you all over my bedroom wall."

Lisa had been approached this way before but rarely by someone with as much reverence shining in her eyes. She was uncomfortable being the object of such esteem and felt unworthy and intimidated by the attention. But this time she sensed there was more than heroine worship involved. "What's your name?"

"Jennifer."

Lisa smiled a smile she hoped would put the girl at ease. "Where did you get so many pictures of me, Jennifer?"

Kevin touched her arm to get her attention. "I'm going to say hello to an old friend," he said. "I'll be right back."

She gave him a quick nod before returning her full attention to the girl.

"Mostly I've cut them from magazines and newspapers when you're flying a shuttle. NASA even sent me one when I wrote to them and asked about you."

Lisa returned Jennifer's pen and paper. "I'll tell you what. Why don't you give me your name and address and I'll send you a better picture of me than the one NASA gives out."

"And you'll sign it?"

"Yes...I promise." While Jennifer wrote, Lisa glanced over at Kevin and noticed he was speaking to a woman who was flushed with embarrassment...or was it pleasure? When Jennifer handed the paper back to Lisa, she folded it and carefully tucked it into her wallet. "I'll send the picture as soon as I get home."

"Thank you." She started to leave, stopped and turned. Her manner serious, her words sincere, she said, "My mom says Mr. Anderson's a real nice man."

Lisa fought the smile that hovered around her lips. "Thank you, Jennifer," she replied as solemnly. "I'm pleased to know that.'' Behind her the luggage belt hummed, jerked and began moving, bringing in the suitcases and boxes from her flight. Across the room Kevin shook his friend's hand, and Lisa noticed that Jennifer was now standing beside the woman. Kevin walked back over to Lisa but stayed only a second before leaving again to retrieve her suitcases. ''Only two?'' he asked, returning.

''Uh-huh.'' She followed him out to the parking lot. ''Did you notice how well I handled that?''

''The autograph?''

''No—letting you get my suitcases.''

He stopped beside a green pickup truck and opened the passenger door. ''I have to be honest, Lisa, I didn't notice until you mentioned it. But that doesn't mean I'm not impressed all the same,'' he quickly added. He put her suitcases into a plastic bag in the back, brushed the snow from his sleeves, took her into his arms and pressed a kiss to the end of her nose. ''Now, who ever said you couldn't teach—''

She leaned back and gave him a warning glare. ''If I were you, fella, I wouldn't carry that sentence one word further.''

''A modern woman to take pity on an old-fashioned man.''

She stood on her toes to return his kiss. ''How is it I constantly forget what you do for a living?''

''There you go, trying to flatter me again.'' He helped her into the truck before going around to the driver's side. As soon as he was behind the wheel, he started the engine and let it warm awhile. Pointedly he stared at her. ''You forgot your seat belt.''

''Oh...right.'' She rummaged for the seat belt, clicked the buckle and gave the strap a tug. ''You may not believe this, but I *always* remember to wear one when I'm not wih you.''

He took her chin in his hand and leaned over to give her a kiss. "I'm glad to hear it.''

They left the parking lot and turned west. After they had traveled several hundred yards down the two-lane road, Lisa turned to him. "Who was the woman I saw you talking to?''

"An old high-school friend.''

Her mouth opened in surprise. "But she looked ten years older than you are.''

"She's had a pretty rough life so far. She and her husband lost their farm the same year I nearly lost mine. Joe, her husband, has been working as a mechanic here in town ever since, trying to save up enough money to get back into farming.''

"They'll never be able to send Jennifer to school...'' She hated to think that the dream she had seen in Jennifer's eyes would die because she couldn't afford to go to college.

"No, but with the grades her mother says she's making, I'm sure she'll be able to get enough scholarship money to get her there.''

They traveled awhile longer in thoughtful silence. Suddenly Lisa eyed him. "You wouldn't be referring to the Anderson Scholarship Fund, would you?''

"Right idea, wrong name,'' he reluctantly admitted.

"I'm impressed,'' she said sincerely.

"Well, don't be,'' he answered more sharply than he had intended. "Giving money away doesn't make me any better than anyone else. I do it as privately as possible to avoid precisely the kind of reaction you just had.''

"I'm sorry, Kevin. I didn't mean—''

He sighed. "No, I'm sorry. I had no right to jump on you like that. All you wanted to say was that you agreed with me." He reached for her hand. "Let's talk about something else. How are things down in Houston?"

"They've been better. If you don't mind, I'd rather save Houston for later." She ran her thumb along the back of his hand, remembering she had once thought a man with hands like his was sure to work outside. "How's Washington?"

"The same as always," he hedged. He couldn't bring himself to tell her about the appointment now, not after she had just arrived. "I've been there almost ten years, through two administrations, and nothing ever changes. With Mike and Caroline gone, my weekends will be different from now on. No more parties with mysterious blond women hiding in their study."

"I hadn't realized it was a common occurrence."

"At least once a month."

"Then I'm delighted they've moved away."

Kevin smiled. He liked her implied jealousy. "Have you seen them since they arrived in Houston?"

"Only Mike, not Caroline. The Peters are having a big welcoming party for them tomorrow night to give everyone a chance to say hi before Caroline starts cutting back on her social life. Cory said Ann has been planning this thing for a month." She fleetingly wondered if the news of the *Orion* would have made it along the underground network by then. If it did, the party would not be the festive occasion Ann had planned. Lisa forced the thought from her mind. "How much farther to the ranch?"

"About twenty more miles." It suddenly occurred to him she might not have eaten lunch on the plane and it was almost three o'clock. "Are you hungry?"

"A little, but I'll make it." She looked out at the gently rolling fields of snow. "I'd like to build a snowman while I'm here—I never have before."

He readily responded to the playfulness in her voice. "There's a real skill involved in the construction—impossible to learn without a teacher guiding you every step of the way, showing you where to place your—"

"This is a hands-on kind of instruction, I suppose."

"Absolutely."

She looked at him for long seconds, her quick reply lost in the warmth that came from his loving expression. "I'm glad I came," she said softly.

He brought her hand to his lips. Because he didn't know how to tell her how much it meant to him that she had come, he simply said, "Me, too."

Twenty minutes later they left the main road and drove up a small hill. "The house is just over the rise," he told her.

As soon as they crested the hill, Lisa saw the barns and outbuildings, and a short while later, the house. It was an old house, two story, farm style in construction with a covered porch running along three sides. Painted white with green shutters and trim, it had obviously been well cared for. She saw smoke coming from the chimney. "I thought you said you didn't have a housekeeper," she said, disappointed they wouldn't be alone.

"I don't. But I do have a mother who comes in and out every now and then to make sure I know how to treat a guest properly. If you'll look further down the road, you'll see the taillights of her truck going over the hill."

"She comes over here...anytime?"

Kevin laughed. "She knows you're here and won't come without calling first."

Lisa felt a blush crawl up her neck. It embarrassed her that her thoughts had been so transparent. "Kevin, your house is beautiful," she said, staring out the window. "I would fight to keep a place like this, too."

He pulled up in front to let her out before taking the truck to the detached garage in the back. She was waiting for him on the porch when he came back around. "You should have gone inside. It's open."

"I didn't know."

He tucked one of her suitcases under his arm, opened the door and stepped to the side so she could enter first.

As soon as she walked in, Lisa felt as if she had come home. In her lifetime only two places had ever given her that feeling, the houses she had shared with her father and brother in Seattle and in Berkeley. Although the apartments she had had since leaving home had all been comfortable, none had felt like this.

The floors were highly polished oak, as were the stair railings, baseboards and ceiling molding. In the living room off to the left, the furniture was a combination of early-American antique and comfortable modern. The curtains were tie back, the rug a rich, thick wool. An opened newspaper lay on the coffee table and a fire burned in the raised-hearth fireplace. From the kitchen came the smell of freshly baked bread. Lisa turned and put her arms around Kevin's neck. "You can keep the tropical island. I'll take this place anytime."

It had been important to him that she like his home. His ranch was an integral part of the man that resided beneath the trappings of a politician. But then, it hadn't been the actual place he wanted her to like. It was the idea. He wanted her to see him as he saw himself, a man more at home in the open spaces than in the halls of Congress. "I think it only fair that we give the island a fighting chance." He held her with one arm, hanging on to her suitcase with the other.

"All right—if you insist." She pressed her lips to his in a quick kiss. "But the island doesn't stand a chance."

"Let's put your things away and feed you. It takes muscle to build snowmen." She followed him up the stairs to a room that was obviously a guest room. "You'll be able to see the sunrise from here," he told her, setting her suitcases at the foot of a twin bed and going over to the window to pull the curtain aside. "If there are any mornings when the sun is out, that is."

Lisa folded her arms and leaned against the wall, looking at him through narrowed eyes. "Would you like to explain this to me?" It had never occurred to her that he had invited her to his home with separate sleeping accommodations in mind.

He turned around to face her. He didn't need an elaboration on her cryptic question. "I wanted you to have options."

"Then the choice of where I stay is mine?"

"Entirely."

"And if I prefer sleeping with you?"

He swallowed. "I would like that—very much."

"Which way?" she asked softly.

"Across the hall."

She crossed the hallway and opened the door to a room containing a king-size bed and dark heavy furniture. Kevin came up behind her. She reached for his arm and placed it around her waist. Leaning her back against his chest, she said, "Looks all right to me...bed's big enough for two, and it's not pressed up against the wall, so I won't have to crawl over you should I happen to want to get up during the night."

He wrapped his other arm around her and held her to him. "I didn't want you to feel pressured."

"I know." His insistence on thinking of her first and his honest, old-fashioned courtliness were slowly dismantling a barrier she had thought impossible to breach. Here she was, a thoroughly modern woman, melting against a man and yearning for him to sweep her into his arms and carry her off into the sunset.

He turned her to face him, cupping her chin and bending to press a kiss to her upturned mouth. The kiss quickly deepened as each of them released a little more of themselves to the other. Kevin reached for the buttons on her coat and took the heavy wool garment from her shoulders. He shrugged out of his own coat and tossed it on the chair beside hers. With a sudden movement he bent down and picked her up in his arms.

Lisa buried her face in his neck, smelling, tasting the essence that was Kevin Anderson. He gently lowered her onto the bed, stretching out beside her and pulling her into his arms. "That was more what I had in mind," she told him.

"You should have said something earlier."

"At the airport?"

"God, no. I would never have made it home." He opened the top of her blouse and touched his lips to the hollow at the base of her neck. A hint of perfume remained from the spray she had applied that morning, enticing him with its elusive aroma. He followed the deep vee opening, tracing a thin, moist line with the tip of his tongue to the valley between her breasts.

Lisa sighed. She had ached for this moment since leaving him in Washington. He had awakened something in her while they were together that was good and wonderful. Her hands slid along his shirt, feeling the smooth texture of the fabric and the hard muscles beneath. She tugged on his shirt to free it from his jeans, and her hands explored the bared skin.

Kevin finished unbuttoning her blouse, smiling when he saw the seductive wisp of lace that covered her breasts. He pressed his mouth to the peaks beneath the lace and breathed warm kisses along the creamy skin that mounded above the covering. Lisa moved against him, softly sighing her encouragement, touching him with growing boldness. He found the hook and released her bra, sweeping it away with impatient hands. Gently he captured an exposed nipple with his teeth, and his tongue caressed, tasted, taunted.

Lisa's breath caught in her throat as tremors of sensation radiated through her. A warmth, a tingling, a need was building with a quickness that astounded her. He had created a hunger that went beyond temporary satiation. Instinctively she knew the yearning that suffused them would go far beyond what was happening between them now. She would want him, she would need him more than she had ever needed anyone. What she had known before was nothing compared to what she and Kevin would share.

As if it was a ritual, Kevin slowly removed Lisa's clothing and then his own. His broad flat hands touched and possessed with unrestrained fervor, with bold and delicate strokes. She sighed her pleasure and cried out her readiness. Moving onto his back he sat up and leaned against a pillow he placed against the headboard. He brought her to him, grasping her knees and pulling them up to straddle his waist. The movement, the tempo of their lovemaking he relinquished to her as he bent his head to take her breast into his mouth. Lisa shifted her hips and guided him into her. She reveled in his sigh of pleasure as she moved against him. His hands cupped her buttocks and supported her, establishing a rhythm that soon carried them to an explosive climax.

As they slowly descended Kevin held her, whispering words of love, pressing tender kisses to her throat, her eyes, her lips. She sighed contentedly and snuggled against his chest. "For someone who doesn't get much practice, you do a credible job, Mr. Anderson." She could feel the chuckle vibrating in his chest.

"You're my inspiration."

"Why, thank you." She pushed her hands against his chest and sat up straight. "I've always wanted to inspire someone about something."

Kevin ran his hands along her thighs. "Have I ever told you how beautifully I think you're put together?"

"You mean how well the collective parts make up the whole?"

"Something like that." His hands slowly traveled from the sides of her legs to the inner thighs, where, with each stroke, he moved a little higher. "I particularly like your breasts, and the way the nipples respond when you're excited...like now."

If he had suggested earlier that she could want him again so soon after they had made love she would have told him it was impossible. But she would have been wrong. Almost imperceptibly she moved to allow his hand the prize it sought as he moved ever higher, ever more erotically up her thigh. "Looks like lunch will have to wait," she murmured breathlessly.

"Maybe even dinner," he said.

CHAPTER TWELVE

THE NEXT MORNING the sun was shining brightly when Lisa woke up. It took her several seconds to realize where she was. When she did, the significance of a sunshiny day made her smile contentedly. Carefully, so that she wouldn't wake Kevin, she rolled over. He was staring at her, love in his eyes, a smile on his lips.

"Good morning," he said.

"It is, isn't it." She snuggled into his side. "Is this a snowman kind of day?"

"Even a snowwoman, if you're so inclined."

"Do you have carrots and coal and—"

"A hat and, if I look hard enough, I could probably come up with a corncob pipe."

"Then what are we waiting for?"

He threw back the feather quilt and let her feel the cold air. "Still anxious to get going?"

She made a dive for the covers. "Haven't you ever heard of central heat?"

"Personally I like getting up to a cold house. It helps me to get moving in the morning."

"I'll tell you what." She pulled the covers up to her chin. "*You* can get moving and *I'll* wait until the fire's going."

"But it's your job to bring in the wood." He snatched the quilt from her loose grasp.

She sat up and glared at him. "Mark my words, Senator Anderson. I'll get you for this. When you're least prepared, I'll be there."

He reached for her robe and tossed it to her. "Last one downstairs has to make the coffee."

"Oh no, you don't. I demand bathroom privileges first."

Kevin reached for his clothes. "Fair enough. I'll meet you in the kitchen." He caught the back of her robe as she walked past and drew her to him for a kiss. "That's the best night's sleep I've had in years."

"Sleep?" She smiled. "I don't remember doing any sleeping last night."

He kissed her again. "Let me be the first one to tell you how much you're loved this morning."

"The first and last, but who's counting?" She headed for the door, stopped and turned. The teasing twinkle left her eyes. "I love you, Kevin Anderson. You're everything I had given up hope of ever finding." She left before he could see the uncharacteristic moisture pooling in her eyes.

By the time she was dressed and downstairs, Kevin had a fire burning in the living room and one in the kitchen stove, and the air was filled with the heady aroma of freshly brewed coffee. Lisa stood in the doorway, inserting the post of her heart-shaped gold earring into her earlobe. "You may talk tough, senator, but you're a marshmallow inside."

"Strictly self-defense. I was beginning to think you were never coming down."

"What's for breakfast?"

"Oatmeal."

"Ugh!"

"You can think of something better?"

"Just about *anything* is better than oatmeal."

"Well, be my guest. The kitchen is all yours."

She put her hands on her hips and shook her head. "I hope you don't think you're fooling me with that old oatmeal trick."

Kevin pointed to the counter, where an economy-size box of old-fashioned oats sat waiting.

"All right, all right. I give up. I'll cook something."

He gave her a satisfied smile, just a little short of triumphant. "Anything you come up with is fine with me."

Later, after pancakes and bacon, they cleaned up the kitchen, then bundled up to go outside. Lisa was ready first and went out on the porch to wait for Kevin. Expecting that the sun would have warmed the day, she was stunned when frigid air hit her in the face like a wall of ice. She sucked in her breath and let it out again, creating a minature cloud. Houston could get cold in the winter but never like this, especially not with the sun shining.

Kevin joined her. "Ready?"

"I'm not sure. Is it safe to go out in weather like this?"

"Once you get moving you'll forget all about the temperature."

"Promise?"

He grabbed her hand and headed down the steps. "How big do you want to make this thing?"

"Right now? Twelve inches sounds pretty good."

He bent down and gathered a handful of snow. Packing it tightly, he stared at her menacingly.

"You wouldn't dare..." Still he stared at her. In self-defense she gathered her own snow and pressed it between her hands. It fell apart.

"You have to squeeze it with your fingers at the same time you're working it with your palms so you're getting compaction all the way around."

She tried again. This time the snowball stayed together. Smugly she tossed it up and caught it.

"I have no idea what your intentions were when you made that," he said, "but I'll show you what you're supposed to do now." He leaned over and started rolling the ball around, picking up more snow as he went.

Lisa tried to do the same. Her efforts didn't work quite as well, but she refused to be discouraged and continued to roll the lopsided ball of snow in ever-widening circles. Kevin watched her for a while before returning to his own work. As he walked around the front yard, pushing the growing ball in front of him, he laughed happily to himself. Four weeks ago he couldn't have imagined—under any circumstances—doing what he was doing now. Nor could he have imagined feeling the way he now felt. He had forgotten what it was like to be in love. Loving someone was what made life worth living. It added the spark that made the difference between ordinary and special.

When the base of the snowman had grown to neary three feet in diameter, Kevin brought it back to where Lisa was working on the middle section. "What do you think?" he asked. "Big enough?"

"Oh, no. Let's make a great big one." She had forgotten the cold in her enthusiasm.

"Okay," Kevin said slowly. "Why don't we trade off for a while?"

She looked from Kevin to the ball of snow he had made and back again. She shrugged. "Sounds fair." When a reasonable push failed to budge the ball, she braced herself and tried again. Still it refused to move.

Brushing the snow from her gloves and casually adjusting her jacket, she gave him a sheepish grin. "As far as I'm concerned, this looks like a good size right here."

They worked steadily for the next half hour, completing the project. With the hat, nose, mouth and eyes—which had to be realigned several times to satisfy Lisa—in place, they stood back to admire their handiwork. "Something's missing," Kevin said. "Wait here, I'll be right back." He returned with a piece of an old yellow blanket and wrapped it jauntily around the snowman's neck. "Now he really belongs to us."

Lisa put her arms around Kevin's waist. "I believe you have a touch of the romantic in you."

"It's the company I keep that inspires me." He kissed the tip of her nose, which was bright pink from the cold. "There's one more thing for you to learn today before I take you inside to thaw you out." He took her hand. "Follow me. We need fresh snow to make an angel." They went around to the side of the house. "Lie down on your back."

She stared at him, her eyes wide in disbelief. "You can't be serious." But she could see that he was. Reluctantly she laid in the snow. "Now what?"

"Spread your legs."

"Now wait just a minute—" She laughed.

"And do this with your arms." He held his arms straight out, shoulder high, then dropped them back to his sides.

Still laughing, Lisa followed his instructions. "Now what?" He helped her up and had her stand back to see what she had done. "Well, I'll be...it does look like an angel."

Kevin swept her up in his arms. "Time to go inside."

She didn't argue. Now that the clouds were drifting in and the sun had disappeared, the cold had permeated her clothing and was on its way to her bones. They stood on the porch and brushed most of the snow off themselves before going inside to take off their jackets and boots. Lisa's teeth began chattering as she pulled her damp jeans off. She hadn't realized how cold she was until the warm air of the house surrounded her like an enticing blanket. She went to stand by the fireplace but still couldn't stop trembling. Finally Kevin insisted she go upstairs and get into a tub of hot water.

"Only if you'll come, too," she told him, following him across the room.

"You can't possibly think I'd turn down an offer like that." He took her to the bathroom with the old-fashioned claw-foot tub. While the water ran he helped her to undress the rest of the way and to get into the water, promising to come right back to join her. When he returned he was carrying a big mug of hot chocolate. "This will take care of the inside."

"Has it occurred to you that trying to get me warm is becoming a habit?"

He unbuttoned his shirt. "Not an unpleasant one."

"Not for you, maybe," she said, laughing.

"Trust me," he said, his voice husky. "This particular episode will end pleasantly for you, too."

She felt a warmth spread through her that had nothing to do with the water or the chocolate.

Two hours later Lisa was standing at the kitchen window staring out at the angel she had made in the snow. In the quiet, while she waited for Kevin to come in with more wood, her thoughts drifted. She grew pensive as the devastating news about the *Orion* came back to her, breaking through the barrier she had managed to construct with Kevin's love. She felt as if she had been gliding free of worry in a beautiful, unspoiled land and suddenly her wings had broken and she had come crashing back to earth.

She tried to hide the change in her mood when Kevin returned, but he immediately saw through her subterfuge. "What's happened?" he gently prodded, taking her into his arms.

"Not now," she breathed, leaning against him. "I'll tell you later."

He held her away from him and looked into her eyes. "Are you sure you don't want to talk about it now?"

She had never been so sure of anything. For all of Kevin's love and understanding, this one thing still separated them. What she needed now was someone to commiserate with her and feel the loss as poignantly as she did, not someone who would feel justified in saying, "I told you so." She knew Kevin would never do such a thing, but she also knew that he had every right to do so, and that hurt almost as much. "Yes, I'm sure."

He held her close, not wanting her to see the fear that had come into his own eyes. He had experienced the same premonition he had had in the restaurant, only this time it was even stronger. *He couldn't lose her.* Not now. Not after it had taken so long to find her.

Lisa fought her despair with the mundane. "Are you going to feed me lunch?" Perhaps by doing something she could shake the feeling.

"How does soup sound?"

"With big slices of your mother's homemade bread, smothered in butter."

"I have a feeling that inside this small person I'm holding is a big one struggling to get out."

"And she gets downright mean whenever I ignore her."

When the meal was ready they put it on trays and went into the living room to eat by the fire. After they finished, Kevin broke the companionable silence by asking, "Why an astronaut? Why not a physics professor like your father or a computer genius like your brother?"

She stretched her legs out in front of her and stared at the orange flames. "Timing mainly. I was just finishing my doctorate in biology and thinking about what I was going to do with it when I read a job-search bulletin on one of the boards at Stanford and saw that NASA was recruiting astronauts. In the beginning I applied as kind of a lark, but the closer I came to being hired, the more important the job became. By the time I actually made the last cut, I was the most gung-ho recruit they'd ever had. It's been that way ever since. I can't imagine going back to civilian life, it would seem so—"

"Ordinary?"

She thought about her feelings for a minute. "No...I don't think that's it. It's hard to describe something like space flight to anyone who's never experienced it. I'd call it an addiction, but the word has too many negative connotations." She struggled for better words. "I love what I do...if someone were to tell me I could never fly again, I would be devastated. I realize the day will come when I'll have to retire, but I honestly feel I'll be able to accept that retirement because it will come as part of the natural progression of things." She glanced over to Kevin. "There's an excitement to being a part of something as important as exploring space that's pervasive. It controls everything you do or feel or say until eventually that excitement is as much a part of you as your heart or lungs or mind. Few outsiders understand that part of an astronaut's makeup. And because others don't understand us, at times it tends to make us rather clannish.''

Kevin had the distinct feeling she was trying to tell him that no matter how intimately they knew each other, he would always be an outsider. He didn't care for the message. He considered commenting but decided to hear her out first.

''If something was to happen to the space program,'' she said softly, almost to herself, ''I'm not sure where I would go or what I would do. Because of the demands put on me as an astronaut, I haven't kept up with what's happening in biology. My doctorate would be useless without years of study to catch up, and I question whether or not I would want to make the effort.'' She cradled her chin in her hands. ''The idea of giving up on something as important as space exploration is beyond my imaginings. So much good for everyone has come out of the program. The medical breakthroughs alone—''

Before he could bite back the answer to what he considered a clichéd excuse for scientists' pompous assertations that they had a right to the purse strings of an entire nation, the words were spoken. ''The greatest medical breakthroughs have occurred because of wars. There's nothing like having thousands of terribly wounded young men to practice on to come up with wondrous new methods of treatment. The ends don't always justify the means, Lisa.''

"That was a cheap shot. How could you compare—"

Kevin recoiled at his own insensitivity. "I'm sorry." What in the hell was he doing? All she wanted was for him to listen to her, not espouse his own views. But he had heard the arguments before, over and over again. They were self-centered and myopic, and it always seemed that those who spouted them were never the ones willing to compromise. It was their way or none at all. "Lisa, we shouldn't be doing this...not now." If he allowed this kind of argument to come between them, how was he ever going to tell her about the appointment?

"Yes...we should," she said softly. "This is precisely the right time for us to get this out in the open...before things go any further between us than they already have." She brought her knees up and leaned her elbows on them. "I have a feeling we made a terrible mistake when we decided to postpone what we both knew was inevitable."

Her voice held such despair, such hopelessness, it frightened him.

"I know I can't expect your wholehearted support for what I believe in..." In her mind she knew; in her heart she had not yet accepted the idea. "But I have to feel that at least you're not aligned against me."

"Lisa, why do you insist on putting what's basically only a difference of opinion on a personal level?"

"Because that's exactly where it is. You don't seem to understand that it's impossible to separate who I am from what I do, Kevin. They are one and the same. I've been trying to tell you that all along."

"And is that how you see me? Is the man I am so closely meshed with what I do in Congress that you can't distinguish between the two?"

"Yes," she reluctantly admitted to herself, to him.

His heart thudded heavily in his chest. "Then I don't understand why you're here."

"Because I truly thought we could come to an understanding."

Kevin felt as if he were going to be sick. "You can't possibly be trying to tell me that you thought you could change my feelings about funding for NASA by sleeping with me." He covered the hurt with anger.

Lisa's head snapped up. "I know you don't believe that. You can't."

"What am I supposed to think? What kind of understanding did you have in mind?" Could she know about the appointment? Piece by piece his world was falling apart.

"I wanted you to see the space program on a personal level, not as facts and figures on someone's balance sheet."

"When the bottom line on that sheet is a $7.5-billion annual budget, I *have* to look at the figures. It's my job." He started to say something about the cost overruns of the latest shuttle but switched to a less volatile example. "Why won't you at least try to see my side of this?" He held out his hands imploringly. "Lisa, there's enough waste in the Pentagon's spare-parts program each year to fund the head-start program for disadvantaged preschoolers six times over. This waste has become so insidious, it's such an accepted part of the system, that the Pentagon doesn't consider the problem to be anything more than one of public relations."

"I don't care about the Pentagon's waste. I care about NASA. I care about a shuttle that could have turned into a death trap because the contractors were so intimidated by cost overruns they took shortcuts. I care about seven special people who were damn near killed because of tightfisted men in Washington whose imaginations and visions of the future are controlled by the narrowness of their minds and fanaticism over balanced budgets. This country's budget has never been truly balanced. Why now? And why put the responsibility on the back of NASA? We pay our way in the good we do for all mankind."

"How long have you known about the *Orion*?" he asked, suddenly understanding her impassioned outburst.

"What difference does it make?"

"I was just wondering whether or not you'd had time to completely think the whole thing through or if you were still reacting on a purely emotional level."

She stiffened, and her eyes grew cold. "What are you trying to imply?"

"You've looked in the wrong direction for your villain. This is what I've been attempting to get through to you all along, Lisa. When you fail to demand the same standards for government spending as those in the civilian marketplace, you leave yourself wide open for this kind of thing to happen. Has anyone made a thorough audit of the expenses and profits of these contractors or really looked into the reasons for the cost overruns and whether or not the corner cutting was to keep the company solvent or if it was to pay bigger bonuses to the men at the top? Those narrow-minded men in Washington you spoke of didn't screw NASA, the contractors did!"

"But without the tight fist, they never would have felt the necessity."

"Your solution would be to turn the other cheek, to ignore the unconscionably obscene profits?"

"It's a fact of life, Kevin. That's the way big business operates in this country. Your precious cost-savings measures are never going to hurt those men at the top. They're going to hurt people like Frank Jenkins or Sandy Williams...or me someday." She dropped her hands between her knees in defeat. He would never understand. They were too far apart to ever come together. "One other thing you seem to be forgetting," she added, unable to give up without one last shot. "NASA employs thousands of taxpaying people. What are you going to do with them when they've lost their jobs?"

Kevin took a deep breath, trying to calm the frustration, the anger that sapped his reason. Why couldn't he make her understand that he didn't want to destroy NASA, only to make it more accountable? "Lisa, there are—"

She stood. "I don't think we should go on with this." She started to leave, but Kevin reached out and caught her arm.

"There's something you have to know." He would give anything for a way to keep from telling her about the appointment, but to delay any longer would only make its impact more lethal. "When the new session opens in January, I will be on the appropriation committee for NASA."

Her eyes grew wide, and she pulled her arm from his grasp. "How long have you known this?"

"A few days."

"Why didn't you tell me before now?"

"I was waiting for the right time."

"And you thought *now* was the right time?" She felt her world collapsing around her. With Kevin on the committee the space station was doomed, if not the entire program. She moved to the doorway, reeling from the impact of his news. "I can't stay here any longer, Kevin." She had to get away, to think, to hide the hurt.

"Lisa, don't do this."

She stared at him, her eyes glossy with pain. "It's been done, Kevin. The minute you accepted the appointment you chose for me. I can't believe you didn't know what it would do to our relationship if you were on the committee. You dealt yourself all the cards—now you can play them as you see fit. But I won't be around to watch."

"Lisa, you're wrong."

"Am I? If you had any intention of instigating a long-term relationship with me—of our having any kind of relationship—how were you planning to avoid a conflict-of-interest charge? Wouldn't your votes for or against NASA be rather suspect when you were sleeping with one of their lady astronauts?" Her words were filled with bitterness.

Kevin felt as if she had hit him. How could he have missed something so basic? "I didn't think. It never occurred to me."

"Do you have any idea how hard that is for me to swallow? If I've come to know anything about you these past few weeks, it's that you're methodical and that you always think things through carefully." She could feel a tightness behind her eyes and knew tears weren't far away. She would not let him see her cry. "It's over, Kevin." She left him to go upstairs to pack her suitcase.

Kevin stood in the middle of the room, too stunned to immediately follow. In ten minutes they had gone from lovers to adversaries. He couldn't let her go. But were there any words that would keep her? He had been so blind not to have seen what accepting the appointment would do to her. God, he couldn't lose her, not now. Not after learning how worth living his life could be again. He went upstairs after her.

Lisa looked up from her packing to see Kevin standing in the doorway. In the short time she had been alone her anger had faded into a numb acceptance. "I think we both knew all along that things could never work out between us," she said, staring at the neatly folded clothes in her suitcase, unable to look at him as she spoke. "It's better that we end it now, before either of us gets hurt." How easily she spoke the lie. She would hurt for a long time to come, a very long time.

"I thought you were a fighter," he said quietly.

"Some things aren't worth fighting for."

Her words, the uncompromising way she said them, hurt so badly he was stripped of the ability to reply.

Lisa felt the blood drain from her face. She hadn't meant to say that. It wasn't true. When she looked up to tell Kevin so, he had turned and was walking away. "Kevin..." His name came out a choked whisper. She heard his footsteps on the stairs. Tears she could no longer fight spilled from her lashes. She started after him, then stopped. It was better for both of them that she let him go.

BY THE TIME KEVIN RETURNED from taking Lisa to the airport it was dark. His headlights swept the house as he made the final turn up the driveway, illuminating the snowman with the now-mocking smile. The telephone rang when he entered the house. He picked up the receiver, telling himself it was foolish to hope it might be Lisa, yet unable to stop his racing heart. It was his mother.

"I made some apple pies today and thought you and your friend might like to come over this evening to have a piece." Her voice was cheerful, excited.

Kevin wearily leaned his head against the wall and ran his hand through his hair to the back of his neck. "You're about four hours too late, mom. Lisa's gone back to Houston." He was too tired to make it sound any better than it was.

"Oh...I'm sorry to hear that."

"Yeah...me, too."

There was a long pause, followed by a sad sigh. "If you feel up to it, why don't you come on over for supper tonight? There's plenty."

"Maybe tomorrow. I've got some thinking to do tonight."

"I understand." Again there was a pause. "Kevin, you never were a quitter. If she's important to you, don't let her go."

His half smile was genuine, if tired. "Sometimes it's a little more complicated than that."

"Nonsense."

"Tell dad I'll be over to help him with the feeding tomorrow."

"You can change the subject, but you can't change the facts. That bed of yours is going to seem mighty cold tonight."

"Good night, mom."

She told him good-night, and that she'd save a pie for him. After he hung up, Kevin went to the cupboard and took down a bottle of brandy he had purchased for nights in front of the fire with Lisa. He poured a generous amount in a highball glass and went into the living room. Three hours and three glasses of brandy later, he reached a decision, and sleep came easier than he had thought or his mother had predicted.

CHAPTER THIRTEEN

WHEN LISA RETURNED to Houston, a profound sadness made simple tasks complex and complex tasks impossible. After the second day of wandering around her apartment like an animal struggling to find its way out of a maze, she decided to seek forgetfulness in work.

The next morning, as she neared Johnson Space Center, she realized she could not use her job as an escape this time. There were too many people at the center who knew she should still be in Kansas. The last thing she wanted to do was answer their questions. She made a U-turn and drove into Houston, telling herself that maybe if she could make the outside of her body feel good, it might do something to help fill the vast emptiness she felt inside.

For a few hours her ploy seemed to work. She wandered from store to store in Post Oak Galleria trying on clothes in the most exclusive departments of Neiman-Marcus, Marshall Field's and Lord & Taylor—departments she would normally only wistfully wander through. But now, with studied casualness, she ignored price tags.

Several of the dresses, slacks and sweaters she tried on appealed to her, but her final choice was a designer suit more expensive than anything she had ever owned. She rationalized the purchase by telling herself the garment was not only beautiful but practical—just the right outfit for speaking at luncheons or attending afternoon receptions.

As she walked down the mall, congratulating herself on her refusal to give in to the black mood that had followed her home from Kansas, she was abruptly stripped of her pretense of normalcy. In a store window stood a broadly smiling mannequin, a yellow scarf draped around its neck. As if drawn by invisible forces, Lisa slowly walked over to the display. Her hand came up from her side and pressed against the cool glass; her breath caught in her throat. The terrible emptiness she had carried around with her for three days returned with a vengeful vindictiveness.

On the plane home she had fooled herself into believing the ache would be no more or less than it had been when she called off her marriage or broke her engagement. But she was wrong. There had been pain and a feeling of loss back then, but there had also been the comfort of knowing she had made the right decision. This time it was as if the decision to leave hadn't truly been hers. Because of who and what she and Kevin were, there had been no choice for either of them.

She pressed her forehead to the glass and closed her eyes, seeking the small comfort she hoped acceptance would bring. If only she could hate Kevin or find the energy to be angry with him. But despite her sincere belief that he was wrong, even naive in his idealism, she had discovered she begrudgingly admired his courage to fight for his convictions. Had he yielded to her and changed or modified his beliefs, her respect for him would have been eroded, and she knew the loss of her love would have inevitably followed. A crushing sorrow filled her. There was no solution for them. What a cruel hoax life had played on her to allow her to finally find the man who could love her as she was—accepting the hard-nosed, ambitious person who lurked inside the diminutive frame—and then put an impenetrable barrier between them. Turning from the window, she headed for her car, forgetting her plans to search for a blouse to go with her new suit.

When she arrived home she took her suit from the box and hung it up in the closet. As she started to close the door she caught a glimpse of the broken television. She stared at the set, considering the hours of mindless entertainment it represented. Never before had she resorted to using television to blank out the world. But then never before had she felt such a great need. Lifting the portable up by its handhold, she took it out to the car and drove to the repair shop.

THE MORNING AFTER LISA LEFT HIM Kevin got up early, arriving at his parents' home before sunrise. He joined them for a big country breakfast, throughout which they all purposely and sometimes awkwardly avoided discussing Lisa. As soon as they were finished eating, Kevin went out to the barn with his father to load alfalfa onto the back of the truck to take out to the cattle.

They worked in a companionable silence, concentrating on the loading, moving quickly in the cold morning air. Finally it was Harold who broke the silence. "Your mom tells me your friend's gone home already," he said, hiking a bale onto the tailgate.

Standing up in the bed of the truck, Kevin took the bale and stacked it on top of another. He wasn't surprised his father had asked about Lisa, only that it had taken so long. If he told him that he'd rather not talk about her, his father would respect his wishes, but it would only be a postponement of the inevitable. "Things didn't work out as we had hoped they would."

"I see," he said thoughtfully. He stopped to undo the top button of his red plaid jacket. "She's gone for good, then?"

"It looks that way. Unless I can come up with something that would change her mind. Right now I wouldn't give much for my prospects, but I haven't given up completely."

He tossed another bale to Kevin. "What seems to be the problem?"

Rarely was his father so persistent in his inquisitiveness. "Did mom put you up to this?"

"We talked some last night, but she doesn't know I planned to bend your ear today."

"Well, I know you're only trying to help, dad, but there's nothing to be done. Like I said before, I haven't completely given up hope. But with the way things are, I can't help but feel it's pretty much over between Lisa and me."

"Sometimes getting things out in the open helps work 'em through."

As an only child, Kevin had been the recipient of enough love and attention for a dozen children, but rarely had his father offered advice or pushed a subject beyond his son's willingness to respond. He sat down heavily on one of the bales and stared at Harold, who had gone back to loading. "Maybe getting things out in the open would help." He sought a parallel situation involving his parents that might help his father to understand what had happened between him and Lisa. "What would you have done forty years ago if you had asked mom to marry you and she had said yes, but only if the two of you lived in the city?"

Harold lifted his hat to scratch the top of his head. "Are you trying to tell me Lisa won't move to Washington? Is that what's keeping the two of you apart?"

"No..." He tried again. "Lisa is a special kind of woman...she's more like a man really." That was as convoluted an image as he could possibly send to his father. He searched for a way to encapsulate her personality. "If Carry Nation were ever reincarnated, she'd probably come back as Lisa." Kevin inwardly groaned. Comparing Lisa to the famed temperance agitator would only confuse him more.

"But I can't see where that would pose such a problem. You've never been much of a drinker." His voice was patient as he valiantly tried to understand his son's ramblings.

"It's not the cause I'm talking about, dad. It's the kind of woman. Lisa has a passion and a belief in what she does that would match old Carry at her bar-busting best."

Harold readjusted his hat. "And she can't handle your budget-cutting philosophies," he said, understanding finally dawning.

Kevin smiled. He was constantly surprised at how closely his parents followed his career. "Actually, it's more than that. I think we might have made it if I hadn't accepted the appointment to the Senate Commerce, Science and Transportation Committee."

Harold greeted the news with a low whistle. "I suppose congratulations are in order." He paused to think about Kevin's news. "I don't understand why you took the job if you care as much for Lisa as I think you do."

"I spent most of last night wondering the same thing myself. At the time I guess I thought we could work it out." He combed his hand through his hair. "I really don't know what I thought," he reluctantly admitted.

Long seconds passed. "And how come you don't give up the appointment now that you know what effect it's had?"

As usual, his father had gone directly to the core of the problem. "I spent a lot of time last night thinking about that, too. I've been in Washington almost ten years, dad, doing a job I never wanted." His voice dropped to a low whisper. "Trying to make up for what happened to Angela and Christine and never feeling as if I were succeeding." It was the first time he had admitted that he had been trying to pay penance for their deaths, and it was as much a revelation to himself as it was to his father.

Harold flinched, and the color drained from his face. "I had no idea you were still carrying that around with you," he said. "I thought you had accepted that it was nothing more than an accident a long time ago."

"I thought so, too. But I've had to take a good hard look at myself lately and this is the only thing that makes sense. Last night I realized that accepting the appointment is far more than just a continuation of wearing the hair shirt I seem unable to shrug off. It means I will finally have a chance to do something that will make the time I've spent in Washington worthwhile."

Harold shook his head, his eyes filled with sadness. "How could I have been so blind not to see any of this before? Your mom and I raised you to take responsibility and not to shirk your duty, but somewhere along the line we must have failed if we didn't teach you that there was a time to let go and to get on with your life." His voice cracked. "Kevin, you never owed Christine or

Angela a thing past your grief at their deaths. You were a good, loving husband and father and you gave of yourself every day they were alive. There was nothing that said you had to keep on after they were gone." He let out a dispirited sigh. "Have you received no pleasure at all from the work you've been doing all this time?"

Kevin hesitated before answering. He gave his father's question as much consideration as if it was the first time it had been asked. He dug deep into his memories, searching for the triumphs and disappointments, the loneliness and friendships he had experienced because of his job. He was surprised with the answer. "There were some good times and some exciting and challenging times. I think eventually I'll look back with good memories and feel that what I did was worthwhile and important." He stared at the tops of his boots, idly noting how far the toes had curled up over the years. "But I'll also remember that never once when I got off the plane in Washington did I feel as if I were going home."

"It seems a good hard look at what you're going to do with the rest of your life is long overdue."

Kevin looked deeply into his father's eyes. He was relieved to see acceptance and understanding there. He had feared his father would be disappointed to learn that he was seriously considering leaving politics. "That's pretty much the conclusion I came to last night."

"And what about Lisa?" he prodded.

Kevin grinned. His father had the tenacity of a hungry mosquito. "I thought it was daughters that fathers worried about getting married off."

"Don't try sneaking out the back door on this. I know it sounds strange for me to be going on the way I am when I haven't even met the gal yet, but anyone who can make you look the way you did when you got off that plane has my vote sight unseen. Giving up has never been the Andersons' style. I sure don't want to see it start with you."

"I don't have any intention of giving up, even though I did say that it appeared things were over between us. But I do have some serious thinking to do before I can approach Lisa again. Nothing's changed since she left yesterday. And even though my gut instinct is to say the hell with everything else and pretend nothing else matters, I know that if I went after her now, before I can offer some kind of solution to what's keeping us apart, it would only widen the breach between us."

Harold straightened and stretched, then reached for another bale. "Well, I've got plenty of work around here to keep you from going crazy while you're thinking things out." He tossed his son a meaningful look. "Just don't go letting too much time pass before you make your move. If I hadn't taken your mom to the altar when I did, there were plenty who would have taken my place."

As THE DAYS SLOWLY PASSED, eventually adding up to a week, and then two, Lisa realized she had harbored a secret hope Kevin would call her. A constant raging battle between her mind and her heart consumed her waking hours. Intellectually she accepted the finality of their parting, emotionally she couldn't let go. She kept reminding herself that time was the great healer. She simply had to wait things out. She managed each day by promising herself the next would bring a lessening of the pain, that soon she would begin to feel a numbness and then there would be nothing.

The last week in November Sandy Williams arranged a blind date for Lisa without telling her she had done so until the day of the date. They were in the cafeteria at the center when she broke the news.

"You did *what*?" Lisa managed to say, choking on a bite of her hamburger.

"I promise you, he's perfect for what ails you, Lisa. He's uncomplicated, a terrific dancer, and has this magnificent centerfold face and body that you have to see to believe. But best of all, there isn't a chance in the world you'll get seriously involved with him. He's perfect for a mindless night out on the town." She put her turkey sandwich back on her plate, peered inside and took out a slice of pickle. "Who in their right mind would put dill pickles on a turkey sandwich?" she grumbled, ignoring Lisa's scathing stare.

"You had no right to do this without saying something to me first," Lisa said, struggling to keep from shouting.

"And if I had?"

"I would have told you—"

"That you wouldn't go. Face it, Lisa, we've been friends long enough for me to know how you think. You left me no options. You've been running around with big sad eyes and your chin on your chest for almost a month now. It's time to cut your losses and move on. Obviously you've met your match in the stubborn department. And since Kevin's not going to break down and call you, and there's no way you'll ever call him, the only thing left is to work him out of your system."

Unable to take another bite, Lisa tossed her half-eaten hamburger back onto her plate. Despite a lack of hunger she had decided it was time she forced herself to eat. The weight she'd lost since leaving Kevin had hollowed her cheeks and created dark circles under her eyes, making her look exhausted all the time. Just that morning Frank Jenkins had stopped her in the hallway and asked if she was sick. Next it would be the physician who monitored the astronauts' health. "I agree with everything you've said. But going out with one of your 'hunks of the month' is not the answer."

"Then what is?"

"Haven't you heard? Time heals all wounds. All I need is to put a few months between me and Kevin and I'll be fine."

"My, my...who thought up that clever bit of wisdom?"

"You're just going to have to call this guy and tell him the date's off."

"I can't."

Lisa glared at her. "And why not?"

"I don't have his number."

"Then go over to his house."

"Can't."

"Why?"

"I don't know where he lives."

She threw her hands up in exasperation. "What did you do, flag him down on the freeway?"

"Not quite. He's the brother of a friend of a friend."

"Why didn't you just take out an ad in one of those singles' newspapers?"

"Calm down, Lisa," she said, looking around to see if they were attracting attention. "It isn't as bad as it sounds. This guy is only in town for a few weeks. He happened to mention that he wanted to meet some

people while he was here and I told him I knew someone who could show him a good time.''

"My God, Sandy," she gasped, "you didn't. With
that kind of lead-in he's probably expecting—"

"No he's not. I purposely emphasized what a nice
person you are. I told him you had a few problems and
weren't looking for anything permanent—that you just
wanted a few laughs and maybe a chaste kiss or two. He
assured me you fit in perfectly with his needs. He's been
gone from this area for five years—"

"Gone for five years?" she repeated. "As a guest of
which prison?"

"Wrong guess."

"Where then?"

"College," she mumbled.

"What?"

She let out a resigned sigh. "He's been in Ohio, going
to school.''

Lisa's eyes narrowed ominously. "Just how old is this
Adonis of yours?"

"Twenty-two or twenty-three, I'm not quite sure. But
he looks a lot older," she added hastily.

Lisa leaned back in her chair and groaned. "I can't
believe you did this to me. How could you fix me up
with someone who's two-thirds my age? You've done
some nutty things before, Sandy, but this tops all of
them by a mile." She threw her napkin on the table. "I
don't care how you do it, but one way or another, you
will get me out of this date."

Sandy grabbed her arm to keep her from leaving. "I
really can't. My friend is out of town, so I can't get his
friend's phone number to call Jason and cancel out."

"Jason? His name is Jason?" Lisa sunk back into her chair. "He's a jock, isn't he?" With a name like Jason, he had to be a jock.

"I'm not absolutely sure..."

"Sandy—*spill*."

"He plays football."

"Plays?"

"He's on the injured reserves for the Denver Broncos."

She sighed, rapidly growing resigned to her evening. "You could at least have gotten me someone who played for the 49ers."

"Next time."

Lisa leaned across the table. "Listen carefully, dear friend. There isn't going to be any next time. If the slightest urge strikes you to do something like this again, I would suggest you take two aspirin, go to bed and call me. I'll list the reasons your efforts will not be appreciated." She paused, letting the knowledge that she was going out with a man ten years her junior sink in. "Why did you wait until now to tell me?" she wailed, already knowing the answer.

"Because I knew if I told you sooner, you'd find a way to squirm out of it."

Lisa eyed her. "I think I just have. When Jason arrives tonight for his date, you're going to be the one who's there to greet him, not me."

"I can't."

"I know how you operate, Sandy. You're counting on the fact that I don't have it in me to stand up some poor guy who's as much one of your victims as I am. Well, I have news for you. I'm dumping this whole thing right back in your lap. From now on Jason is your responsibility."

"Nice try, but it won't work. I'm leaving for the Cape in an hour."

Lisa finally accepted the fact that she was cornered. "I'll get you for this."

Sandy smiled triumphantly. "No you won't. You'll thank me."

JASON CLARK ARRIVED at Lisa's apartment at exactly seven-thirty. He was precisely as Sandy had described him. From the top of his head, covered with thick black hair, to the tip of his toes, shod in lizard-skin cowboy boots, he was the perfect material for a centerfold layout. In between head and toe was a six-foot-two-inch body with muscles that bulged through a navy-blue sport coat and tan slacks. He didn't look the twenty-two or twenty-three Sandy had said; he looked eighteen.

Briefly she wondered what he had been told about her. Jason Clark was definitely not someone who needed anyone to fix him up with a blind date. All he would have to do was walk down the street and he would have willing females following behind, like cats to cream.

After they had introduced themselves Lisa said, "Sandy failed to mention where we were going."

"Any place is fine with me." He shoved his hands in his pockets and grinned self-consciously. "Well, almost any place. I have this shoulder separation, so I'd just as soon stay off mechanical bulls."

Lisa realized he was as ill at ease about their date as she was. "Why don't you let me fix you a drink while we figure out someplace to go?" She resisted an impulse to ask him if he was old enough to drink.

Responding to her easygoing manner, he visibly relaxed. "That would be great. Do you have any beer?" He followed Lisa over to the kitchen.

"Have a seat." She indicated the bar stools. She served him a beer and herself a glass of wine. Leaning her elbows on the counter, she looked at him. "Tell me, Jason, exactly how did you get roped into this date?"

His neck turned bright pink. Slowly the color reached his face. "My girlfriend dumped me a month ago and my brother decided I'd moped around the house long enough so he arranged—"

"You don't have to tell me any more, I can fill in the rest for myself." She had decided she liked Jason Clark. His tendency to blush and his openness reminded her of her brother. "Do you play gin rummy?" she asked impulsively.

He blinked. "Yeah, as a matter of fact, I do."

"Good. How about if I fix us something to eat and we spend the evening playing cards?"

"I think I should tell you I'm a pretty good gin player," he warned.

Lisa smiled. "I've been known to win a game or two myself."

Jason shrugged out of his jacket and hung it on the back of the stool. "What can I do to help with dinner?"

SIX HOURS LATER, Lisa was at the front door telling Jason good-night. The evening had been a good one for her, the first since Kansas. After an initial awkwardness she and Jason had developed an easy rapport that included healing laughter. He told her about Suzy, the girl he had been engaged to and whom he still desperately loved. Lisa listened quietly, realizing because of her own situation that he wasn't asking for platitudes or advice, only a friendly ear. By the end of the evening she had added him to the list of friends she would make a special effort to see.

She moved about the living room, straightening cushions and returning the chairs they had used while playing cards to their proper places. Humming slightly off-key to a song being played on the radio, she smiled to herself as she remembered Jason's tale of what he went through the first day he reported to the Broncos' training camp. She felt good for the first time in weeks and congratulated herself for coming through yet another disillusioning, disappointing love affair, if not unscathed, at least intact.

The last of the dishes were washed and put away, and feeling pleasantly tired she headed for bed. Once under the covers she discovered she wasn't as ready for sleep as she had first thought, so she opened the drawer of her nightstand for a book of slightly boring short stories she kept there solely for the purpose of putting her to sleep. Her newly constructed shelter of good feelings and hope that she was at last on the road to recovery shattered like flawed crystal. Lying beneath her book were the clippings Kevin had sent to her a month and a half ago. As if she had no control over her actions, she reached for them.

She sat up, leaning her back against the headboard. For a long time she held the clippings on her lap, neither looking at them nor touching them. How naive she had been to believe she was on her way to getting over Kevin. She would carry his memory and the warmth and tenderness of the love he had given her for a long time to come. They had been together such a short time. For a while she had thought it a blessing, but now she felt terribly cheated. If she must endure the bitterness of what might have been, shouldn't she have been entitled to more of the sweetness?

Slowly her hands traveled to the slick surface of a magazine page. She touched the handwritten script at the bottom, her eyes too misty to make out the words. She blinked away the moisture. The one thing she had not done since returning to Houston was cry. She had held her grief inside as if it were something precious, something to be guarded and protected.

Her gaze focused on the top picture, a group of people at a party, smiling, laughing, having a good time. "From now on," he had written, "I will never attend a party without thinking of you." She swallowed. Slowly she moved the page aside to look at the next.

A huge chocolate-chip cookie, broken in half, dominated the page. In bold red letters the manufacturer claimed its product was as moist and chewy as homemade. "I don't believe a cookie that comes from a bag or a box will ever taste homemade. A good cookie is one-quarter love, one-quarter how it smells when it's baking and only the rest ingredients." Lisa's mouth twisted in a sad smile. When she had called Kevin the day after receiving his package of clippings, she had told him she had a recipe for chocolate-chip cookies that would knock his socks off. He had teased her by saying no one could make a better cookie than his Aunt Evelyn but that he was willing to let her try.

The next clipping was from a newspaper. It was a feature article that highlighted several prominent scientists and gave their predictions on what life would be like twenty-five years in the future. "I read this yesterday morning while I was eating breakfast. All I could think about was you and how my feelings about the future have changed since we met."

A tear rolled down Lisa's cheek and landed on the newspaper. Why was she doing this to herself? It was insanity to purposely sit there and torture herself with what might have been. Not to mention that her behavior was masochistic. She covered her face with her hands. Oh God, when would the pain lessen? Great heaving sobs racked her. When would there be a day she wouldn't think of Kevin? Would there be a time she didn't have to fight the compelling urge to forget what separated them and go to him just to ease the terrible emptiness that haunted her?

Up until then, whenever she had almost broken down and started to reach for the phone, an overpowering fear had stopped her. She was too much of a realist to ever, even in her darkest moments, believe that either of them could truly change who and what they were. They might agree never to discuss their differences, but someday, somehow those differences would surface, and when they did, they would do so with a destructive fury. What she and Kevin had shared was too special to risk such an ending.

Through the tortured thought process she had used a hundred times since returning to Houston, she convinced herself she had made the only choice possible. After such reasoning sleep should have come easily, but it didn't.

THE NEXT MORNING Lisa was on her way out the door to pick up groceries and run errands when the phone rang.

"How'd it go?" Sandy asked, skipping the usual small talk.

"Better than I had expected," Lisa reluctantly admitted. "Jason's a nice kid."

"Kid? How can you call someone like Jason a kid?"

Lisa, too, was surprised at her choice of words. "I still can't believe you thought we were—"

"What I thought was that you would at least respond to him on a physical level." Frustration edged each word. "For crying out loud, Lisa, Jason is an exceptional example of the male of our species. Didn't he do anything for you at all?"

Lisa felt as if Sandy had hit her. For the first time she realized she had crossed an age barrier, one that separated her from Jason and his generation as surely as if they were on different planets. She felt strangely old, apart. "I felt like his older sister," she said, dumbfounded as she recalled how easily she had slipped into the role.

Sandy sighed. "That was not the intended plan."

"From now on you're just going to have to let me work this out on my own."

"I'll be back in Houston on Tuesday. How about if we go out for pizza and a movie?"

"Just the two of us?"

"Don't worry, I've learned my lesson."

They settled on a time and place and told each other goodbye. After she hung up the phone Lisa walked over to the gilt-edged mirror that was hanging by the front door. She stared at her reflection, looking to see if there was any physical evidence that marked the mental change she had experienced. She was the same. No new lines or sagging jowls. Still, there was something different...an indefinable maturity shining from her eyes.

She had always looked on aging as most other scientists did, an inevitable result of being born. How she would look as an old woman or whether she would age "gracefully" had never bothered her or caused her concern. She accepted her appearance as a matter of genes, nothing more. What did bother her, she suddenly realized, was knowing that the choice of whether or not she would ever have children was being irrevocably taken from her by the aging process.

She had asked Kevin how he felt about having children but had never told him her feelings, primarily because every time the thought surfaced she would send it under again, telling herself there would be plenty of time to consider it later, when her life was in less upheaval, when there weren't so many other important things going on. She needed to talk to someone— someone who would understand the fears and doubts that raced through her mind. Without hesitation she knew that the someone she needed to talk to was Caroline.

Groceries forgotten, she headed for the Websters'.

CHAPTER FOURTEEN

AS PREPARATION INTENSIFIED for Lisa's next flight, and with the distraction provided by the holidays, December passed more quickly and more easily than November had. Lisa saw Jason Clark twice more before he returned to Denver. Both times they played cards at her apartment and ruminated over loves lost. Whenever possible, her Sundays were spent watching the 49ers play football on the Websters' television, which was hooked up to a satellite dish left by the previous owners.

The day before Christmas she flew to Berkeley to be with her father and brother's family, then flew home the day after. January came and with it the announcement of Kevin's appointment. The response at the center was milder than she had anticipated, the general feeling being that the makeup of the committee had pretty much stayed the same and the voting would go as it always had. The Super Bowl took place in mid-January while she was in orbit; she won the pool by betting on the 49ers to win by seventeen. When she arrived back in Houston after an uneventful mission she learned that Caroline had been hospitalized. That afternoon she went to visit her.

Lisa hated hospitals, the smell, the tension, the way people walking down the halls avoided eye contact. Cory hadn't remembered Caroline's room number so She stopped by the nurses station to ask. Lisa side-stepped a gurney carrying a woman who was being returned to her room from surgery and patiently waited while a young girl experimented with the procedure of turning a wheelchair in the middle of the hallway before Lisa found 513. The door was partially open. Lisa knocked lightly and entered as soon as she heard Caroline's voice. Sitting on every flat surface were vases filled with flowers. It seemed that every size, every shape, every type of flower was represented. "I hope you're getting a kickback from the florists in town," Lisa said.

Caroline laid her paperback down on the shelf her stomach made. "Mike has this thing about bringing me flowers. He has since the first day we met." She held out her hand. "Welcome home. How was the flight?"

Lisa came over to her and gave her a hug. "Not nearly as exciting as what's been going on here. How are you feeling?"

"Pregnant. Very, very pregnant. I now know what a queen bee must feel like. People keep bringing me food and I just keep getting bigger and bigger."

Lisa brought a straight-back chair over beside the bed and sat down. "Did something special happen to put you in here?"

"No, the doctors just thought it was about time for me to get off my feet. It seems this way I'm more likely to carry the babies longer, and the longer I carry them, the better their chances."

"Did you get everything done that you wanted to do before you came here?"

"Pretty much. Mike's having a ball finishing up the rest. He's painted and papered and bought enough baby clothes for ten kids. I don't see how he's getting anything else done."

Lisa knew Mike's work load had been back-breaking since the release of the information about *Orion*. NASA had been receiving relatively little publicity in the past few years, but the *Orion* fiasco had created an up-surge. Since resuming his old job as spokesman for the shuttle program, Mike had not had an entire day off work.

As he had in the past, he deftly handled the news conferences, turning what could have been a public-relations disaster into a general feeling of sympathy toward the program. Several magazines had run articles on the *Orion's* crew members and their "daring" rescue, and thanks to his unceasing efforts there were several more in the works.

"Where is he now? I was surprised he wasn't here when I came in."

Caroline's smile faded. "You don't know?" she breathed.

"Know what?" Lisa asked warily, responding to the look in Caroline's eyes.

"He's with Kevin."

"In Washington?"

Caroline shook her head.

"Kevin's here?" She felt as if a band was tightening around her chest, making it difficult to breathe. "In Houston?"

"He's been here for three days now."

Lisa struggled to give the impression the information meant nothing to her, but she failed miserably. "Why?" she finally managed to ask.

"It has something to do with his appointment."

"How long..."

"Two or three more days." She reached over to take Lisa's hand. "He's come here every day with Mike."

When Lisa didn't respond, she added, "Around this time, every day."

"Oh...I see." Lisa stood. "I'll be sure to come back earlier tomorrow. We can visit then." She walked toward the door, stopped and gave Caroline a half smile. "I know this is a foolish question, but is there anything I can bring you when I come back?"

"Thanks for the offer, Lisa, but Mike would be crushed if I didn't ask him."

"I understand." She shoved her hand in the pocket of her gray wool slacks. Her hand made contact with one of the primary reasons she had come. "I almost forgot," she said, walking back over to the bed. She took five mint silver coins out of her pocket. "I took these with me on the flight. They're for the babies— their first gift from their honorary aunt."

Caroline took the pieces of silver from Lisa's outstretched hand. She looked at one side and then the other of the plastic-encased coins. "They're beautiful," she exclaimed. "Thank you." Her expression changed from pleasure to alarm as she glanced at the door.

Lisa didn't have to ask what had caused the abrupt change. She could feel Kevin's presence as surely as if he had touched her. She closed her eyes and took a deep breath before turning around and forcing a smile she didn't feel. "Mike..." She swallowed. "Kevin..." Standing in the doorway in a tweed sport coat, light-brown slacks and rust-colored cashmere sweater, his hands resting in his pockets, Kevin looked like an ad in a travel magazine designed to get young unmarried women to tour Sweden.

Mike broke the tension by coming across the room to give Lisa a hug. "Welcome home," he said. "I heard you did an excellent job, as usual."

"Thank you." She had the most peculiar urge to cling to him, seeking refuge from the storm swirling around her.

Still holding her hand, he leaned over to kiss Caroline. "How are you doing, beautiful?" he asked, his voice a low caress.

Caroline smiled. "I'm doing fine."

"What's this?" He picked up one of the coins.

"A gift from Lisa. She took them up with her into orbit."

Mike studied the pieces of silver. "They're proof pieces, aren't they?"

"Yes. I picked them up when I was in Denver awhile back."

"I've always wanted to get into collecting them. Now I have a good reason. Thanks." He gave her hand a squeeze. "And since the babies can't thank you, I'll do it for them, too." He gave her a kiss.

"You're welcome." She had to get out of there. Kevin's presence made it hard for her to even think. "I hate to bring presents and run, but there's someone waiting for me..." She could tell by the looks on their faces that no one believed her. She started across the room and realized she could not get out the door without making contact with Kevin. To leave without speaking would be confirmation of her growing need to do just that. Only by feigning normalcy could she ever hope to convince him she had recovered from their affair. "How are you, Kevin?" she asked, surprised at how natural her voice sounded.

"I've been better," he said softly, intimately.

The words, the way he spoke them, nearly destroyed her aloofness. He wasn't playing the game by the rules. He had no right to look at her with such longing in his eyes. "And the new job?"

"I've done things I enjoy more."

The liquid sound of his voice attacked her defenses. "Well...it was nice to see you again." How completely insipid she sounded.

Speaking so that only she could hear, he said, "*Nice* isn't the word I would have chosen for the way I feel about this meeting, Lisa. Seeing you again has put a knot in my stomach the size of a boulder. If there weren't people around us, I would take you in my arms and hold you against me until the knot disappeared."

Her heart pounded in her ears. What was he trying to do to her?

"Just because I let you leave me without doing anything to try to stop you doesn't mean that I've given up on us. If our time apart has taught me nothing else, it has taught me that what we had when we were together transcends any ideological differences we might have."

"Don't do this, Kevin." She was standing so close she could smell his cologne and see a muscle twitching along his jaw. "Please...don't." She had honestly thought the pain of their parting was lessening. It had been two and a half months, and lately there had even been a few times when she was so deep in work she hardly thought of him at all. But she had been wrong...so wrong. Seeing him had plunged her back into the abyss. The pain was as bad as it had been the day she left.

Kevin moved aside to let her pass. He had seen all he needed to see. Despite her words and actions she still loved him. He watched her as she hurried down the hall away from him and disappeared around the corner.

Feeling an odd mixture of elation and anguish, he crossed the room to give Caroline a kiss. "You look like you've put on a little weight since I saw you last."

She smiled. "Thanks, Kevin. You always did have a knack for saying just the right thing."

"I only wish."

"She won't see you?"

"I didn't ask."

"Why? It's obvious the two of you still care for each other."

"Right now there are some pretty formidable roadblocks standing in our way."

"You mean the committee thing?"

"That, and a few other things." He punctuated his words with an ironic laugh. "Whenever I dig a hole, I dig it deep."

Mike eyed Kevin. He had never seen him look more miserable. Once again he kicked himself for being the one who had gotten Lisa and Kevin together in the first place. He should have known better. They were so much alike, so vulnerable, so passionate and unbending in their beliefs; it was inevitable sparks would fly between them. Still, everything might have worked if Kevin hadn't accepted the appointment. It was the one thing Lisa had been unable to handle. He pulled another chair over to Caroline's bed. "Have a seat," he said to Kevin.

"Thanks, but I don't think I'll stay long tonight. You two haven't had a chance for any real time alone this week, and I have some paperwork I need to finish while everything's still fresh in my mind."

"You have your key?" Mike asked, checking to make sure Kevin could get into the house without him.

"Yes..." He patted his pocket. "Right here."

"I'll see you at home then. Go ahead and eat without me. There's plenty of food in the refrigerator." Mike walked Kevin to the door. "If you need anything you can't find, give me a call. I'll be here for a couple of hours before I head back to the center." He spoke in a low voice, not wanting Caroline to know he still had work to do that night after leaving her.

"I'm sure I'll be fine," Kevin said before heading down the hallway in the same direction as Lisa.

Mike returned to Caroline. "Every time I see those two I can't help but think how easily we could have wound up the same way." He took her hand and brought it to his lips. "I can't imagine my life without you, my love."

She gave him an impish grin. "It was a good thing I wasn't the stubborn type."

He laughed. "You could have taught those two something about stubbornness."

She tugged on his hand. "I want you to sit down and prop your leg up while you're here."

"It's noticeable, huh?" For the first time in months the injury he had sustained several years ago when ejecting from a T-38 was bothering him again. The damage to his leg had marked the end of his career as an astronaut and inadvertently led to his meeting Caroline.

"Only to me. I doubt anyone else could detect you were favoring one side. But if you don't slow down," she warned, adopting a stern tone, "you're going to be limping soon."

"Why is it you won't believe me when I tell you I'm not overdoing things?"

She gave him a look that told him she wasn't fooled by his protestations. "You're the worst liar of anyone I've ever known."

He decided the best way to get the focus off himself and the work load he was carrying was to shift the subject back to Kevin. "You'd have been proud of your cousin today. He did a hell of a job with those budget people. Every time they started to hedge on something, he caught them and brought them back in line."

"And knowing Kevin, he did it with grace and charm. He's always been like that. Even when we were kids, I could be furious with him and he could still get me to do his bidding."

"Too bad Lisa's immune."

"I don't think he's completely given up on her yet. He's said a couple of things this week that make me wonder if he isn't just biding his time."

"Such as?" The romantic in Mike jumped on the news.

"Well, for one thing, he's been talking about what cattle ranching in the Houston area is like as opposed to Kansas."

Mike sat back in his chair and let out a low whistle. "Do you think he was seriously considering something or just idly wondering?" The ramifications of such a move were far reaching.

"I don't think he knows himself. The whole thing came about because of an article he saw in the newspaper when he came to visit me. It was one of those times where one thing leads to another and then another. He wound up leaving early so that he could check with a land broker to see what grazing land was going for around here. He tried to convince me that his interest was only curiosity, but I know him too well to believe he would do that kind of investigating on a whim."

"Do you suppose he's seriously thinking about getting out of politics?"

"I wouldn't be surprised. He's never shown the same enthusiasm for the life-style that we saw in the other elected officials in Washington. And despite running for reelection twice, I don't believe he's ever wanted the job."

"Still—you can't ignore the fact that he accepted this committee thing and that he's working at it like a man with a purpose. He must have realized what—"

Caroline let out a bubbling laugh.

"Did I say something funny?" Mike queried, completely confused by her odd reaction.

"No..." She reached for his hand and placed it on the side of her stomach. "One of our brood has the hiccups again. Every time it happens I get the giggles."

Mike gently pressed against her abdomen. He was rewarded with the rhythmic movement of his unborn child. A smile suffused his face. Then, as always, a twinge of fear for Caroline and the babies modified his happiness. He knew the next six weeks would be a continuation of the past weeks, a nerve-racking combination of terror and exhilaration, like walking a tightrope across the Grand Canyon.

Caroline leaned over to kiss him. "Obviously he has his father's appetite," she said. "Let's hope he's not such big a worrier."

AFTER LEAVING Caroline and Mike, Kevin headed for the front entrance of the hospital to get a taxi, anxious to be alone with his thoughts. The minute he stepped from the elevator, he saw Lisa standing in the lobby talking to Cory and another woman. He tried to make it to the front door without being seen but was stopped when Cory called out a greeting. Kevin glanced up in time to see the expression on Cory's face when he realized what he had done. Quickly he looked from Lisa to Kevin and back again. Unable to gracefully avoid going over to talk to them, Kevin joined the threesome.

"Kevin, I don't think you've met my wife, Ann."

Kevin took her hand. "I'm glad to meet you, Ann. I've been hearing wonderful things about you for years from Mike and Caroline."

"And I've heard a lot of nice things about you, too." She smiled. "From several sources. How is the investigation going?"

She was the first person to pointedly ask him about the work he was doing at the space center. "Slowly. I won't have any real idea of what I've got though until I'm home and have a chance to sort through everything." It was an evasive answer, but he wasn't prepared to give anything more concrete.

"Cory says you've been doing quite a job. How much longer do you think it will take?"

"I'll probably be here a few more days..."

Lisa tried to avoid looking at Kevin while he talked. Frantically she sought a plausible reason to leave. Being near him was torture. Although she fought it, she found herself responding to him on a physical level that was almost impossible to control. She was afraid that if she stood there much longer she would reach out and touch him. The ache to be in his arms, the need to have him respond to her were tearing her apart. "Excuse me," she blurted out. "I have to go...there's someone waiting for me."

"I have to leave, too," Kevin said, desperate to get away, needing to be alone to think about what was happening to him. Before coming to Houston he had convinced himself he could see Lisa, and still maintain the distance necessary for both of them. Even knowing how important it was that their relationship remain above suspicion didn't help. His feelings went too deep to respond to rational thought.

While he waited in front of the hospital for a cab, Lisa drove by in her Mustang. She was almost to the end of the driveway when she stopped and backed up to where he stood. Rolling her window down, she looked up at him. "It seems impossible for me to forget I know you. Can I give you a ride somewhere?"

"I'm staying at Mike and Caroline's house."

"Get in. I'll take you there."

"Are you sure you want to do this?"

Lisa hesitated. She thought she detected a note of warning in his voice. "All I'm offering you is a ride, Senator Anderson. Nothing more."

"Then it would be better for both of us if I took a cab."

The look he gave her left no doubt that he meant every word. Before she capitulated to the inner voice that demanded she respond to him, she forcefully looked away and said, "Suit yourself." Without a backward glance she drove away from him.

TWO DAYS LATER she was in the administration building at the center looking for Mike when she ran into Kevin again. He was walking down the hallway toward her, alone. Her heart started to beat heavily in her chest, her mouth went dry and she felt as if the floor had disappeared from under her. Taking a deep breath, she continued toward him, determined not to give in to her urge to flee. "Still here, I see," she said, forcing a lightness into her voice.

"Today's my last day."

"And then it's back to Washington?" Thank heaven for small talk.

"California."

She caught herself before she asked him why he was going to California. It was none of her business. "I'm sure you'll enjoy your trip out there. California's a beautiful state."

"I'd like to see you before I leave."

"Why?" She was quickly losing her battle to remain aloof from him.

"There are some things I would like to discuss with you." His voice was low and intimately beckoning.

"Kevin, I've been thinking about our relationship a lot since we ran into each other the other day at the hospital. I realize we can't go on cringing every time we see each other. Not only is it awkward for us, it's hard on anyone who happens to be near us at the time." She stopped to take a breath and to slow her rapid-fire delivery. "Since we're bound to run into each other from time to time now that the Websters live in Houston, I feel we should try to overcome this awkwardness. I'm willing to do whatever it takes to put us on neutral ground." What she didn't tell him was how anxious she was to stop hurting, or how keenly she still felt his loss. Knowing him had left her lonely, whereas before she had simply been alone.

"Do you honestly feel it's possible for us to be neutral in our feelings toward each other, Lisa?"

His voice held a tenderness, a poignancy that stripped away her defenses. "It's either that or nothing. Do you really want to force me to leave every time you're around because I can't stand to be in the same room with you?"

"I won't accept that you feel that way. What we had was too special to let it sink into neutrality. I waited a long time to find you. Do you think I'm going to let go so easily? Passions that burned as brightly as ours did deserve better."

"You have no choice, Kevin. Didn't you learn anything from our little fiasco in Kansas?" Her words held a plea for him to understand how hard it was on her to have to go over their argument yet again.

He stared at her for long seconds before taking her arm and leading her into an empty conference room. Closing the door behind them, he jammed his hands into his pockets. "I'll tell you what I learned from our time together in Kansas. I learned what it's like to wake up in the morning with you by my side and what pleasure it gives me to watch you as you slowly wake up and turn to me with love in your eyes. I learned what it is to laugh and to smile and to feel good inside doing something as simple as rolling a ball of snow around the ground."

Lisa leaned her back against the door, wishing she could pass through the wood and escape, knowing his words would haunt her for days and months to come.

"Do you know that the snowman we built stayed outside my front door the entire time I was home, reminding me of the morning we spent together every single day I was there. Snows came and softened the shape and buried the scarf and hid the smile, but the form remained...and so did the memories."

She covered her ears with her hands. "Stop it, Kevin. You're only making things worse."

He caught her hands and held them by her sides. "Worse?" He laughed humorlessly. "Hardly, my dear Lisa. *Worse* is taking a bath and remembering having you there with me, how your skin felt as I passed over it with soapy hands, how your breasts filled my hands, how—''

She tried to pull away from him but he held her. ''How your lips felt,'' he said softly, his words hardly more than a whisper against her cheek.

With a tiny moan of surrender Lisa lifted her mouth to meet his. Her arms went around his neck and their kiss deepened, expressing a hunger logic couldn't destroy. She was caught in a maelstrom of emotion, of wanting, craving, but it was a journey down a dead-end road. Her hands left his neck and pushed against his chest. ''Congratulations, Kevin,'' she said, unable to hide the anguish that gripped her. ''You proved you can still arouse me. If that was your objective, you've won. If you thought that by arousing me you could convince me that none of the other matters, you've lost.'' She didn't realize there were tears running down her cheeks until he reached up to wipe them away.

''What would you say if I could find a way for us to resolve our differences?''

She fought the tears until she couldn't anymore. She was exhausted with a battle that had raged inside of her since she had seen him at the hospital two days ago. She felt as if she was fighting for her own existence in a confrontation her heart wanted her to lose. With a sob she said, ''Why can't you understand, there is no way.''

Kevin gently pulled her into his arms. ''I promise you I'll find a way, Lisa.'' He wasn't sure how he would fulfill his promise, he only knew that it was the most important he had ever made. Tenderly he held her face cupped between his hands. ''And I'll also promise you that until I can come to you with a solution, I'll leave you alone.'' He released her and opened the door for her to leave him. Unable to watch her as she walked down the hallway, he remained in the room until he was sure that she was gone.

KEVIN POSTPONED HIS TRIP to California when he learned that a bill he had cosponsored was to come up for a vote sooner than he had anticipated. He returned to Washington and the never-ending paperwork. His new position put a welcome drain on his time and energy as he continued to gather material and sift through reams of reports on NASA's far-flung operation. He was pleasantly surprised at the cooperation and response he received to his inquiries. Because of his work load the days passed relatively easily. The nights, however, often seemed interminable.

In late February his mother called to tell him that his father had fallen from the truck while feeding cattle and had broken his leg. Kevin took the next plane to Kansas.

"How's he doing?" Kevin asked, giving his mother a quick hug as she greeted him at the airport. Dark circles had appeared under her normally sparkling eyes.

"Dr. Winchester insisted he stay at the clinic hospital," she said, her voice steeped in exhaustion. "He says he wants to keep a close eye on your dad just in case pneumonia starts to set in. I told him Harold had had a bout a few years back, and he didn't seem to like hearing that."

Since Kevin had only brought a carryon with him, they went directly to the car. "And what did dad have to say about staying at the hospital?"

"He didn't complain too much. The doctor gave him some pretty strong medicine for the pain, so all he wants to do is sleep."

"How bad was the break?"

"Clean through," she said softly.

"How did it happen?"

"He told me he was in the back of the truck and got his leg caught under a bale of alfalfa. When he tried to get free, he lost his balance and fell over the side. It was a good thing he landed on one of the bales he'd already unloaded. He could have frozen before we found him."

"Where was Marvin?" Marvin Turner was the year-round employee who lived on the ranch.

"He'd gone into town to pick up some parts."

"How long was dad out there?"

"Close to four hours. He'd just begun feeding, hadn't even broken the ice off the water yet."

Kevin flinched. The pneumonia his father had had six years ago had left some scarring and a predisposition to contracting it again. Although he was concerned about his father's broken leg, the possibility of pneumonia frightened him much more. He drove to the hospital, located on the far side of Crossroads, faster than he normally would have traveled on icy roads.

As they entered Harold Anderson's room, Kevin immediately knew his worst fears had been realized. His father had the flushed look of fever, and his sleep seemed unusually restless. He walked over to the bed and lightly touched his hand to his father's forehead. It felt hot.

His mother came up beside him. "I guess it's a good thing Dr. Winchester insisted he stay," she said, acceptance in her voice. She shrugged out of her coat and laid it over the back of the chair. Her hand stole into her husband's as she settled down beside him in a chair. Without raising her intent gaze from Harold's face she spoke softly to Kevin. "Why don't you go on to the house and see if Marvin needs any help. We'll have to see about hiring someone extra for a while, so I guess you could be thinking about that, too, if you've a mind.''

"Do you have anyone in particular you want me to contact?"

She thought a minute. "I think the Taylor boy went back to school this last fall..."

When she didn't continue, he realized she was no longer concentrating on hired help but on the man beside her. "I'll do some scouting around to see what I can find out."

She nodded absently, lost in a world of her own.

Kevin leaned over to press a kiss on the top of her head. "I'll be back in a couple of hours. Call me if there's any change."

On his way through town Kevin stopped at Dr. Winchester's office. A nurse immediately took him into a large room filled with functional furniture where Carl Winchester sat behind a desk, studying a medical journal.

Tall and lean and only two years past his residency, Carl Winchester was the youngest physician most of the people in Crossroads had ever seen. To many of them, this dark-haired intense stranger in their midst was still in the process of proving himself after a year and a half in the community.

He stood and came around his desk to greet his visitor. "Kevin...I'm glad you stopped by."

"Is he as bad as he looks, Carl?" Kevin asked, skipping the usual social rituals.

Carl leaned against his desk and folded his arms across his chest. "I was with your father about an hour ago when the first signs of pneumonia started to set in. I've put him on a new antibiotic that's been highly successful in older patients. I'm hoping it will work as well with him."

"It took him a long time to shake his last bout."

"I've been going over his file and the treatment he received then, and considering the circumstances, he responded quite well. From what I can tell, your father didn't go in to see Dr. Evans until he was a pretty sick man."

"And then only after my mother threatened to leave him."

"I don't want you to get the idea that just because we've gotten in on this in the beginning that it won't be as hard to beat as it was six years ago. Your dad has a badly broken leg, he's suffering from exposure and his lungs are scarred. He's well on his way to a classic case of double pneumonia. Now on the plus side, he's in remarkable shape for a man his age, and I get the distinct impression that he believes there's a lot of living he has yet to do."

Kevin smiled. "I take it he gave you a hard time about putting him in the hospital?"

Carl chuckled. "Let's just say he wasn't too keen on the idea."

Kevin thanked him, said he would keep in touch and left instructions that told where and how to reach him should an emergency arise.

The following week became a blur as he divided his time between the ranch and the hospital. He had made phone calls to an ever-widening circle of neighbors and still hadn't been able to find anyone he felt capable of taking over the running of the ranch when it came time for him to return to Washington. Twice during the week his father had reached a critical stage but had rallied.

Rose spent her days sitting by Harold's side, quietly talking to him, telling him about the trips they would take when he was well, describing in detail the places they would see, reading to him from *National Geographic* about exotic locals and the earth's oddities they would one day wonder over together.

Midway into the second week, on a crisp, clear morning, Kevin was driving through town on his way to the ranch after dropping his mother off at the hospital when he spotted a familiar face among the schoolchildren waiting at a bus stop. He smiled and waved at Jennifer Kennedy and drove on, lost in the memories of the last time he had seen the soft-spoken girl with her mother at the airport. He wondered if she was pleased with the photograph Lisa had sent, never doubting Lisa had remembered.

Earlier that morning he had read in the paper that she was one of ten people chosen to be the first crew for the space station when it was completed the following year. Knowing how much the assignment meant to her had made it even more difficult for him to resist calling to congratulate her.

His thoughts drifted back to Jennifer and the airport and how happy he and Lisa had been on that special afternoon. Fleetingly an image of Marge, Jennifer's mother, came to him, and something about the memory struck a cord. He tried to capture the elusive thought that filtered through his mind. Another mile passed and still he couldn't seize the thin thread.

And then everything fell into place. Of course! He struck his hand on the steering wheel. How could he have been so blind? The perfect person to run his father's ranch was Jennifer's father, Joe Kennedy. Hadn't

Marge said they were still trying to put money aside to buy another place of their own?

But how could he ask Joe to give up his job at the station for what was temporary work at best? He was a family man with long-term responsibilities. Even if Kevin was to promise him a year's employment at a better wage than he could ever make at the garage, what would he do at the end of that year?

Kevin mulled the problem over for the rest of the day. When he picked up Rose later that evening he casually mentioned Joe's name on the way home, wondering aloud if he might not be a good choice for someone to help out around the ranch.

She considered Kevin's suggestion. "Joe's a good man," she said, "honest as they come and hardworking as any I've ever known. It's a real shame he can't be doing what he loves best. People like him and your dad have topsoil and cowhide running through their veins, nothing they do will ever get it out." She glanced over at her son, studying him in the light of an oncoming car. "There were times I used to think you were made out of the same kind of stuff, but then you went off to Washington and did so well there I decided I must be wrong."

Kevin reached over to take her hand, which lay on the seat between them. "Maybe my blood just runs a little thinner." He flicked on the turn signal to leave the main road. "Do you suppose dad feels the same way about Joe that you do?"

"As far as I know." She continued to stare at him. "What's this all leading up to, Kevin?"

"I'm not sure yet. I need a day or two to work it out, then I'll let you in on what's been going through my head."

But it didn't take a day or two for him to reach a decision; it took one night. The next morning he knew exactly what he was going to do about Joe Kennedy and his parents' problem of needing someone to help out around the ranch. By the time he was heading for town, he was supremely confident he had made the right decision. He would offer to sell Joe his house and four sections of land, stretching the interest-free payments over twenty years on the condition Joe help manage Kevin's parents' place for the length of the contract. Or, if it turned out that his parents wanted to sell out themselves someday, for as long as they owned their land.

He was surprised at how easily he accepted the idea of selling land he had fought so hard to keep ten years earlier. He suspected his parents would find his decision to sell hard to accept at first, but he was confident that in time he would be able to convince them it was something he really wanted to do.

Later that day, after talking to Joe and returning an hour later for his decision, which was to accept the offer, Kevin felt a peculiar lightness, as if a massive burden had been lifted from his shoulders. Until that precise moment he hadn't realized how strongly his land and house had tied him to his past. He had expected a sense of loss, but there was only the feeling of freedom.

TWO DAYS LATER Harold was far enough along the road to recovery that Kevin felt he could tell him about the offer he had made to Joe Kennedy.

Harold listened carefully to his son's prepared speech as he listed the benefits of having Joe help out on the ranch, how having Joe there would give them time to travel and see all the places they had talked about seeing and how wrong it was for him to hang on to a piece of land he wasn't using. He also told Harold that the deal would not go through if either he or his mother had any objections to having Joe around.

It took every ounce of control Kevin possessed not to try to fill in the silence that followed with yet more arguments in favor of his decision. Finally, when the tension became almost unbearable, Harold said, "I think this is probably the smartest thing you've done in the past ten years."

Kevin let out a pent-up sigh. "I think you may be right, dad," he said softly.

CHAPTER FIFTEEN

LISA WAS TAKING A SHORTCUT across the lawn, going from the administration building to the cafeteria, when she heard someone calling her name. She looked around and spotted Cory running toward her, excitedly waving his arms.

"Mike just left for the hospital," he said, stopping a moment to catch his breath. "Caroline's gone into labor."

"Is she all right? Is *he* all right? Shouldn't someone have driven him there?" Mike had been a walking zombie the past two weeks, lost somewhere between wondering when the quints would be born and being thankful for the time Caroline was able to carry them.

"Ann took him. He was so excited he was incapable of handling a car by himself. I told him I would look for you and that we would follow them to the hospital as soon as possible."

Lisa let out a spontaneous whoop of joy and threw her arms around Cory. "I can't believe after all the waiting, they're really going to be here—today—right now." She grabbed his hand. "What are we doing standing here? Let's get going."

Cory laughed. "It might be prudent to check out first, don't you think?"

"Details," she grumbled, pulling him along behind her.

By the time they arrived at the hospital, Caroline had already given birth to the first baby, a girl. One more girl followed and then three boys. A well-rehearsed medical crew of thirty-five attended the births—along with one anxious father.

An hour later a deliriously happy Mike came downstairs to tell them about Caroline and the babies. "She's doing fine," he beamed, love shining from his eyes and touching everyone in the room. "The newest members of our family weighed in between three pounds, six ounces and two pounds, fifteen ounces. The pediatricians tell me that they are all doing fine and if no problems arise we should be able to take them home with us in about a month."

The waiting room was filled to overflowing with friends, and everyone burst into applause.

Mike basked in their well-wishes. "Caroline sends her love and said to tell all of you that any and all offers to baby-sit will be appreciated and immediately accepted."

Lisa blinked back tears of joy. Her thoughts returned to the discussion she and Caroline had had about having children, and she knew now that Caroline had been right. She had told her that it wasn't the fear of growing older that had guided her decision to have children, it was the love she shared with Mike. This moment represented far more than the renewal of life; it was something special between two people who deeply loved each other. It was a reaffirmation of their commitment to spend their lives together.

They would make wonderful parents, understanding, caring, loving. Lisa ached for what they had. Lately her life had seemed without substance. Previously she had believed she would be half a person without her career, but now she realized she was only half a person with it. Not even the assignment to the space station had made a difference in the way she felt. She looked around the room at the faces of her friends. For the most part they had found the magic combination. They had managed to have both careers and marriages without compromising either. Why was it so impossible for her to do the same?

Two days later when she arrived at the hospital to visit Caroline, Lisa found her friend sitting up in bed, talking on the phone. As soon as she saw Lisa standing by the door, Caroline smiled and waved for her to enter. Looking around the room, Lisa threw her arms up in the air in a gesture that said, "I don't believe this." If the room had looked like a wholesale florist before, it now looked like a jungle. She even had to move a potted plant to find a place to sit.

Caroline held up one finger and rolled her eyes in frustration, signaling to Lisa she would be off the phone soon. "I know it's the opportunity of a lifetime, Ernie but the timing is atrocious. I can't possibly take an assignment now. A month from now is even worse. The babies will be ready to come home from the hospital by then, and I'm not about to welcome them by leaving them."

Lisa crossed her legs and caught her knee between her clasped hands. She looked around the room at the profusion of flowers. The birth of the Webster quints had received national television coverage when Caroline's former coanchor announced the event on the evening news. She wondered how many of the flowers had been sent by fans and leaned over to read the card on an arrangement sitting on the bedside stand. The arrangement held two white and five yellow roses. "When the two of you do something, you certainly do it up right.

All my love, Kevin." Her heart gave a funny little lurch. Of all the arrangements in the room, she would pick the one from Kevin.

She smelled the subtle fragrance of the newly opening buds. A wistful smile tugged at her mouth. Kevin was the only other person she had ever known whose favorite color was yellow. She thought about the way he had looked when he saw her in the sweater she had purchased in New York. She turned from the flowers and started across the room.

"I know," Caroline said, sighing. There was a long pause while she listened. "You wouldn't!" Again there was a pause. "He would do a terrible job." Impatience edged each word. "You couldn't wait six more months? The film crew could be working on the background now and I could fill in the text later." She reached up to rub the side of her neck. "I'll get back to you," she said wearily. "No, that does not mean yes." She said goodbye, firmly replaced the receiver in its cradle and let out a heavy sigh. She looked at Lisa. "Finally they come up with an assignment I've been bugging them to do for two years just when it's impossible for me to take it on."

"I assume that was your old boss in the Washington bureau?"

"Someone higher up yet. He claims the proposal just reached his desk. He's particularly enthusiastic about doing a documentary on the plight of the illegal aliens in Texas because that's how his father came to this country. He married, had children and started his own business before he was caught and deported. After he returned to Mexico he disappeared and was never heard from again."

"And he expects you to leave your hospital bed to start shooting?"

"Not quite, but it's almost as bad. He's willing to give me a month to recuperate with the promise I would only have to work three and a half days a week."

"What are you going to do?"

"I can't see that I have any real choice. I'll stay home with the babies."

"Is the assignment important to you?"

Caroline absently touched her stomach as if seeking something lost. When she answered, her voice took on a solemn enthusiasm. "While I was on another assignment I met a priest in Washington who headed an organization similar to the underground railroad that operated in this country to help free slaves before the civil war. Only today the people he was helping would be classified as illegal aliens. It isn't the fact that their story hasn't already been told by others that I wanted the assignment. I honestly felt I could bring a poignancy to the telling that had been lacking in the research I did."

"Isn't there any way you could get him to hold off for a while so you could do the story?"

"He says because of everything that's happening right now, if they were to wait, the piece would lose its immediacy. It doesn't matter in the least that I'd suggested it a long time ago and I felt it was my story."

An orderly entered the room. "The nurse said you wanted me to take some more of these flowers to the convalescent wing."

Caroline smiled. "Please...it's getting difficult for anyone to move around in here. Just be sure the cards are removed first so that I can thank people." She looked at Lisa. "People's ingenuity never ceases to amaze me. I was listening to the news broadcast when it was announced that the quints had arrived. Not one word was mentioned about the hospital or even the city—only that we had increased the population of Texas by five.'' She swung her arm to indicate the profusion of flowers. ''And yet look at this room. And I've been told there are more yet down in the lobby.''

''It must make you feel good to be remembered. It seems you once told me that the public had a very short memory where newscasters were concerned.''

She smiled. ''I don't want you to get the impression I'm complaining...''

The orderly brought in a cart and began loading vases. He worked his way toward them and started to reach for the roses beside Lisa. ''No, leave those,'' Caroline said, ''and all of these on this side of the room.'' She gave Lisa a sheepish grin. ''I can't part with the ones Mike or any of our close friends have sent.''

For as long as Lisa had known her, Caroline could not mention Mike's name without her eyes lighting up. ''How long have you two been married?''

''It seems like yesterday,'' she said, ''but it's been almost six years now.''

''How have you...''

''Kept the specialness?''

''I guess that's what I'm asking.''

''I'm not sure what formula we've used. All I know is that I love Mike as intensely now as I ever have. I think it may have something to do with being absolutely right for each other, but I can't shortchange the fact that we work very hard to keep what we have.''

''According to Ann, in the beginning you weren't so sure about being right for each other.''

Caroline studied her friend. ''Lisa,'' she said, ''are we talking about me and Mike, or you and Kevin?''

Lisa got up and walked over to the window. She stared down at the traffic on the street below. "I've been doing a lot of thinking lately about what happened between Kevin and me."

"And?" Caroline gently prodded.

"And I've come to the conclusion that like you and Mike, we were two of those people who were absolutely right for each other, but we happened to come together at the wrong time in our lives. Our destiny has been controlled by forces we couldn't overcome." Her faint laugh had a cheerless ring. "I know that sounds rather pretentious but it's true. I understand now—I really always did understand—that Kevin's dedication and belief in what he's doing is every bit as demanding as mine. I could never ask him to give it up, any more than he could ask me."

"And there's no compromising for you two?"

"That's the worst part of all this. If it just involved the two of us, Kevin and I could compromise, but it's our jobs that won't let us. There's no way he can become involved with me again without jeopardizing his position on the committee."

Caroline stared at Lisa, her brow furrowed in puzzlement. "Conflict of interest," she breathed at last, understanding dawning.

When Lisa turned from the window her eyes were moist with unshed tears. "So you see, even though I've finally admitted to myself that Kevin is probably the only man I will ever love completely, I can't go to him without destroying him."

"Maybe after everything settles down..." She didn't sound very convincing.

Lisa touched the side of her finger to her lower eyelid to catch a tear. She forced a smile. "The *Orion* certainly hasn't been the disaster everyone anticipated, has it?" She leaned against the windowsill. "Well, not *everyone*," she admitted. "As I recall, I was the only one who was running around like Chicken Little saying 'the sky is falling, the sky is falling.'"

"Lisa, don't ever apologize for your passionate spirit. In a world where apathy is becoming the dress code of the middle class, you're like a breath of pure mountain air." Her voice grew soft. "I'm sure your intensity is one of the reasons Kevin fell in love with you in the first place."

"I only wish—" Just then Mike came in, interrupting her.

"You're just the person I want to see," he said to Caroline as he came across the room. "I've figured out that our number-two son, James Arnold, was the one with the hiccups. You ought to see him take his food." He bent over to give her a lusty kiss. He nuzzled the softness of her neck and the creamy flesh above her breasts.

"Poor timing, Webster," she said in a stage whisper. "We have company."

He wasn't the least chagrined when he looked up and spotted Lisa. "Ahh, another person I wanted to see." He threw his arms wide to give her a hug. Instead of immediately releasing her, he put his arm around Lisa's shoulders and turned to face Caroline. "Have you asked her yet?"

Caroline grimaced. "Not yet. I was thinking tonight might be a better time."

Lisa's curiosity was instantly piqued. "Asked me what?"

Mike was confused by the message being sent to him by Caroline. "How you felt about being a god-mother," he answered slowly.

Lisa looked from Mike to Caroline. "Is he serious?" she said, her words barely spoken above a whisper as she struggled with yet a new emotion.

Caroline nodded. "But there's something you have to know before you make your final decision, Lisa." When Mike looked as if he was going to help her, she sent him an I'll-handle-this look. "Because it's too much to expect two people to be godparents to five children, we plan to ask Ann and Cory if they would take the three boys and—"

"You and Kevin to take the girls," Mike finished, unable to contain his enthusiasm.

Caroline groaned.

"There wasn't a gentle way to say it, Lisa," Mike said, responding to the stunned look she gave him. "Caroline and I spent the better part of last night discussing this. At one point we even decided not to ask either of you in order to avoid—"

"But we changed our minds," Caroline interjected. "Primarily because we believe that should something ever happen to Mike and me, you and Kevin would love and care for our daughters as if they were your own. The fact that you might do so as single parents doesn't alter how we feel."

"Have you talked to Kevin about this yet?"

Mike answered. "We called him last night."

"And what did he say?"

"You mean besides yes?" Mike could feel the tension in Lisa. It surrounded her like an invisible aura. If just the mention of Kevin's name could do this to her, what must she go through on long lonely nights. Although he and Caroline had not decided to ask Lisa and Kevin to be godparents in order to bring them together, they had discussed the possibility.

Lisa was tired of trying to pretend news of Kevin didn't matter to her. "Did he say anything about me?"

"He asked if you had agreed to the arrangement and sounded disappointed when I told him we hadn't asked you yet."

"Is this kind of thing allowed—two unmarried people..."

"The minister assured us the important thing was the kind of person we chose, not their marital status," Caroline said. "And we both feel you and Kevin are the people we want to stand up for our daughters."

Lisa gave them both a heartfelt smile. "How could I say no?" she said, her voice a choked whisper. Her deep pleasure over the honor they had bestowed on her was tempered only by her fear of seeing Kevin again. With each passing week her defenses crumbled a little more; slowly, brick by brick, her fortress was being dismantled.

A WEEK LATER Kevin was in his office at the Senate building studying a computer printout detailing NASA's budget escalation over the preceding thirty years when his secretary, Nancy, rapped on the door.

"You asked me to remind you before I left this evening that you wanted to go shopping for your godchildren."

"Thanks, Nancy. I'll be through here shortly."

"Uh-huh," she said skeptically. She started to leave then came back. "One more thing, senator..."

"Yes?" He looked up at her over the rims of his glasses.

"I think your parents are real sweethearts."

He laughed. "I'll tell them you like their gift." Earlier that day his father had called to tell him how well Joe Kennedy was doing on the ranch and how much he enjoyed his company. Almost as an afterthought he had added the news that he and Rose had finally settled on a gift for the quints. The first five steers born that spring were to belong to the babies. Profits from their eventual sale would go into the quints' savings accounts to be used for their college educations.

She raised her hand and fluttered her fingers in a wave. "Don't work too late. Remember, the stores are only open until nine tonight."

"I won't," he said absently, already back to work shuffling through papers on his desk, looking for a companion report to the one he had been studying earlier.

"Uh-huh," she humphed, closing the door.

Two hours later Kevin leaned back in his chair, removed his glasses and wearily rubbed the bridge of his nose. Lately the work he had been doing for the committee no longer seemed the grind it had first been. At quiet times like these, a sense of excitement frequently settled in that made the hours disappear as if they had been spent in a pleasant dream. His other committee work had suffered proportionately, but he couldn't bring himself to slow down. There was still a long road ahead of him before he would be through with the NASA budget, and now that he had reached a decision about his future, his time on that road was limited. Never before had he assigned so much of his routine work to aides. But he had become a man with a purpose, and the purpose had become all-consuming. Abruptly the harsh sound of his phone interrupted his musings. It was Mike.

"I was afraid I'd miss you," he said.

"I'll be here for at least another hour or so tonight." He tossed his glasses onto the paper-strewed desk. The shopping would have to wait for another day. "Now that you've had some time to think about it, how's it feel to be the father of five?"

"I'm still not sure the fact that they're really here has settled in yet. I keep standing outside the hospital nursery getting fingerprints all over the glass, repeatedly telling myself that those five little people inside are mine and Caroline's, but it doesn't seem to register."

"Have they let you hold them yet?"

"Yeah..." he said softly. "What an incredible sensation."

"I remember," Kevin replied as softly. The first time he had held Christine was moments after her birth. All pink and plump, she had nestled in his arms and stared up at him, her eyes blinking against the brightness but never leaving his face. Before her birth he had read books that claimed infants could not see clearly, and he knew it was useless to try to dispute the supposed authority of the authors, but to that day he remained convinced his daughter had looked at him with sharply focused eyes. For the few moments he had held her, they had communicated with their eyes and in that time formed a close bonding. "How is Caroline doing?" he asked. "I haven't talked to her since yesterday morning."

"Fantastic. So well, in fact, the doctors are letting me take her home tomorrow."

"I'll bet she's excited. How long has it been since you two have been alone together?"

"Almost three months."

Kevin heard someone talking to Mike in the background and realized he, too, was still at work. When he had talked to Caroline the previous morning she had expressed her concern about the long hours Mike had been keeping at work as well as at the hospital.

"Sorry about the interruption, Kevin. I'd better get to why I called before I have to leave for the press conference. I wanted to let you know that I finally managed to round up that material you asked me for last week. I sent it out by courier this afternoon, so it should be to you by Monday morning."

"Your timing is perfect. I'm at the point where I couldn't go any further without it."

"Let me know if there's anything more you need on the 1978 budget. The information didn't seem to be as thorough as the others."

"I'll be sure to look at it before I do the rest of them." He paused. With Mike's hectic schedule he was reluctant to keep him on the phone any longer than necessary, but he couldn't hang up without asking. "I assume you've talked to Lisa?" His heart felt as if it was in his throat.

"Yes...I'm sorry I didn't say something earlier, but I knew you'd been in touch with Caroline since we asked Lisa and I just assumed she had told you about it."

"She didn't really have a chance. We were cut short when the doctor came in to see her."

"We talked to Lisa the day after we called you. She's agreed to be Margaret and Sandra's godmother."

Kevin heaved a silent sigh of relief. "I'm glad." He had been afraid the situation would be so awkward for Lisa that she would feel it necessary to refuse. "I've had

Nancy clear my schedule for the Friday before the weekend that I'm coming down so if there's anything I can do for you, let me know."

"By then the three nannies we hired will have moved into the house and will be handling most of the extra work. I'm really impressed with the efficiency they've shown so far—the English sure have the right idea about child care. I don't know what we'd do if we couldn't afford help." He chuckled. "I don't even want to consider what it would be like."

"How many people are you expecting at the christening?"

"We decided to keep the ceremony at the church small. Only the principals and grandparents." He paused. "Now the party afterward is something else again. The Webster quints' debut to the world is going to be handled in high style even if their presentation only lasts a short time before they're wisked away to their rooms."

"I'm looking forward to being there."

"Kevin..."

"Yes?"

"You don't have to worry about Lisa anymore. She's doing fine."

Kevin leaned forward in his chair. What in the hell had Mike meant by that? "What do you mean, she's doing fine? I wasn't aware there was anything wrong with her."

"I just meant that she's finally recovering from your breakup. It took awhile, but I think she's solidly back on her feet now."

"I'm...glad to hear it," he said slowly, trying to cope with the panic that gripped him. He started to say something more but Mike interrupted him.

"I hate to do this to you, but I have to hang up or I'll have a room full of hostile reporters when I get to the press conference."

Kevin fought a desperate urge to try to keep him on the phone. He needed to know exactly what Mike had meant about Lisa. Icy fingers of dread replaced the panic. Was it possible he had waited too long, been too confident that their love would endure the months of separation?

For a long time after he hung up the phone he stared out the window, lost in a world where he imagined himself without Lisa. The idea left him physically ill. God, he couldn't lose her...not now.

CHAPTER SIXTEEN

MIKE MET KEVIN at the airport on a Friday evening three weeks later. They had talked several times after their conversation about Lisa's "recovery" but never again about Lisa. Kevin had purposely avoided bringing up her name, preferring to believe they still had a chance to get back together. To that end he had doubled his already concentrated efforts on the upcoming NASA budget hearing.

"Your dad called this week," Mike said, maneuvering through the beginning of Houston's rush-hour traffic on his way through town. "He said his doctor advised against making the trip down for the party, so he and Rose were reluctantly staying home." He chuckled. "Of all the gifts the quints have received, none has come close to theirs for originality...or generosity."

"I'm surprised dad listened to his doctor's advice. I don't think I've ever seen two people who enjoyed kids more than they do. They were both in seventh heaven when Christine was born."

"I suspect your mom wielded a heavy hand in the decision. I understand she told your father he'd return to an empty house if he came down here against the doctor's advice."

Kevin smiled. "She's been using that threat for as long as I can remember. It's her ace in the hole whenever she can't get him to do something she thinks is for his own good." He looked out the window, blindly staring at the cars rushing by. From the minute he had boarded the plane in Washington, he had had trouble catching his breath. The closer he got to Houston, the worse his condition became. He tried to shake his growing dread, and forcing himself to concentrate on something else, he asked, "What are you doing with everyone who's coming from out of town?" The questions was so off-the-wall, his voice so artificially cheerful, he knew he had given himself away.

Mike glanced over at him. He had known Kevin for five and a half years. During that time they had become close friends, and never once had he seen him this nervous. He smiled a private satisfied smile and looked forward again. His ploy was working. Ignoring the obvious, he answered as if there was nothing unusual about the question. "We arranged for several rooms at a hotel not too far from the house. There were a lot of friends here in Houston who offered their spare rooms, but we thought logistically it would work out better all the way around if we had everyone stay at the same hotel."

"Is there going to be a rehearsal tonight?" He was desperate to see Lisa again.

"No—a rehearsal for a christening really isn't necessary. They aren't as complicated as weddings. Caroline and I are taking the godparents out to dinner this evening, however, so there is something planned for you to do tonight if that's what you're asking." Again he glanced over at Kevin, careful to keep his face a mask of innocence. "I hope that doesn't interfere with anything else you had in mind."

"No..."

"Good," he said, another smile curving his mouth. "Caroline's been looking forward to this night for weeks."

THE TWO HOURS Kevin spent at the hotel waiting for Mike to pick him up seemed interminable. It had taken him less than half an hour to shower, shave and dress for the evening. The remainder of the time he had spent pacing his room and then the lobby.

For the past three weeks Mike's "You don't have to worry about Lisa; she's doing fine" statement had echoed like an ominous warning, following him everywhere. His nights had been the worst. Whenever he couldn't sleep, he tried to convince himself he had not been wrong in the way he had handled everything. The road always led back to the same conclusion. He had had little choice in the matter. There had been no other way to handle what had happened between them, and until he could show her that he had found a way, they were at a stalemate.

The biggest frustration of all was that although he had continued to work on the budget recommendation for NASA morning, noon and night for the past three weeks, he still wasn't at the point he felt he had to be in order to approach Lisa with a resolution to their differences.

Kevin continued to pace the lobby as he waited for Mike and Caroline, lost somewhere between gut-wrenching worry and wild elation over the prospect of seeing Lisa again after almost four months.

At the sound of someone calling his name, he looked up and saw Caroline coming toward him. She waved and smiled and hurried her step, throwing her arms wide to accept his embrace as he came across the lobby to meet her. She hugged him, laughing and crying at the same time. When a tear threatened to spill from the corner of her eye, she pulled the hanky from his coat pocket and dabbed the moisture away. "Do you realize this is the first time in my life something momentous has happened and you weren't there?" she gently scolded.

He laughed, holding her close, delighted to see her. "I'm not sure Mike would agree with that, but I'm flattered you missed me."

"It was more than missing you, Kevin," she insisted. "You're the brother I never had—the only one who listened to me and understood what I went through when my parents divorced." Her voice softened. "And the shoulder I cried on when I went through my own divorce."

"Don't tell me my old tree-climbing buddy is going to get all sloppy and sentimental on me after all this time."

She playfully pinched him. "Not a chance. I'm just going through postpartum something or other. I'll be my crusty old self again in no time. I've been told these moments of unbridled schmaltz come with the new territory. All I have to do is hold one of those babies in my arms for one minute and I feel like nurturing everything in sight. Including my favorite cousin if he isn't careful."

"I can tell about the nurturing. The glow you've developed looks fantastic on you." The Caroline he had known all his life had subtly changed since he last saw her. It was more than the dramatic weight loss or the gentle rounding of features that had been sharp before. Something intangible had added a new dimension to her beauty.

She studied him for long seconds. "You're not teasing, are you?"

"No...I'm not." Out of the corner of his eye he saw Mike coming toward him.

"If we dont' get going, Lisa's likely to think we forgot her," Mike said, coming up to them.

"Just when the conversation was getting good." Caroline put one of her arms through Kevin's, the other through Mike's. Looking up at her husband, she said, "He was telling me how motherhood becomes me." She turned to Kevin and winked. "I want you to promise me you'll remember where we left off."

When they arrived at Lisa's apartment, Caroline asked Kevin to go in and get her while she and Mike waited in the car. Since he had anticipated her suggestion, he was prepared. Still, by the time he was at Lisa's front porch, his heart was beating so loudly he was sure she would be able to hear it the minute she opened the front door.

Lisa had been watching at the window for their arrival, anxious, nervous, excited about seeing Kevin, desperately wishing they could be alone together yet grateful for the Websters' company to ease the awkwardness of seeing Kevin again for the first time in four months. With supreme effort at self-control, she waited for Kevin to ring the doorbell. She took a deep breath and slowly opened the door. She began reciting her carefully prepared speech of welcome, but as soon as she saw him the rest of the words wouldn't come out. He looked the way she had so often dreamed he would, a half smile on his lips, his deep-blue eyes filled with openness and warmth, his light-brown hair casually brushing his forehead. He was wearing a charcoal-gray pin-striped suit that gave a new meaning to the word sexy.

She ached to ask him to come inside, to use the cocoon of her apartment to close out the world that had separated them and to forget all that had alienated them, if only for one night. But she couldn't. It wasn't the right time. Others were waiting for them.

Kevin had thought he had prepared himself for seeing Lisa. He had imagined the moment over and over again. But when she opened the door, nothing he had imagined could come close to the actual assault on his sensibilities. Now that she was standing in front of him he was stunned that he had been able to stay away from her as long as he had. An overwhelming need to touch her gripped him. To maintain his shaky control he backed away from her, and in a voice he hardly recognized as his own he said, "Are you ready?"

"Yes," she breathed. "I'll just get my coat and..." She started to walk away when she realized she had left him standing on the porch. "Would you like to come in?"

"Mike and Caroline are..."

"Of course. I'll be right back." She walked over to the chair where she had left her coat and purse. Her hands were trembling so badly she dropped first one and then the other.

Silently Kevin came up behind her. "Here," he said, "let me help you."

Lisa stood very still, afraid to turn around. She could feel his presence in her mind, in her heart, in the air she breathed. "Thank you," she answered, not knowing how to tell him no, reluctant to let him know how afraid she was to have him touch her even in the most formal way.

He held her coat while she slipped her arms into the sleeves. As she did so, her perfume assailed him, creating vivid memories of the time he had held her close, when they had... Hers was a fragrance that had haunted him, one he had never recognized on any other woman.

When her coat rested on her shoulders he automatically reached up to adjust the collar and free the tendrils of soft blond hair. His fingertips touched the back of her neck, and he felt her shudder and jerk away.

Lisa tried to cover the abruptness of her actions by bending to retreive her purse. If she lacked so much control at the beginning of the evening, what was she going to be like by the end? She had a knot in her stomach the size of a bowling ball. How was she ever going to eat dinner?

"I like the way you've decorated your apartment," Kevin said to distract himself from what had just happened between them. They would never be able to make it through an entire evening together if they continued this way.

"It's comfortable but kind of small whenever I have company." She grasped on to the impersonal dialogue as if it was a lifeline. "The Oriental pieces were an afterthought. I'm usually not so adventuresome or creative when it comes to decorating, but I saw a photograph in a magazine of a room that had chairs like these and I liked the way they looked so well I decided to steal the idea." She knew she was rambling but she didn't care.

She was almost to the door and feeling more confident that they would be able to pull the evening off after all when Kevin delivered a line that stole her breath away as forcefully as a physical blow to the midsection.

"I've missed you, Lisa."

His voice held such poignancy, such longing. She almost succumbed but was stopped by the sight of Mike getting out of the car. What they had to say to each other needed its own time. To start anything now when it would be impossible to finish could easily lead to misunderstandings—the very last thing she wanted to happen. "It think we'd better leave now, Kevin."

"You're right." What had ever possessed him to say something like that now? It was neither the time nor the place to try to straighten things out between them. With a studied coolness and a detachment he didn't come close to feeling, he accompanied her out to the car.

A SHORT TIME LATER they met Cory and Ann Peters in the bar at Bonne Cuisine. The restaurant Mike had chosen for their celebration was one of the finest in Houston. The food was superb and the ambience shamelessly romantic. The decor was in mauves and dusty rose, and the waiters wore brown tuxedos and pink carnation boutonnieres. Unless someone happened to be a favored customer of the restaurant or a friend of one of the owners, it could take three months or more to get a reservation. Mike happened to be a friend.

The underlying happiness that had precipitated their celebration and Caroline's anecdotes of Mike's first week of hands-on fatherhood soon dissipated the tension between Lisa and Kevin. Although they were seated next to each other at dinner, it proved easy for them to avoid intimate contact by joining in the lively discussions.

Midway through their meal, a small band began to play dance music. As couples moved to the dance floor,

Lisa thought of another time and place and how her life and her outlook had changed in little more than a year.

The coveted four-star rating given to Bonne Cuisine for both its food and atmosphere was wasted on Lisa as she picked at her meal, the house specialty, Chateaubriand with bordelaise sauce. When their plates had been cleared and Mike insisted everyone have dessert, it was all she could do to even taste the rich white-chocolate mousse with rum.

Noticing her discomfort, Kevin surreptitiously changed his half-eaten dessert with hers at the first opportunity. He had watched her throughout the meal as she took small bites and rearranged food on her plate to make it look as if she had eaten more. Although he knew he was undoubtedly the source of her distress, he hadn't figured out precisely why. On the one hand, she could feel awkward being with him because she had not yet truly put him from her life, but then again, she could be afraid that he would misinterpret any friendly overtures as encouragement for him to pursue her. He preferred to believe the former, but her actions at the apartment made him fear it might be the latter. If only he knew her better.

Mike had not missed the silent exchange between Kevin and Lisa but he was not heartened by it, either. He had been watching the two of them all evening for signs of a thaw, yet they were still no warmer to each other than a native New Yorker and an ardent Californian. He took Caroline's hand. "Come dance with me, my love. They're playing our song."

She blinked and shot him a puzzled frown. "Since when is the theme from 'Hill Street Blues' our song?"

"Every song is our song when I can dance with you and hold you in my arms."

Caroline blushed and gave her friends an embarrassed smile. "Can you believe that? He's been talking this way since I came home from the hospital."

Ann took Cory's hand. "Hospital nothing—Mike's been running off at the mouth that way since the day he met you." She stood and tugged on Cory's hand. "Come on, Romeo, you don't intend to let these whippersnappers show us old folks the way it's done, do you?"

Cory grinned. "Not a chance. Mike calls me daily for pointers."

When they were gone, Kevin turned to Lisa. "Would you like to dance?"

She did but doubted her legs would hold her. "No...I don't think so." For long seconds he stared intently at her, and she was grateful she had decided to wear her red silk dress. The vibrant color would help hide the blush she felt warming her cheeks. "Is something the matter, Kevin?" she finally asked, unable to withstand his scrutiny any longer. "Do I have something stuck in my teeth?"

"Talk to me, Lisa," he said, ignoring her attempt at humor, his voice pleading. "Tell me what it's been like for you since we last saw each other." He knew the timing was wrong but he desperately needed to know what Mike had meant.

She couldn't answer him. Not there; not then. "Another time, Kevin." She had to concentrate on every breath, reminding herself first to take in the air and then expel it. "I agree...we need to talk to each other. The way it is now isn't good for either of us."

Across the dance floor Mike maneuvered so that he could see what was happening at the table. "I think we'd better turn in our matchmaking licence," he said with a sigh. "It appears we've struck out. I thought for sure our little scheme to bring them together would work."

She tilted her head back to look up at him. "Oh ye of little faith. I'll wager those two are in each other's arms before the weekend is out."

"I don't know about—"

"Trust me. I can see it in their eyes. They just have to find some way to scale that stupid barrier they've spent the past six months constructing. Once they do, they'll be fine."

His eyes narrowed suspiciously as he looked at her. "Has Lisa said something to you?"

"You mean do I have inside information?" she asked, her expression innocent.

Abruptly his thoughts switched from Lisa and Kevin to the woman he held in his arms. He looked at her with such love it was almost a physical caress. "I feel sorry for anyone who misses out on what we have. Life is so short, the path so rocky. Without you to share my time here on earth with me, there would be no sunshine in my life."

"Me, too..." she whispered, touching her lips lightly to his.

When the dance was over they returned to the table. The dessert dishes were taken away and second cups of strong Colombian coffee poured. Caroline raised her cup in a toast. "Tomorrow afternoon at the party, Mike and I will have a special announcement to make to everyone," she said mysteriously, "but tonight I wanted to share something personal with my closest friends, something that wouldn't mean a thing to anyone else. As you all know, my mother and father were divorced when I was thirteen. It was one of those nasty affairs that demand people take sides whether they want to or not." Incongruously, she smiled. "Well...thanks to five little babies who were never involved in taking sides, my parents have called a truce to a war that has gone on for over twenty years."

Mike reached for her hand. As a child Caroline had been trapped in the middle of her parents' war and it had left deep scars. "Caroline has left out the best part. Not only have they stopped fighting, they're seriously talking about giving marriage another try."

Kevin leaned over and pressed a kiss to Caroline's cheek. "This should have happened a long time ago," he said, knowing without being told what her parents' reconciliation would mean to her.

She laughed. "If you recall, there was the slight problem of my father's other wife for fifteen of those years."

"This will certainly give the folks back home something to talk about this summer," Kevin said. "It could last into the fall if they actually did go through with the marriage." For twenty years, because of the feuding, people in Crossroads had been forced to decide which half of the Travers clan would be invited to any gathering. Now they could stop.

"Speaking of back home..." The dreamy look disappeared from Caroline's face and she flashed accusatory eyes at Kevin. "Why didn't you tell me you had sold your ranch?"

Kevin could hear Lisa's sharp intake of breath. "I guess I just hadn't gotten around to mentioning it," he replied.

"You make it sound like the sale was an every-day occurrence," Caroline remarked, obviously mystified by his attitude.

"It seemed like the right thing to do at the time." He should have realized Caroline would find out about the sale and would question him.

Noting Lisa's stunned reaction, Mike squeezed Caroline's hand, and she responded immediately.

"I was just surprised you hadn't mentioned it earlier," she said, her voice taking on a purposely calmer tone.

Kevin could have kicked himself for not saying something to Caroline about keeping the sale quiet until he had a chance to tell Lisa. "I'll fill you in on all the details before I leave on Sunday."

Not understanding what was happening, Ann inadvertently added to the tension. "Will selling your land cause problems about your Kansas residency when you run for office again this fall?"

"By law all that's required is that I have a place to hang my hat in Kansas," he hedged.

"Do you think it will make any difference to the voters that you don't—"

Mike could see that Ann was warming up to one of her favorite topics, politics. She was obviously unaware of Kevin's lack of enthusiasm for the subject. "How about postponing this discussion until later when we can all put our feet up on the coffee table and relax? I'm afraid if I don't get Caroline home to bed, tomorrow will be one big exhausted blur for her."

Caroline gave him a puzzled look but went along with Mike's excuse for ending the party. She smiled apologetically. "As much as I hate to admit it, I'm still not back to full strength. It seems having babies took more out of me than I thought it was going to."

Mike signaled for the check. While they waited for the waiter to return, they finished their coffee and talked about the last-minute preparations for the party.

Kevin withdrew from the discussion, concentrating instead on Lisa. Although her behavior that evening had not instilled wild hope in him, neither had it destroyed that hope. Even though the timing was still not what he had been working for, he was more determined than ever that he was not leaving Houston until things were settled between them.

CHAPTER SEVENTEEN

LISA'S ALARM CLOCK went off at six-thirty the following morning. She tapped the snooze alarm and rolled back over to her other side to catch an extra ten minutes' sleep, but all she succeeded in thinking about was Kevin. The news that he had sold his ranch had left her dumbfounded. She had to find a way to talk to him today. They couldn't go on the whole weekend the way they had so far, and she wasn't about to let him return to Washington without telling him how she felt.

Before the alarm could sound again she turned it off and got out of bed. The first thing she did was go to the closet to take out the clothes she would wear that day. The price tag still dangled from the sleeve of the burgundy designer suit she had purchased the week she had returned from Kansas. She had gone shopping for a blouse to go with the suit three days ago and had chosen one in a soft-pink crepe de chine. She hadn't spent as much time looking for just the right article of clothing since high school, when she'd searched for a prom dress that would make the boy who had not asked her to go with him sorry that he hadn't. She smiled at the memory. She hoped she had better luck impressing Kevin than she had the high-school football hero.

She walked into the bathroom and started running hot water into the tub. As she sprinkled in bath salts the air filled with fragrant steam. She stared at the colored crystals lying on the bottom of the tub and gave an ironic smile. The way her luck had been going lately, Kevin would be allergic to bath salts.

WHEN LISA DROVE UP to the church three hours later, the aura of self-confidence she had worked all morning to attain disappeared like early-morning mist. The first person she saw as she swung into the parking lot was Kevin. He was standing outside on the walkway, a baby in his arms. A lump filled her throat as she watched him holding the pink bundle, his face suffused with a smile of pleasure.

Lisa took a deep breath, left the car and walked over to him. "What are the two of you doing out here?" she asked, succeeding in her efforts to make her voice sound normal.

"It seems our goddaughter to be is the outdoor type," he said, chuckling. "She was putting up a real fuss when we were inside, but the minute I brought her out into the sunshine she was as content as a cow in clover." He gazed at Lisa, their differences temporarily forgotten in the specialness of the morning. "I hate to admit this, but when I walked out that door with this little charmer I was sorely tempted just to keep on going and take her home with me for a nice long visit." He readjusted the blanket which a light breeze had blown across the baby's face. "Do you think they'd notice if one was missing?"

She smiled, grateful for the easy familiarity he offered her. "I'm not sure about Caroline, but Mike would be on your trail in a second. What you really need is one of your own." She winced. Would she never learn to think before she opened her mouth?

He gave her an intense look, as if trying to discover if there was a hidden meaning behind her comment. "I think we should probably go inside," he finally said.

Lisa followed him up the steps, fervently wishing she could buy back the past sixty seconds and live them over. When she looked up she was relieved to see Caroline standing by the door. She came toward them, giving Lisa a hug before peeking at her sleeping daughter. "How in the world did you manage that?" she whispered to Kevin.

"It's an old family secret."

"Then how come I don't know about it?"

"It's from the Anderson side."

"Well, I don't want you to leave town until you teach it to me." She slipped her arm through Lisa's. "Come inside. There are some people I want you to meet."

The people Caroline introduced Lisa to were both her and Mike's parents and the minister. She decided that she would have had trouble placing Caroline with her mother and father, but Mike bore such a strong resemblance to both his parents she felt she could have picked them out of a crowd. The quints obviously had an interesting mixture of genes in their background. If they were true to the two generations that had preceded them, inheriting their strong personalities and stubbornness, they were going to be a real handful as they grew up. She glanced over to Kevin and wondered what a child of theirs would look like. The thought brought a curious sense of panic that she might never find out, but her musings were cut short when the minister indicated it was time to begin.

After the ceremony Lisa was reluctant to relinquish her new godchild. Margaret Ann Webster tipped the scale at just over five pounds. With her whisper of downy brown hair and dark-blue eyes, toothless yawn and tiny hand wrapped around Lisa's index finger, she had irrevocably captured her godmother's heart. She looked so small in her long white christening gown, yet already a steely determination showed through whenever she was displeased about something.

Although the idea of having five babies to care for at the same time intimidated her, having one was enormously appealing. She tried to convince herself that the powerful maternal feeling she was experiencing was a natural consequence of the day's events, but she knew better. What she felt was the culmination of thoughts and images and ideas that had been a part of her all along. She no longer questioned whether or not she wanted a child of her own—she did. And she wanted Kevin to be the child's father. She wanted it all—the home, the hearth, the loving glances, the knowledge that when she returned from a space flight there would be someone waiting for her who cared deeply that she had been gone.

As they left the church she decided it was time to go to Kevin. If she continued to wait for the perfect opportunity for them to speak to each other, it might never arrive. She waited patiently while he helped put the babies into their car seats in Mike's new station wagon. After he closed the door she went up to him. "Would you like to ride with me to the party?"

The smile left his eyes as he looked at her, a stunned expression on his face. He had been looking for an opportunity to talk to her but thought she would be resistant to the idea. He wasn't sure how he should feel about her being the one to make the overture. "Yes, I would," he said softly. "But I can't. I'm driving the grandparents over."

"Oh...I see."

He moved closer to her. "But before I leave on Sunday I want to talk to you. We have some things to work out between us."

Everyone, everything disappeared for her except Kevin. He was all she could see or hear or feel. She noted the slightly nubby texture of his lightweight wool suit, the soft sheen of his brown silk tie, the way his hair brushed against the top of his ears, his powerful hands, the compelling look in his eyes. "Yes..." she said at last. "We do have to talk to each other. We can't go on like this."

"What about tonight?"

She nodded.

"After the party?'

Again she nodded.

He reached out to touch the side of her face with the back of his hand. He wanted to tell her how much he had missed talking to her but decided it best to wait until they could be alone.

Somehow, with concentrated effort, Lisa was able to drive the three miles to the Websters' sprawling ranch-style house without incident. She followed Mike and Caroline into the house and out to the large backyard, where almost two hundred friends and relatives were waiting for them, all eager to see the quints, most of them for the first time.

Mike handled what could have been a troublesome situation with his usual aplomb. He introduced each of the babies in turn, explaining the necessity to make their stay at the party as short as possible. After the nannies had whisked their new charges off to their rooms, Mike rapped for attention and informed everyone he had another announcement to make.

"As you all know, Caroline's rather unusual pregnancy made it necessary for her to take an extended leave of absence from her network news anchoring job. While this allowed us to move back to Houston and be with all of you good people, it left her career in limbo. Since anchoring the evening news was never something she wanted to do in the first place, she says she wasn't too upset about leaving, except that her absence put her out of the running to do what she really wanted to do—in-depth investigative reporting. I'm sure some of you have seen the short segments she's had on the evening news. They were really fantastic. She has a deft touch when it comes to getting people to open up."

Caroline rolled her eyes and shook her head. "Would you please just get on with it before you put everyone to sleep with how wonderful your wife is?"

He put his arm around her shoulder and held her close to his side. "To make a long story short—"

"Oh, please do," she groaned.

He had to wait for the laughter to die down before he could continue. "In order to take on a particularly important assignment she has had in the works for two years, Caroline is going back to work. And as of this Friday I am officially on leave from NASA for the next six months so that I can stay home with the quints."

There was an instant of stunned silence and then spontaneous applause. Mike leaned over to whisper in Caroline's ear. "It seems I've found a way to be a hero in my own time."

"To me you always have been," she whispered back.

Across the patio Sandy Williams stood beside Lisa watching the exchange. "Those two could make you believe in happy endings," Sandy said, sighing.

Lisa's gaze swept the crowd, looking for Kevin. "Don't tell me your redheaded psychiatrist is finally wearing you down."

She laughed. "He's still giving it the old college try."

"Isn't that him over there signaling to you?"

Sandy looked to where Lisa pointed. "He probably wants to tell me how Mike's decision to stay home with the babies is going to have a positive effect on them when they're teenagers."

"You're kidding."

"Of course I'm kidding," she said, popping a mushroom stuffed with shrimp and crab into her mouth. "I'll catch you later."

A waiter walked by with glasses of champagne on a tray. Lisa took one and absently began wandering around, surreptitiously looking for Kevin. She had seen him earlier when he took one of the babies from Caroline and followed the nannies into the house, but she hadn't seen him since.

Two hours passed and she still hadn't seen him. Her need to talk to him had grown steadily and she was unable to force a lightheartedness she didn't feel or engage in small talk anymore, so she drifted into the house. Desperately needing a few minutes of solitude to think about what she would say to him later, she went into the study and closed the door.

She had made such a terrible mess of things with Kevin, and now that they had finally agreed to meet with each other, doubts assailed her like barbed arrows. If need and want counted for anything, she and Kevin were a shoe-in. If logic and the Senate Ethics Committee were given voting privileges, they were in deep trouble.

She walked over to the window and stared outside. The most puzzling thing that had happened in the time she had known Kevin had been the transformation in the way she felt about being an astronaut. None of the passion or dedication had diminished, but the way she viewed her job had. She had come to understand why Kevin's assertions that she looked at the space program with myopic eyes were true, and because of him and what he had shown her, she now had a broader picture of the world around her. Nothing would ever stop her from fighting with her last ounce of strength for the continuation of the space program, but at least now she was beginning to see it was possible for economic guidelines to be established without the program's wholesale destruction. Her gaze searched the people milling around outside. *Where was he?* They had so much to say to each other and so little time.

A charged feeling of anticipation swept over her, touching the wisps of hair on the back of her neck. Behind her she heard the door open and then softly close.

"Mind if I join you?" Kevin said, his voice deep, husky.

Her mouth went dry and she tried to swallow. Slowly she turned to face him. "I hope you didn't think I was going to offer to leave like I did the last time and let you have the room all to yourself." He had taken off his jacket and tie and rolled the sleeves up on his shirt. His hair looked as if it had been finger combed; his eyes were penetrating, sensual with their stark desire. As he stared at her, his gaze touched her as intimately as if he had made love to her. He continued to watch her as he slowly shoved his hands into his pockets and leaned against the door.

"I've been looking for you," he said, the tone implying he had looked a lifetime.

The corner of her mouth twitched in a nervously attempted half smile. "I'm not much good at parties."

"Then leave with me, Lisa...now."

The air was becoming too heavy for her to breathe. "I know a place...it's small but I think you'll like the way it's decorated."

"Oriental accents?"

"One or two."

"Quiet?"

"Yes...."

"Private?"

"Yes...."

"I'll get my coat from the nursery and meet you at your car."

"I'll tell Mike and Caroline we're leaving."

He looked at her for long seconds, his hunger etched in the lines radiating from his eyes and the taut set of his jaw. "They already know."

A warmth spread through her. "I'll meet you at the car then."

After he had gone she continued to stare at the door for a moment, unable to move. She tried to remember the layout of the house, seeking an escape route that would avoid the celebrants. She didn't need to see her reflection to know there was a look about her that would give her feelings away. And those feelings were so intensely private, she didn't want to share them with anyone.

By leaving through the garage side door then out the backyard gate, she made it to the car without being noticed. Kevin was waiting for her. Her hands trembled when she reached inside her purse for the keys. Grasping the brass ring between her fingers, she held it out to him.

"No," he said, "you drive."

She nodded and unlocked his door before going around to the driver's side. After she had started the car she turned to face him.

He returned her gaze, waiting expectantly for her to say what was troubling her. It was everything he could do to keep from touching her. She looked so incredibly beautiful. In the slanting rays of the afternoon sun her gold hair created a soft halo around her face. Her mouth was moist where she had licked her lips, and slightly open in an innocently erotic invitation; her eyes flashed a challenge that caused his blood to race.

"Your seat belt..." she said.

Slowly a smile traveled from his eyes to his lips. "You may not believe this, but I always remember to wear one when I'm in my own car."

She pulled out into traffic. "I'm glad to hear it," she said softly.

There was no other conversation between them during the drive to her apartment, each of them privately struggling with the words they would use to try to convince the other that their lives were meant to be lived together. When she unlocked her front door Lisa was convinced she would never be able to communicate to Kevin what was in her heart. There were no words to express such intense feelings, and without the words, how could she make him understand that she had changed?

Kevin followed her inside, closing the door behind him.

"Would you like something to drink?" she asked as she walked over to the sofa and laid her purse on the end table. She started to unbutton her jacket. When Kevin didn't answer she turned to him to see why and found him staring at her.

"No...I don't want anything to drink." He came over to her. Gently moving her hands aside, he finished pressing the pearl buttons through the buttonholes. "Did you think about me when you dressed this morning?"

"Yes...in a way I even bought these clothes especially for you, although I didn't realize it at the time." Where his hands accidentally brushed her body she felt a pleasure that bordered on pain.

He slipped the jacket over her shoulders, the silkiness of the lining making a sensual sound as it slid against her blouse. The resulting static electricity made the crepe de chine cling softly to her breasts and Kevin caught an alluring trace of perfume. It was everything he could do to keep from pressing his face into the valley between her breasts. His craving to hold her, to make love to her had increased with every heartbeat until he could think of nothing but how it would feel to have her lying beneath him. "Lisa..." he choked, his voice in a husky whisper. "Lisa..." His hands cupped the sides of her face. Slowly, tenderly he drew her to him. "My God, Lisa, I need you more than I have ever needed anything in my life. I need your warmth. I need your love. I need you *now*. Please don't ask me to wait."

With a tiny cry she put her arms around his neck and kissed him. Their lips met in an explosion of sweet surrender. The necessity to talk to each other, to work out their problems, to find a way for them to come together intellectually as well as emotionally disappeared in a maelstrom of physical hunger. It had been so long, the memories of sleepless nights so poignant, and the love that burned inside them so powerful that they could deny themselves no longer.

Kevin's hands swept the length of her back, her sides, the fullness of her breasts. His lips tasted the honey of her skin as they caressed her neck, her temples, where her pulse throbbed at the base of her throat.

Silently Lisa led him to her bedroom. Their need for each other precluded the slow gentle lovemaking they had shared when they had come together before. This time their hunger had been honed to a desperate sharpness, which controlled their actions, determining a pace that left no room for carefully removed clothing or seductive kisses. When their clothes were discarded, Kevin caught Lisa to him, lifting her up to straddle his waist. He held her suspended there for the sheer pleasure of feeling her nakedness against his own, then slowly he lowered her until they made intimate contact.

Lisa caught her breath as she felt him enter her. He moved to the bed. In a tangle of arms and legs, touching and caressing, sighs and whispered words of passion, they made love to each other. Quickly they climbed a wondrous peak then gently slid down the other side. Afterward Kevin held her in his arms, stroking her, reveling in the quiet pleasure of having her against him.

"I love you, Lisa," he said, his cheek resting against the top of her head. "I love you today...I will love you tomorrow...I will love you always."

"I think I tried a lot harder than you did to stop the loving," she reluctantly admitted. She placed her arm around his waist, and when she spoke, her voice caught in her throat. "What are we going to do? I can't go on without you anymore. When I told you that I wanted to talk to you, I thought I had worked out a solution. But I realize now that it was only a temporary one at best."

"What was your solution?" Not until that moment had he known how much it would mean to him that she had planned to meet him halfway.

"I wanted you so badly I was willing to suggest we have a tacky, clandestine affair...just as long as we could be together. But I realize now it would never be enough." She turned so that she could prop herself up on her elbows to look at him. "I want to be your wife, Kevin. I want to live with you out in the open. I want to have your child."

For a long time he stared at her, unable to speak. If he had allowed himself a wish for their coming together again, he would never have dared let it be one so complete. If the wish had not come true, the disappointment would have been too painful. "Oh, my beautiful Lisa," he whispered. "I love you beyond words." Tenderly he held the sides of her face and kissed her lips. "If I told you that there was a way for us to love each other without restrictions, would you marry me this coming fall?"

"I would marry you this afternoon...this minute."

"Then you can consider yourself officially engaged."

"How.."

"This coming November I will no longer be a senator so there will be nothing standing in our way. No one else knows about this yet, so we'll have to keep our engagement quiet for a while. It's important that the work I'm doing now remain above suspicion.''

She caught her breath. "Kevin...you can't...not because of me...I won't let you.''

"Lisa, listen to me carefully. From the very beginning I've been honest with you about how I feel about politics. Although I passionately believed in what I was doing, I had no passion for any of it. My first love has always been ranching.''

"But you sold—''

"And it not only felt good to sell the ranch in Kansas, it felt right. I finally realized there were too many memories for me there. I need a fresh start. My abilities may be a little rusty after a ten-year hiatus, but I think you should know that I'm a damn good rancher. If you hadn't been a part of my decision, my first choice would probably be to buy another spread near Crossroads simply because it's country I'm familiar with. But there's a part of me that's excited about the challenge of raising cattle in Texas.''

"Kevin, I can't let you sacrifice so much for me. I'm afraid that if I do, someday you'll regret what you've given up and it will affect our marriage. You'll have to let me give something, too.''

"You haven't been listening to me, Lisa. I'm not sacrificing anything. If you recall, even George Washington called it quits after he'd served his time in office. Besides, I've stopped carrying the banner alone. It's time to turn things over to others. More and more politicians are beginning to see the sanity of controlled spending. There are better and more effective leaders ready to take my place."

He ran his fingers down the side of her face. "I've gone so long without love in my life, Lisa, I realize now that I was beginning to wither away inside. Home and family are important to me. More important than anything else." He gave her a lopsided grin. "Do you have any idea what you did to me when you said you wanted to have my child?"

"Kevin...I love you so much." The words seemed so inadequate for the way she felt, but they were the only ones she knew.

"There's one more thing."

"It couldn't be important."

"It has to do with the committee and the work I've been doing on it for the past four months."

"You want to tell me what you're going to do to NASA's budget for the next year, and I don't want to hear about it right now."

"It's important that you know."

She grimaced. "Couldn't we talk about it later?"

He caught her to him. "Are you trying to tell me the tiger hasn't truly changed her stripes?" He nuzzled her neck, moved higher and caught her earlobe between his teeth. "What happened to all the talk about facing up to our differences?" he teased, knowing she was afraid of what he had done to the budget and reluctant to face what would surely be a disagreement between them.

"It takes time for the paint to dry on us tiger types," she said with a sigh, turning her head to allow him better access to the sensitive places behind her ear.

He could wait to tell her. He knew she would balk at the series of checks and balances he had suggested NASA implement before any more money was allocated to the space program, but he also knew that after the initial explosion she would see the fairness he had worked so hard to instill into the budget.

"Kevin?" she murmured.

"Hmm?"

"How big are the cuts?"

He chuckled. "We'll talk about them later." He stopped her protest with a lingering kiss.

"Maybe not even until sometime tomorrow," she sighed as she moved deeper into his embrace.

Author **JOCELYN HALEY,**
also known by her fans as **SANDRA FIELD**
and **JAN MACLEAN,** now presents her
eighteenth compelling novel.

DREAM OF DARKNESS

**With the help of the enigmatic Bryce Sanderson,
Kate MacIntyre begins her search for the meaning behind
the nightmare that has haunted her since childhood.**

Together they will unlock the past and forge a future.

Available in NOVEMBER or reserve your copy for September
shipping by sending your name, address and zip or postal code, along
with a check or money order for $4.70 (includes 75¢ for postage
and handling) payable to Worldwide Library Reader Service to:

Worldwide Library Reader Service

In the U.S.:
Box 52040,
Phoenix, Arizona
85072-2040

In Canada:
5170 Yonge St., P.O. Box 2800
Postal Station A,
Willowdale, Ontario M2N 6J3

DREAM—01

She fought for a bold future until she could no longer ignore the...

ECHO OF THUNDER

MAURA SEGER

Author of Eye of the Storm

ECHO OF THUNDER is the love story of James Callahan and Alexis Brockton, who forge a union that must withstand the pressures of their own desires and the challenge of building a new television empire.

Author Maura Seger's writing has been described by *Romantic Times* as having a "superb blend of historical perspective, exciting romance and a deep and abiding passion for the human soul."

Available in SEPTEMBER or reserve your copy for August shipping by sending your name, address and zip or postal code, along with a cheque or money order for—$4.70 (includes 75¢ for postage and handling) payable to Worldwide Library Reader Service to:

Worldwide Library Reader Service

In the U.S.:
Box 52040,
Phoenix, Arizona,
85072-2040

In Canada:
5170 Yonge Street, P.O. Box 2800,
Postal Station A,
Willowdale, Ontario, M2N 6J3

ECO-A-1

EYE OF THE STORM

MAURA SEGER

A powerful portrayal of the events of World War II in the Pacific, *Eye of the Storm* is a riveting story of how love triumphs over hatred. In this, the first of a three-book chronicle, Army nurse Maggie Lawrence meets Marine Sgt. Anthony Gargano. Despite military regulations against fraternization, they resolve to face together whatever lies ahead.... Author Maura Seger, also known to her fans as Laurel Winslow, Sara Jennings, Anne MacNeil and Jenny Bates, was named 1984's Most Versatile Romance Author by *The Romantic Times*.

At your favorite bookstore now or send your name, address and zip or postal code, along with a check or money order for $4.25 (includes 75¢ for postage and handling) payable to Worldwide Library Reader Service to:

WORLDWIDE LIBRARY READER SERVICE

In the U.S.:
Box 52040,
Phoenix, AZ 85072-2040

In Canada:
5170 Yonge Street,
P.O. Box 2800,
Postal Station A,
Willowdale, Ont. M2N 6J3

EYE-E-1R

The final book in the trilogy by

MAURA SEGER

EDGE OF DAWN

The story of the Callahans and Garganos concludes as Matthew and Tessa must stand together against the forces that threaten to destroy everything their families have built.

From the unrest and upheaval of the sixties and seventies to the present, *Edge of Dawn* explores a generation's coming of age through the eyes of a man and a woman determined to love no matter what the cost.

COMING IN FEBRUARY 1986

EDG-H-1

*You're invited to accept
4 books and a
surprise gift* **Free!**

Acceptance Card

Mail to: Harlequin Reader Service®

In the U.S.
2504 West Southern Ave.
Tempe, AZ 85282

In Canada
P.O. Box 2800, Postal Station A
5170 Yonge Street
Willowdale, Ontario M2N 6J3

YES! Please send me 4 free Harlequin Superromance® novels and my free surprise gift. Then send me 4 brand new novels every month as they come off the presses. Bill me at the low price of $2.50 each—a 10% saving off the retail price. There are no shipping, handling or other hidden costs. There is no minimum number of books I must purchase. I can always return a shipment and cancel at any time. Even if I never buy another book from Harlequin, the 4 free novels and the surprise gift are mine to keep forever.

134 BPS-BPGE

Name _____ (PLEASE PRINT)

Address _____ Apt. No.

City _____ State/Prov. _____ Zip/Postal Code

This offer is limited to one order per household and not valid to present subscribers. Price is subject to change.   ACSR-SUB-1

Just what the woman on the go needs!

BOOKMATE

The perfect "mate" for all Harlequin paperbacks!

Holds paperbacks open for hands-free reading!

- **• TRAVELING**
- **• VACATIONING**
- **• AT WORK • IN BED**
- **• COOKING • EATING**
- **• STUDYING**

Perfect size for all standard paperbacks, this wonderful invention makes reading a pure pleasure! Ingenious design holds paperback books OPEN and FLAT so even wind can't ruffle pages—leaves your hands free to do other things. Reinforced, wipe-clean vinyl-covered holder flexes to let you turn pages without undoing the strap...supports paperbacks so well, they have the strength of hardcovers!

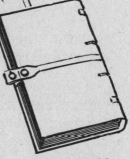

Snaps closed for easy carrying.

Available now. Send your name, address, and zip or postal code, along with a check or money order for just $4.99 + .75¢ for postage & handling (for a total of $5.74) payable to Harlequin Reader Service to:

Harlequin Reader Service

In the U.S.A.
2504 West Southern Ave.
Tempe, AZ 85282

In Canada
P.O. Box 2800, Postal Station A
5170 Yonge Street,
Willowdale, Ont. M2N 5T5

MATE-1R

What readers say about SUPERROMANCE

"Bravo! Your SUPERROMANCE [is]...super!"
R.V.,* Montgomery, Illinois

"I am impatiently awaiting the next SUPERROMANCE."
J.D., Sandusky, Ohio

"Delightful...great."
C.B., Fort Wayne, Indiana

"Terrific love stories. Just keep them coming!"
M.G., Toronto, Ontario

*Names available on request.